PRAYER FOR TH

He's back! Or rather. . . . *she's* back

"That's right, trust in the Lord. Let Him be your guide and strength," uttered Mrs Clifton fervently.

"Please Mum," he begged. "Leave me be."

"I don't know what's the matter with you. What are you rolling your eyes about for? " Her voice began to rise becoming more strident. "Tony, you're not listening. *Tony!*" Mrs Clifton's agitation was apparent.

Tony appeared to blank his mother out. He was becoming confused, angry and...dangerous. His chair scraped backwards as he leapt up. His hands clenched tightly at his side. The twist of his mouth showed pain and hatred.

His mother hissed, "Remember St Mark, chapter twelve verse twenty-four." Her tone altered becoming more reverent as she continued,

"And Jesus answering said unto them, Do you not therefore err, because ye know not the Scriptures, neither the power of God?"

A low rumbling roar began deep in Tony's throat, softly at first, gradually building up to a terrifying howl like a demented demon denied the right to destroy.

A nurse moved quickly to Tony's side, talking slowly, calmly. He nodded at Mrs Clifton,

"I think you'd better go... *Now.*"

Prayer for the Dying

Elizabeth Revill

Edward Gaskell *publishers*
DEVON

First published in 2000 by
Edward Gaskell publishers
Cranford House
6 Grenville Street
Bideford
Devon EX39 3DX

ISBN: 1 -898546 -41 -X

Prayer for the Dying

Elizabeth Revill

Printed & Bound by
Lazarus Press
Unit 7 Caddsdown Business Park
Bideford
Devon EX39 3DX

For Andrew and Ben

1

THE HAPPENING

A blinding flash of light stabbed behind Holly's eyes. She convulsed and shuddered as pictures from a newsreel stuttered and formed behind her eyes. Her slender shoulders heaved uncontrollably as the film came into focus and she saw the subtly lit passageway leading off from a thickly carpeted stairwell splutter into view.

A magnified vision of a strong, oak hardwood door loomed before her and opened, secured by a safety chain. A young, but sad face peered in between the space of door and durn. Recognition glimmered in those wistful eyes and a smile spread across the melancholy features lighting that face with more power than a pyrotechnic display on a festive celebration night.

Holly followed the figure with the watcher, whose eyes like hers, were locked on the girl's face. Holly gasped as she saw a look of delight change into one of terror as the girl noticed the knife.

Holly gagged, drowning for lack of air and as abruptly as the psychic stage had been lit, it faded to blackout.

She sat up in bed, threw off her bed covers and stretched for the safety of the light that would chase away the menacing shadows that had congealed in the corner, clumping together to threaten and disarray.

The light flooded her bedroom bringing with it an initial twinge of pain to her eyes. Her chest rose and fell rapidly in time with her racing heart and she flicked back a tendril of her hair that had slicked and stuck in the sweaty sheen that had spread across her face and downy upper lip.

It had happened again!

Holly remembered the tremors of last night's dream when the sheets wrapped around her, clinging like mud, rendered her limbs useless and immobile. *She* had been behind the eyes of the watcher observing that same young woman whose terror she had felt so acutely tonight. Through a substantial chink in the curtain viewed from a tree-top position, *she* had seen her laughing with a friend, *she* had heard her say goodbye, *she* had stared when she reached for the bottle and *she* had sympathised with the young woman who sobbed inconsolably. *She* had watched with the watcher.

What did it mean?

Ever since Holly could remember she had been sensitive to atmospheres. She had been aware when things were going to go wrong. She had known when there was going to be a death in the family but the strength of her ability was accelerating. More and more she was seeing things that didn't only affect her family, but that of total strangers. She was receiving images of the suffering of others. The power was growing and she didn't like it.

"I heard you call out – are you OK?" asked Paul in a concerned voice as he opened the bedroom door.

Holly ran lightly across the room to him and pulled him close.

"I need a hug."

"Did you dream again?"

"Yes."

"What did you see?"

"It was like a continuation from last night. Only this time the watcher went to the door and went in. There was a knife."

"You still don't know if it's a man or a woman?"

Holly shook her head and nuzzled her face through his open shirt into the thick mass of blond chest hair.

Paul released her arms that had been locked around him. He held her by the wrists with one huge hand and looked down at this diminutive creature who he loved so deeply. She gazed up at him, her huge dark eyes veiling her fears.

Paul stood six feet two in his stockinged feet, a viking of a man, broad shouldered, slim hipped, blond cropped hair and full beard that was more ginger than fair. His voice was deep and resonant with a slightly throaty quality that had come from years of smoking Old Holborn.

"I stopped you working. I'm sorry." Holly said flatly.

"I wasn't concentrating too well. I was just about to stop for a drink. Put your robe on and come and join me."

She hesitated fractionally, "Please...!"

"Please," he affirmed and grinned. "Headache gone?"

"Not too bad now. The sleep helped even if I did have a bad dream," She arched her back, cat-like and soft footedly moved to her bathrobe hanging on the door and covered her striped nightshirt with an over-large, soft towelling, peach wrap.

"How's it going?"

"Could be worse – come and see. I value your opinion."

Paul was an architect. He was in the middle of designing an all purpose conference centre that was to be built in the extensive grounds of *Fontaines,* an impressive five star hotel on the outskirts of Worcester.

They went downstairs through the warm sitting room with its log fire spilling its cheery flickering glow tinting the sheepskin rug an oily linseed yellow.

They passed through the dining room and into the annex which doubled as Paul's studio and study. It was here he worked and here he painted for relaxation.

A watercolour of the city of Birmingham at night rested on the easel. Muddy hues of the street lights breaking through foggy gloom, seeped on to the canvas. Holly stopped to admire it.

"You've really captured the mood of the city's streets. All those people scurrying through the evening dusk, yet isolated and lonely. There's tremendous feeling in this picture...."

Holly crumpled over as if she'd been hit in the stomach. She dropped to her knees.

"Blood," she whispered weakly.

"Blood dripping from the ceiling, flowing like scarlet ribbons. The walls bleeding and crying."

"Where?"

"I can't quite see... No....!"

Holly sobbed convulsively. Paul was at her side.

"Holly....HOLLY!" He tried to raise her to her feet.

"A knife – bread knife – serrated edge. Blood.. blood ......"

Holly shuddered and slipped into unconsciousness.

Mrs Clifton wiped the blade on the hygienic white towel and stuffed both into her roomy canvas bag. A smile began to play on those thin, pale lips that had once been crimsoned with artificial colour. Her unblinking eyes swivelled carefully around her surroundings.

There were no tell-tale marks, no incriminating signs. Her surgically gloved hands tugged at the tea cosy hat ensuring that not a hair would fall from her head. She beamed at her ingenuity in encasing her shoes and feet in the outdated, small, plastic galoshes reserved for the rain and she resisted the urge to sing.

She looked out from the shelter of the curtains in that shaded front room. The street was silent. The windows of the flats opposite were in darkness, with drapes drawn against the night. Her hooded snake eyes scrutinised the church on the island surrounded by cherry trees waiting to bud. Her lids dropped reverently and she comforted herself with a word from the Scriptures, Psalm 25:

"Consider mine enemies; for they are many;
and they hate me with cruel hatred.
O keep my soul and deliver me: let me
not be ashamed; for I put my trust in thee."

She curtseyed briefly in the direction of the tall church spire where religion stood, blocking the moon's light from the houses in its path and soundlessly she left.

The door clicked softly behind her and she melted away into the mystic shadows, padded around the corner, the collar of her coat up, masking her face from view. She emerged onto the busy main road with people too busy to notice, going about their evening business, lost in their own little worlds.

She shuffled down the once gloriously leafy lined avenue with the trees now brutally hacked, ugly and stunted from cruel pruning. Gone was the copper beech that once stood magnificently at the roadside – removed to make way for progress, road widening and increased automation. There was no place for sentiment in industry and no place for sentiment in Tony's mother's heart.

She crossed the busy Monument Road junction, past the shops and St Paul's sixth form college and into the Oratory which she had not visited for many years. She dipped her fingers in the Holy water crossed herself and slipped into a pew, her bony knees resting on a blue tapestry footstool, bowed her head in supplication and prayed for deliverance.

Before leaving she lit a candle, then retreated into the night.

"Come *on* Holly – this is getting serious."

"I know. I know. But why Paul? Why now? Why am I being plagued by these... these happenings?"

"I don't know sweetheart. You've always been sensitive."

"But not like this! The odd family death I could cope with – but *this* – this is full scale murder. It's like a private screening of a film. It's like I'm a giant TV receiver for the film channel on Sky and they're all horror movies!"

"OK. OK. Calm down. Let's reason this through. You've always been aware of a sixth sense?"

"Yes."

"Only now it's become heightened – exaggerated. Maybe due to your car accident in November. That's when all this started wasn't it?"

"Yes, after those two lads ploughed into me and shunted me up the road into that wall and I smashed my head on the windscreen. Then I started having those vivid dreams. But we know all this," said Holly hopelessly.

"Bear with me. You picked up on that serial murderer –

11

The Crooning Killer some papers dubbed him – but I thought things had settled down since his capture?"

"They did – They had! Now it's started again. But somehow I feel – feel this is something to do with those deaths."

"P'raps you ought to see someone – get some help."

"Have everyone think I'm nuts? No thanks."

"Look, let me have a word with Colin."

"Colin Brady? He'll think I'm cracked."

"No he won't. He's a good friend. Besides he's interested in the paranormal. He's even conducting research into the connection between head injuries and increased psychic abilities. He may be able to help."

"I don't know – maybe it'll go away. Maybe I *am* only dreaming."

"Did you only *dream* about the murders in November and through Christmas?"

"No."

"Well then?"

"But wasn't Colin involved in Tony Clifton's psychiatric assessment?"

"So what?"

"Well...." Holly sighed in exasperation. She was feeling weakened by the visions. She reluctantly nodded. "OK. Speak to him – but not now. Wait until morning."

"I'll call him first thing. You could do with some cheering up I'll invite him and Marcie over for drinks. OK?"

Holly smiled half-heartedly, "I need a drink. Is there any wine in the fridge?"

"Yep – a whole box full."

"Good. Then I'll pour a glass and come and see how your design is progressing."

Tony sat at the battered chessboard looking beyond his playing partner to the door by the nurses' station. It wouldn't be long now. She would be here, in her woollen tea–cosy hat and drab, grey coat, her face pale, her only colour from the network of thread veins that redly criss-crossed her cheek bones giving a rouged appearance.

Tony knew every inch of her face, her darting tongue, elemental eyes that seemed to see and know everything. He shuddered.

"Your move," quavered the voice of George Harper.

Tony picked up his Queen's Knight and jumped it, "Check."

George rubbed his bristly, emery chin and puzzled for a moment before moving his king to safety.

"Your Mum coming today, then?" He asked.

The glimmer in Tony's steel blue eyes hardened and he blinked in acknowledgement.

"And you?"

"I don't get no visitors on a regular basis. If I'm lucky one of the students from the college will come to see me. There's one I really like. Pretty little thing with huge eyes, name of Tammy. Proper little singing voice; plays the guitar a treat. Sometimes she and her friend, Babs come and entertain us. I'm allowed out in the grounds with her. Just to walk around. No nurse – nothin'. At my last review they said they were thinking of moving me to a low risk ward. Mind you, they've been saying that for some time. They're talking about care in the community now. I just do as I'm told."

Tony listened, walks outside, care in the community, they all sounded good to him. He needed to convince them that he wasn't a threat. Time. It would take time.

The electronics on the door beeped as the punch pad was operated. A nurse entered and Mrs Clifton padded in behind him, her feet silent on the polished floor.

The Shuffler rose up from his chair and trotted after her rubbing his hands together like Uriah Heep, muttering obscenities under his breath. Mrs Clifton stopped and turned to face the gaunt faced schizophrenic. Her tongue lashed at him raising a welt on Tony's heart as he listened and remembered similar verbal beatings.

The Shuffler stopped, spat on the pitted parquet floor. Mrs Clifton's strident voice spoke out:

> "I will send swarms of flies upon thee and
> upon thy people and into thy houses,
> Exodus 9 Verse 21."

"Hello Mum," Tony's mellifluous tones lifted in greeting to his mother.

George Harper raised himself out of his seat, "We'll play later Tony, all right?"

Mrs Clifton settled herself in George's vacated chair. She picked up George's King's Bishop and moved it effectively protecting the king and threatening Tony's Queen.

A muscle in Tony's cheek started to pulse spasmodically as Mrs Clifton made herself more comfortable.

"How are you?" She asked perfunctorily in her thin, reedy whine.

Tony automatically responded, "Fine Mum, fine."

"Good. I'm glad. That's one little detail I don't have to worry about. All the loose ends are gradually being tidied, make no mistake."

"What do you mean?"

Her thin tones dropped conspiratorially, "Like Athaliah, mother of Ahaziah, if my son is dead to me then I will arise and destroy all the seed of those responsible." The words gushed from her and as she talked, mother and son played chess together.

> "Let the lying lips be put to silence,
> which speak grievous things proudly and
> contemptuously
> against the righteous."

Her whisper became more fevered,

> "For I have heard the slander of many;
> fear was on every side:
> while they took counsel against me,
> they devised to take away my life."

"Mother, why are you quoting psalm 31?"

"For your deliverance son, for yours and mine. We *will* be together again."

Tony's eyes shrouded with mist as he felt himself being caught up on the sticky strands of the web of his mother's rhetoric. But, before he allowed himself to be cocooned in her poisoned silk casing, he saw everything with startling clarity. He understood what she was. He understood what she was doing and he saw a way out.

Holly was shivering uncontrollably. Paul had her seated in her favourite soft easy chair. She gratefully sipped a glass of iced water.

"How are you feeling?"

"OK," she smiled hesitatingly. "Paul, I'm frightened."

"I know sweetheart, " he attempted to reassure her by gently squeezing her hand, "I know."

"The ferocity of these visions... They're so draining. I've no control over them. They just happen."

"Look, I realise it's difficult but you must try to put it aside until we can speak to Colin. If anyone can help, he can."

The forensic science team were going through the upstairs flat in Lyttleton Road with meticulous skill.

The flash bulbs of police cameras had ceased their popping and the pathetic, lifeless form of Amy Calcutt had been bagged and removed to the city's morgue.

Detective Chief Inspector Allison's craggy face was stern. He grimaced at the thought of informing Amy's parents, currently on holiday in Spain, a vacation booked before their daughter had become innocently involved with a serial killer, a break that Amy had urged them not to cancel.

Allison hated this part of the job. It had been bad enough breaking the news to Janet Mason's mother, telling her of the murder of her only child.* Now, he had the same dirty job all over again, that of telling the Calcutts of their only daughter's

* See *Killing Me Softly*

15

death. Amy's brother Steve, numbed with shock, had just been driven home in a patrol car.

DCI Allison tapped his fingers impatiently on the back of a chair when his sergeant Mark Stringer radioed that he'd just arrived at the murder scene.

Allison's gravelly voice cut through the normal police routine.

"I'll leave you to finish up here. I'll expect a report ASAP. Pooley, you're in charge."

Allison manoeuvred his huge bulk through the door frame, lumbered down the thickly carpeted passageway to the stairwell and tiled hallway, through the huge oak door of Holly's dreams and down the tarmac path to the waiting car.

"I don't understand it.... such a frenzied attack. No apparent sexual motive. Why would anyone want to target Amy?"

"Revenge?" queried Stringer.

"For what? Her boyfriend is inside – Who would want her dead?" Allison continued almost to himself, "We'll need to review the files – all Clifton's victims – their families, friends, associates. Oh and Mrs Clifton, she's worth a call. Damnation! I thought we were over the worst."

"Do you think his mother had anything to do with this?"

"Could have. She idolises her precious son. But I must admit although she's a strange old biddy, she seems harmless enough."

"She gave Taylor the creeps," rejoined Mark.

"Yes, but he's young. An impressionable copper- he could have got her wrong. Still, no stone must be left unturned. Get Pooley on to it when he's finished here or better still let Taylor do the footwork. He knows her. We'll head back for the station."

Mark Stringer started the car and turned out into the Hagley Road, past the Norfolk Hotel and headed towards the town and Steelhouse Lane Police Station.

Allison ripped the wrapping off his Mars bar without his usual fervour and munched his way through it in an almost mechanical manner. It was going to be a long night.

Ronnie Soper looked about him. It was one of those grey days when nothing much was happening on the streets. He always had his eyes open for an opportunity to improve his standard of living. There was a smart BMW parked a little way down the road. Ronnie watched and waited. Every Wednesday, its owner parked the car at the same time and went into the wine bar at Five Ways shopping precinct; he popped out to make a phone call at about 1.00 pm then went back to the bar and didn't usually leave until about 2.30 pm. Ronnie was sure that this Wednesday would be the same. He'd been watching this car, in this area, for the last six weeks. Now was the time to make his move.

Ronnie was small for his fourteen years. He was thin and scrawny with a mop of crow black hair. He had a mischievous looking face with a permanently impish expression. His colour was a pasty, unhealthy white, making the dark mole that grew just above his lip, under the left side of his face, stand out. The little whiskers that protruded from it were long enough to make it look as if a small spider had settled under his nose.

Ronnie glanced nervously about him then walked nonchalantly up to the vehicle. He tried the handle, front passenger side...nothing. He slid his hand inside his coat and took out a length of flat plastic. In less than a minute Ronnie was sitting inside the BMW, screwdriver at the ready. He neatly removed the stereo CD radio. He looked over his shoulder to the back seat which was covered in a smart leather coat. Ronnie grabbed this and the brown paper package the coat was concealing.

Whistling cheerily, he was on his way and off to 'Uncles' to see what he could pick up from the pawnbroker for his latest haul, as long as he could steer clear of the EWO who was on his trail as Ronnie was a persistent truant.

Ronnie smiled cheekily, they would have to be up early in the morning to put one over on him. Truanting? He'd got it off to a fine art.

He'd always register, then midway between class and the assembly hall he'd make himself scarce. He'd be back on the school site for his free lunch, afternoon mark and then be away again. At least that is what he had always done in the past but now his tutor and teachers had become wise to him. He'd been forced to stop registering but still left home early enough in the morning to give him time to dodge the school traffic, taking refuge in the Gents' loos at the shopping precinct.

He was safe from the cottagers who tried their luck with him in there. They had suffered too many kicked shins and knew better, leaving him alone.

Ronnie darted into those loos now. He locked himself away in the third stall to examine his booty.

He swore in exasperation as he looked at the radio CD.

"Coded!" he hissed under his breath. That was annoying. That meant he'd have to take it to Fred in the jewellry quarter to have it decoded before he could sell it on. Fred would want his cut and that would lower his profit margin. Still, he had the leather – he could pick up a few bob for that. But what was this?

Ronnie removed the brown paper and string. He gasped and his eyes stretched to their limits as he unrolled the aging, crumbling canvas and gazed on an ancient fine quality oil painting in the style of an impressionist such as those he'd seen in the Museum and Art Gallery.

He knew he was in possession of something valuable – he knew that possession could cause him trouble. His gut instinct told him it wasn't safe to keep it, but how could he safely be rid of it?

DCI Allison sat hunched over his files reading Amy Calcutt's last statement to the police. He leaned back in his chair and rubbed the bridge of his nose with his huge fingers. He was tired and nothing seemed to make any sense. Why should the ex-girlfriend of a serial killer, a girlfriend who had absolutely no knowledge of his involvement in the murders which at the time had sent terror through the hearts of the people of Birmingham, be struck down now? And why in this manner?

Amy had helped the police considerably in gathering evidence, pinpointing dates for which Tony had no alibi and reporting on Tony Clifton's state of mind within their relationship.

Amy had been sympathetic to Tony's mother believing that she had been wronged both by Tony and herself, that she had been as much of a victim as Amy herself had been. But now Amy was dead, horribly murdered and the frenzied stabbing had much in common with the original murders but as yet no obvious sexual gratification.

Greg Allison pressed his intercom.

"Maddie – get some tea in here please and tell Mark when he arrives to report to me."

"Sir."

Allison continued reading the report in front of him. At least there had been one stoke of luck, a perfect thumb-print had been found on a teacup on the kitchen table next to Amy's body. A fresh print that *didn't* belong to Amy. Fingerprint files were currently being checked. If the offender was known to them they'd soon have a name. Allison was pleased, but he had a gut feeling. It wasn't going to be as simple as that.

The driver of the BMW whistled as he emerged from the wine bar. It looked like rain – he'd make his call and retrieve his leather from the car before returning to the bar.

He stepped into the glass booth with its BT messenger symbol blowing a fanfare. The call didn't take long, just routine. He walked back towards his car and looked with horror at the ill-fitting door, so clearly unlocked. One glance was enough to tell him his CD cassette radio was missing, but more importantly so were his leather and package.

A stream of expletives fell from his lips and were taken away by the wind as the first drops of rain fell.

Allison groaned – too many things were happening too fast. He had too much to deal with and his case load wasn't getting any lighter.

Greg Allison stared hard at his office door, then rose from his seat, lumbered to the window and perused the familiar sight of activity at the General Hospital opposite, always busy. An anguished sigh escaped him. There was a soft knock and the door opened.

Allison saw the reflection of his young sergeant in the glass of the window through which he had been staring, surveying the scene outside.

He turned around slowly to face Stringer and raised one of those bushy, hammock meshed eyebrows that had been pulled and teased into shape. No words were necessary from Allison so Mark explained,

"You're not going to like this, sir. But, we've got a match on the print."

"Yes?'

"It's Clifton's."

"Mrs Clifton?"

"No, Tony Clifton."

"That's impossible!"

"I know – but it is – "

"Dammit he's inside – isn't he?"

"Safe and sound."

"Then how....? Are they sure?"

""Positive, look – see for yourself."

Mark tossed the enlargements of the prints onto Allison's desk. Allison returned to his seat and examined them.

"Looks identical."

"They are. Forensic are sure."

"How can that be?"

Mark shook his head, "Beats me. I said they'd have to offer all possibilities – see if the prints could be lifted and transplanted onto an object – anything like that. I have to say sir, it would have to be some kind of technical whiz kid to pull a stunt like that. Or..."

"Or? Don't tell me Clifton did it."

"Not unless he's escaped in the last twenty four hours."

Allison thrust forward his pugnacious chin. "Why are things never straight forward?" He slammed his meat cleaver hands on the desk top spilling the remains of a cold cup of tea that had skinned and stained the inside of the cup.

"What else have they come up with?"

"Nothing. Flat's as clean as a whistle. Not a trace of anything else. No one seems to have seen or heard anything."

The phone's impatient ring interrupted the conversation. Allison growled into the receiver,

"Yes?"

He listened quietly for a number of seconds before speaking, "You'd better get in and see me." He replaced the receiver. "Brady," he said in response to Mark's questioning gaze. "Some garbage about a woman seeing this death."

"A witness?"

"Not exactly."

"What then?"

"A clairvoyant."

Mark stared in disbelief at his boss who lumped into his seat and gazed across the room.

"If it hadn't come from Brady I wouldn't give it any credence at all. But..."

"But?" probed Mark.

"I don't know. It all seems fanciful rubbish but I've a lot of respect for Colin – least I can do is hear him out. He's coming in this afternoon at 2.30. Will you be around?"

"I'll guarantee it. Sounds interesting."

"Don't hold your breath. All this supernatural tripe....."

"You never know. Look at Peter Hurkas. He's helped the police on many an occasion. And that famous woman psychic in America..."

"Yeh, yeh. We'll see. Now any more on that antique fraud?"

2

FAST CHANGES

The car screamed into the gutter, its wheels spinning furiously in the mud. The front door passenger side flew open and a body was bundled out onto the deserted street. The door slammed shut and with a squeal of rubber on tarmac the vehicle raced off.

The motor screeched around the corner sending a shower of water over a bent old woman wheeling a supermarket trolley full of carrier bags and an old clothing bundle. She swore and shook her fist at the disappearing automobile and wiped her mud spattered face with a red, ragged handkerchief. Her thinning, grey hair blew in the breeze that stirred in the tree lined avenue.

She picked her way along the road foraging in the bins that intermittently rose up from the concrete, whose once hungry mouths were now over-stuffed and dribbled their contents down their shiny plastic bellies. She stopped when she saw the crumpled heap on the pavement and peered cautiously around her.

Scurrying like a rat to its hole, the old woman darted to the still mass and deftly searched it. Finding nothing, she hurled a stream of abuse into the air and spat angrily into the road. She turned on her heel, wrapping her patched and frayed coat tightly around her. She wiped her nose on the back of her ravelled sleeve, muttered some more obscenities and carried on with her patrol, ferreting in each bin she passed.

Finding an old pom-pom hat that had seen better days and had been discarded on a wall, she thrust it on her head. She poked at the stray wisps of hair, tucking them out of sight, and wheeled her trolley towards the glare of the shop lights and city centre.

Behind the old woman, the mound of clothing on the pavement moved, groaned, sat up and examined her cuts and bruises, then scrambled to her feet before, she too, proceeded towards the city lights. As she began to wander the pedestrianised streets of the city centre, she attracted many curious glances but no-one approached her or spoke to her to see if they could help. The usually friendly town by day changed character at night and ordinary folk were afraid of the consequences of getting involved.

She stumbled her way up New Street, Paradise Street past the library complex and crossed over the main road by the old National Provincial Bank and across to the Hall of Memory where she settled on a wooden bench. She was wearing a faded, Indian style cotton dress, rope sandals, head scarf and a short grey duffel coat.

She shivered involuntarily in the cold wind and tried to rest her black, bruised eyes.

PC Taylor was on his way to Steelhouse Lane Police Station. He was on the night shift with PC Parkhouse and they had some time to kill; so had stopped off at the cafe wagon for a burger and a hot chocolate. They crossed the road by the New Rep and paused fractionally by the bill boards advertising the latest play, 'A Man For All Seasons.' PC Taylor looked with interest at the names of the stars, and noted the performance times. It would be good to go and see a really classy show. He'd have to check the duty roster and see if there were any seats available on his night off.

The younger constable's feet clattered on the concrete path, home to a number of wooden benches placed for people's comfort, overlooking the gardens belonging to the Hall of Memory. He paused momentarily and took a cursory look around, whilst Parkhouse still studied the show photographs on the hoarding.

How Birmingham had changed, even in his short lifetime. Gone was Bingley Hall which his mother told him had enter-

entertained with circuses and exhibitions, to be replaced by the superb New Symphony Hall. This Birmingham was shinier and glossier, but with its sprawling masses, mixed culture and sheer size, Birmingham's crime rate was still rising. The force needed more men. There was too much to do, too many case loads to work on. He sighed, he was becoming far too cynical. Something to his left caught his eye; a fluttering newspaper or rag perhaps?

Another tramp? It was such a cold night, David Taylor didn't have the heart to move her off. Perhaps a friendly warning and some money for a hot drink and bite to eat would be more in order. Then at least he would have seen her off and if she returned after she'd eaten, he wouldn't be there to see it.

He slowly approached the shaking bundle of what appeared to be mud soaked rags and touched her lightly on the shoulder. She recoiled from his hand as if she had been burnt and huddled into a tight lump on the corner of the bench. She stared at him with frightened, swollen eyes. Her face was grazed and there was an ugly, raised purple welt across her left cheek. He was surprised to see how young she was, possibly only twenty-four or twenty-five years old. He spoke gently to her,

"It's not the sort of night to be out alone. Haven't you got a home to go to?"

The young woman shrank further into the corner, almost as if she were trying to disappear. Her eyes, he noticed, in spite of their puffiness, were a startlingly bright green. He put his hand in his jacket pocket for some money and she flinched as if he was taking a stick to beat her.

"Please, I only want to help. Look, here's some cash. Get yourself some hot soup. You look as if you could do with it."

Eyes that had witnessed some extraordinary horror, fastened on his outstretched hand. She gingerly moved her bruised and bloodied legs from under her and tried to stand. The effort was too much and she fainted on to the cold stone floor.

David Taylor radioed for help, "PC54216 reporting, I've got a young woman, white, aged about twenty-four who needs an ambulance. I'm at the Hall of Memory, Birmingham Rep side. Make it quick."

PC David Taylor shouted for Parkhouse, who came running. They both shifted their feet in the cold and waited. Parkhouse wanted to keep moving, and offered,

"I'll walk down to the road keep a look out and direct the ambulance when it arrives. I'll be within earshot if you need me."

Taylor nodded and then tried to make the young woman as comfortable as he could. He took off his jacket and made a pillow out of it for her. He stared hard as he lifted her head onto the make-shift cushion.

Although her face was dirt streaked and bruised there was a wild beauty about her. In ordinary circumstances she would be described as strikingly attractive. Her head lolled on to one side and she groaned.

"I say, I say, are you all right?" the young constable asked, "The ambulance won't be long, you'll soon be safe. We'll look after you."

His breath clouded on the frosty air. He looked across at the New Rep, down to the roadside where Parkhouse was waiting, then back to the Celebrity restaurant. His eyes took in the Symphony Hall. It was quiet and closed, just the neon lights of its name heralded its existence.

The blaring sound of a siren broke the silence and within a few minutes an efficient team had removed the young woman and whisked her away to the General Hospital. PCs Taylor and Parkhouse continued on their beat, counting the minutes until their duty ended.

Back at Steelhouse Lane, Detective Chief Inspector Allison bit hard into his Mars Bar savouring the melted chocolate and enjoying the stringy strands of caramel that stretched from his lips. The phone jangled for attention. He struggled to swallow the mouthful of chocolate then gruffly answered.

"Chief? Chief? Is that you?" asked the polite, well cultured tones of his detective sergeant Mark Stringer.

Greg Allison hurriedly gulped and managed a reply, "What's the problem?"

"Got a floater. The canal just down from Ronnie Scotts. Doesn't look like a suicide or an accident. Thought you should know, could be Dan."

"Dan?" Greg Allison sat rigidly, momentarily shocked into stillness.

Dan Fletcher was one of Allison's snouts, getting on in years but reliable. Allison pushed his heavily set body forward onto the desk, "Are you sure?"

"Can't be sure of anything, sir. But it looks like him."

"Follow it up will you? Call me back. It doesn't matter if I've gone home, call me there. I shall be leaving here in just under an hour."

"Sir." Mark recoiled at this instruction. No-one hated the city morgue more than he did. His years on the force hadn't quelled his feelings of nausea whenever he was forced to visit. It was something he had never hardened himself to, the one aspect of his job he loathed.

Allison replaced the receiver and lay his Mars Bar on the desk, its tempting delights no longer attracted him. He rubbed his hand across his brow and frowned. He pushed the switch on his intercom.

"Maddie can you get me everything we've got on Dan Fletcher? Oh and a cup of coffee too, please."

Allison waited for the acknowledgement and twisted his mouth from side to side, scraping his broad hand over his chin sprouting with bristles, Dan? Why would anyone want to get rid of Dan?

Mark Stringer took a gulp of air before steeling himself to mount the steps of the city's morgue and speak to Hurst, or whoever was on duty at this Godforsaken hour.

The light burnt hot and muddy through the frosted glass of the Coroner's Office. Mark rapped lightly on the door.

"Enter," shouted tones that Mark recognised. He pushed

against the heavy door that finally yielded under his weight and came face to face with an efficient looking Hurst.

"What can I do for you?" asked Hurst, one eyebrow raised, surprised to see Mark at this late hour.

"You have a floater; male; about sixty-eight; must have come in about an hour ago?"

"You're a bit early. He's on ice, ready to do in the morning. I'm bushed. Just completing some paper work for Susan and then I'm off. It's been a long night."

"No possibility of anything now? Chief's waiting."

"He'll have to wait. Can't perform miracles. Go on Mark, clear off before you're sick."

Mark nodded gratefully and exited before the first rise of bile hit his throat.

Doctor Milman slipped his right hand into his pocket and spoke to the young woman in the hospital gown in front of him.

"Well young lady, it looks like you've taken quite a battering. No internal damage, thankfully. But if this blow or kick here," he gestured to a point just below her rib cage, "Had been an inch further this way, you'd have been looking at a ruptured kidney."

Her green eyes followed his movement but she said nothing.

"Now," he said a little more gently. "The police are waiting to ask you some questions so at least you can tell me your name?"

The young woman hesitated and furrowed her brow.

"I...I don't know."

"What do you mean?"

"I can't remember." Her voice grew louder with alarm, "I can't remember!" Her eyes grew wider and they began to fill with a wild panic. "I'm...I'm..." The struggle she had with herself was apparent.

Steven Milman placed a comforting hand on her shoulder.

"Look, you've had a terrific beating. The amnesia is likely to be only temporary," he paused. "You'll have to see the police. They've been waiting to interview you. I'll explain your condition. We'll keep you in for observation; who knows, by tomorrow you'll probably have remembered everything." He smiled reassuringly at her.

She looked stunned and embarrassed.

"Tell you what – bet you've got a favourite name."

"Favourite name?" She stared blankly at him.

"Yes, a name you've always liked."

"I'm not sure..."

"Well, now is the time to use it. Any name you've fancied – use it until you remember your real one. " He looked hard at her.

Speaking with more confidence than she felt, she replied, "Judy. I've always liked the name Judy. I don't know how I know – but some how I do."

"Well, there we are. Judy it is then." The corners of Steven Milman's mouth twitched in a quick half smile. He stared at her a little while longer before pulling the curtain around her bed and leaving. He signalled to the waiting copper, spoke quietly to him for a few minutes then strode briskly out of the ward.

DCI Allison stirred his tea vigorously,

"OK Mark. What have we got?"

"Too much to do – as usual."

"Let's see.... Amy Calcutt is dead – stabbed to death in a frenzied attack. No apparent sexual motive. Clifton's thumb-print is on the coffee cup, but Clifton is safe inside on a closed ward. Right?"

"Right."

"Dan is found as a floater – We're still awaiting the PM report.* Vencat is on the loose – sightings coming in from all over the country. And we have a young woman, an amnesiac found in the city centre in the early hours of the morning with no means of identification. No hand-bag, all the labels cut out of her clothing.."

"Someone went to a great deal of trouble to make sure she couldn't be identified."

* See *Killing Me Softly*

"Don't forget the antique fraud and the Handsworth, racially motivated stabbing last night."

"Plus all the usual crap – burglaries, car thefts, muggings...."

"OK. OK. - Brand is still dealing with the antique fraud. Let Woodward continue to pursue Vencat. We'll stick with the Calcutt killing."

"What about the stabbing in Handsworth?"

"Leave preliminary investigations to the locals for the time being. The Calcutt killing will have to take precedence. So, what have we got?"

"No sign of forcible entry."

"She knew her killer?"

"It's a possibility or someone had a very plausible reason for being admitted."

"Try contacting that friend of hers..." Allison clicked his fingers impatiently as he searched for her name.

"Sheena... Sheena Blakewell," Mark supplied.

"Sheena..." affirmed Allison,"See if she can shed any light on this.... help account for Amy's last hours."

Allison lumbered to the door and opened it as Mark replied, "Right!"

"Maddie!" growled the DCI walking back to his desk. "Are all the Clifton files here?" he queried, thumping his huge hand on the work surface making the pile of reports jump.

"All the police files. Psychiatric reports are with Brady." Maddie answered.

"And I'm seeing Brady at 2:30 – " He glanced at his watch – "Exactly two hours time."

Ronnie Soper watched while Fred decoded the CD radio cassette player.

"What code do you want keyed in?"

"I don't – Can't you leave it so the customer can fix his own code?"

"I can. I just thought it would seem more legit. if you picked a code, one you could remember. Should save a lot of questions.

Anyone would really think it *was* yours. They certainly wouldn't believe it was hot."

Ronnie paused before answering,

"That makes sense. OK."

"Got any number in mind?"

"I expect my birthdate is as good as any. At least I won't forget that," and he reeled off a number which Fred duly keyed in.

"Got a buyer?" said Fred pointedly, "That's a smart leather you've got there."

Ronnie thought for a moment. He'd taken the leather on impulse. 'Uncle' wasn't over keen on buying clothes. Maybe he could do a deal with Fred, then he wouldn't have to pay for the decoding. He'd already had half a mind to set up something of the sort.

"Sure is. Do you like it?"

"Looks cool. What size?"

Ronnie looked at the label, "Forty-two."

"My size."

"Do a deal?"

"What are you suggesting?"

"The coat for the decoding," Ronnie licked his lips, a habit he had when thinking about money, "And fifty quid."

"You gotta be joking!"

"Come on. It's an expensive leather, you said so yourself. It must have cost at least three hundred pounds and it looks brand new."

"It's also quite individual – recognisable. I'd be taking a risk. I'd have to do something to it, to personalise it. That'd cost." Fred's eyes narrowed greedily, "Besides you should get a ton for the player. It's top of the range."

Ronnie hesitated, "Forty quid?"

"Call it twenty and you've got yourself a deal."

"Done! You drive a hard bargain."

Ronnie pulled a face but inside he was smiling. Fred didn't know but Ronnie would have given the coat to him in exchange for the decoding. Ronnie had noticed that it was a speciality leather and didn't want the fag of being stuck with it and now he was up twenty quid on the deal. Nice one! He'd also checked the pockets and amongst the till receipts, phone numbers on odd scraps of paper and a couple of business cards, he'd found a roll of notes yet to be counted. This was turning out to be a very good morning's work indeed.

What he was less happy about was the canvas which he'd safely stashed until he could decide what to do with it. But for now things were looking good.

Holly gasped, light flooded her eyes in the same familiar fashion that heralded another vision. She buckled and groped for a seat waiting for the happening.

A cool breeze lifted the strands of her hair in an otherwise still room that had begun to alter. The walls transformed to breathing living matter which pulsed and rippled. A vein that threaded across the membrane of this heaving tissue began to fill and swell. The colour suffused and changed, manifesting itself in a pulsing drip. The walls haemorrhaged, every pore filled and burst in a red stream. The network of capillaries that fed the main artery crossed the ceiling and blood dripped. Then the room started to cry. Holly let out a howl.

What was she to see this time?

Colin Brady shook Allison's hand vigorously before sitting opposite the big man.

"Right Colin, you've got me intrigued. What's all this about?"

For a moment it looked as if Colin wasn't going to reply, then the dapper little man hooked his fingers through his hair and leaned forward.

"I have a friend, a close friend and following a car accident where she sustained head injuries she seems to have an acutely developed sixth sense." He stopped.

Allison sensing encouragement was needed prodded, "Go on."

"You may or may not know but I'm making this subject, head injuries and increased psychic awareness, the focus of a special study – I'm writing a paper on it. But that's by the by. However, when she began to have premonitions I naturally became interested." He paused again and watched Allison's face closely looking for some clue to the Chief's thoughts. He saw none. Allison's face was impassive. He sat and waited for Colin to continue.

"When the killings started.... that November, Holly..."

"Is that her name?" interrupted Allison, "Holly what?"

"Let's just leave it at Holly for now. "

Allison nodded and Brady continued.

"She began having these visions. 'Happenings' she called them. She felt Janet Mason's terror. She saw Annette Jury's death through his eyes. She witnessed Sandra Thornton's attack and Natalie Blakeney's death. At first, there were a lot of jumbled images and some very physical things that happened to her. By the time I found out about her experiences Clifton was captured – but now...."

"Now?" Allison prompted.

"Now, it's happening all over again."

Neither man spoke. The silence was loud and screaming. There was a soft knock on the door that gently opened. Maddie's voice sliced through the taut strings of tension.

"A reporter from the Post is in reception. He wants information on last night's murder."

Brady raised one eyebrow and looked at the Chief.

"He'll have to wait. Tell him there'll be an official statement at six o' clock."

"Sir."

"And Maddie,"

"Sir."

"Get some tea in here."

The door closed quietly and Brady spoke,

"So there *has* been a murder."

"Murder, stabbings, beatings, traffic accidents," Allison

stopped and changed his tone,

"What did she see?"

Brady tried to faithfully represent the images Holly had seen and her subsequent terror. As he described the heavy oak door, passageway and thickly carpeted stairwell, Allison saw it all in his mind's eye. He recognised the upstairs flat and the young blond whose eyes had opened wide with fear.

Brady hesitated, his voice deepened with urgency,

"You know don't you? – You're familiar with the place I'm describing and you know the girl?"

"Amy Calcutt."

"Clifton's girlfriend?"

"The same."

"And is she dead?"

"Last night – murdered, a frenzied knife attack. You do realise that someone with such detailed knowledge of the crime will have to be interviewed?" Allison waited. He sensed that Brady had more to say, "There's something you're not telling me." It was more of a question than a statement. Brady nodded.

"Holly I can vouch for – She has her alibi but she also told me one detail that I'm certain the police wouldn't reveal to the general public. One of those tid-bits that would only come up at a PM – a detail of prime importance in your hunt for the killer."

"And what would that be?"

"On the nape of the neck, underneath the hair, a small piece of flesh has been removed. Small but distinct..."

Allison waited.

"In the shape of a cross. Am I right?"

Allison frowned, "I can't tell you that. Although I agree it's just the sort of detail that we would keep to ourselves but the fact is, we don't know. I haven't had the PM report yet. But I'll tell you something else, if that proves to be the case I really must talk with her, and soon."

"I know – she's expecting to anyway."

Once more PC Taylor found himself outside that house in Sparkbrook from which he'd fled when he was checking witnesses' statements in the hunt for the serial killer. How well he remembered Birmingham at the time, gripped by fear of the atrocious murders which hit the headlines in that awful November, through Christmas and New Year until the killer's subsequent capture.

Now, he was here again. Even in the crisp, cool sunshine looking at the freshly brushed path, spotlessly scrubbed step, shining letter box and gleaming windows which set this house apart from its dingy neighbours, David Taylor felt a small prickle of fear winkle its way into his stomach and grow into a stabbing lance of terror. He rang the bell and waited.

He heard the slop, slop of slippers flopping off at the heel as each step approached the front of the house. Finally, the door opened and Mrs Clifton peered out suspiciously,

"Yes?" her thin, reedy tones questioned.

"PC Taylor, Ma'am. You said to drop by if I was ever in the area. Good for a cuppa you said." He sounded more cheerful and confident than he felt.

Recognition gleamed in those slit-like cobra hooded eyes. She pulled the door open wider and grinned at him drawing back her pale lips revealing her yellowing teeth.

David Taylor forced a smile as he followed her into the dark house past the cross with its fairy lights and into that room of religious gloom.

"I remember you. You're the copper who lives with his mum.... A good boy is a Godly boy," she recited.

He tried to settle himself in the moquette Queen Anne chair facing the spitting gas fire while the dead eyes of Christ looked down benevolently at him. The cloying sweetness of the air filled him with trepidation and he longed to run out, back to the safety of the spring sunshine and the street.

"Now let me see, white and two sugars – is that right?"

"Just one sugar please."

"I haven't any lemon cake, but I've made some apple

muffins. You must have some. I'll warm them up. They're lovely with cream, " she added in her nasal whine.

"Thanks, that'd be.... nice."

Already, the joss stick perfume was sending his head
spinning. He knew he had to suppress this inner revulsion or
he'd never find out anything. He willed his trembling hands to
be still, but they continued to shake uncontrollably.

She called out from the kitchen to him.

"Still with your mum then?"

"Yes – I am." He tried to sound bright and interested.

"Not met a special girl then?"

"No, not yet," and inexplicably the face of the girl with the
impossibly green eyes popped into his head.

"At least I don't think so," he added as much for his own
benefit as for hers.

"So there might be someone then?"

"Yes...no...well not exactly."

"Ah I see," she hissed knowingly as she brought in the tea
tray and apple muffins, "You've met someone!"

And almost as a way of gaining her confidence and encouraging her to talk, David Taylor found himself telling Mrs Clifton
all about the young amnesiac he'd found at the Hall of Memory.

"Well that's a strange tale, " she muttered sympathetically, "a
real mystery. I'll say prayers for her tonight. Have faith and
believe; for it is said:

> "...without faith *it is* impossible to please him:
> for he that cometh to God must believe that
> he is, and that he is a rewarder of them that
> diligently seek him.
> Hebrews Chapter eleven
> Verse six."
> Seek help from the Lord and believe
> and He will bring you comfort.
> He has all the answers."

Taylor took a swift gulp of tea that scalded his throat. He hastily replaced his cup as he spluttered and coughed.

Mrs Clifton was at his side. She offered him a handkerchief in the corner of which was a small embroidered black cross. He accepted it gratefully and the glass of water presented so quickly to him.

Mrs Clifton watched him, a smile beginning to tug at the corners of her mouth. She liked this young copper. She didn't know why. She just did.

"What's your name?" she enquired.

"Taylor ma'am."

"I know that. I mean your *Christian* name." She emphasised the word Christian loading it with hidden meaning.

"David."

"Ah...David," she smirked superciliously, "And do you resemble our King David? Was he a man after God's own heart or indeed, an adulterous brigand?"

Taylor had no idea what she was talking about and just shrugged his shoulders.

"No matter. It's a good strong name."

"That's enough about me Mrs Clifton, what about you?"

"Grace...You can call me Grace, and I'll call you David."

"Well, Grace," he said the name with difficulty. "How have you been coping?"

"Miserably well," she replied, "But surviving. It was such a shock, my Tony an' all but I told him. I warned him the Lord would find a way of making him his own, just like Jonah. I just didn't expect it to be like this."

"What about friends? Neighbours?"

"Most of them moved away years ago. There's not many round here that associate him with me. There's the Singhs next door. They've always kept themselves pretty much to themselves, but they've been ever so kind to me since the story broke in the press and they realised it was *my* Tony. Yes, they've been really kind. Had me in for a curry you know? Our church has said prayers. We pray for his deliverance from Satan for it is truly the work of Lucifer that has forced him to this."

Taylor tried to steer her back to the subject in hand.

36

"What about Tony...Grace?" The name still didn't come easily to his lips. "How do you feel now?"

"He's still my son. A mother is always a mother, no matter what. He's still my boy."

"Do you see him at all?"

"I visit when I can. That place he's in. It's corrupt, full of lost souls abandoned by God. It's pitiful. But if God can find it in his heart to forgive him, then who am I to question such Divine deliverance?"

"What about his victims?"

"It's terrible. I really feel for them, but they're with the Lord now."

"And Amy?" David Taylor watched her face closely. There wasn't a flicker, not a muscle stirred.

"Dear, sweet Amy, such a lovely girl. It's just a pity Tony didn't meet her sooner. None of this might ever had happened... come on eat your muffins before they get cold."

PC Taylor gave a half smile and forced a piece of muffin into his mouth. It was surprisingly delicious.

"What's that you've got there, Ronnie?"

Ronnie Soper jumped and flushed guiltily as the hand of the EWO came to rest on his shoulder.

"Nothing," he drawled. "I just found it."

"Yes, but where? And what is it?"

Ronnie sucked his breath in through his cheeks before replying.

"I went down there to take a leak," he gestured to a short alley, "and this package was on the concrete by the bins. The paper looked too new to be rubbish and the packet looked as if it hadn't been opened, so I picked it up for a butchers."

Julie Flemming extended her hand and reluctantly Ronnie gave her the parcel. His mind was racing – He was *nearly* in serious trouble. He soon would be, if she managed to take him to school. Similarly, as soon as she saw what was in the package.

That was a bit of quick thinking on his part saying he'd gone for a Jimmy Riddle.

"Go on Miss – open it, " he urged. "Maybe it's something valuable and we'll both be rich. Go on."

Julie Flemming was not taken in by this wide eyed, innocent act and refused to take her grip off the boy's shoulder. She handed the packet back to him.

"Tell you what, Ronnie. It's your treasure. *You* open it."

Ronnie frowned, for a minute he was flummoxed. *She* should have opened it there and then. He could have given her the slip. There were plenty of alleys into which he could disappear amongst the back to back houses of Ladywood. He started to pull back the paper, half revealing the transparent polythene wadding covering the canvas when another idea occurred to him.

"Look Miss," he called excitedly, "It must be something special. It's all protective wrapped."

He feverishly tore some more of the thick, stiff paper and made a pretence of clumsily losing his grasp as he struggled to hold on to it.

Julie Flemming's grip relaxed when he bent forward to retrieve the falling parcel. He felt her fingers only lightly touching him. He seized his opportunity. He streaked forward as if on starting blocks, down the alley, on top of the dustbins, over the wall and he was gone.

The Educational Welfare Officer blinked in frustration, grabbed the paper package and swore.

"Just wait Ronnie Soper – You haven't won yet."

She gazed curiously at the plastic wrapping and proceeded to remove it. She like Ronnie gasped when she saw the rolled up canvas.

The place for this was with the police. Julie Flemming walked briskly to her metallic grey Volvo and headed for Steelhouse Lane Police Station.

David Taylor was off duty. He'd handed in his report of his visit to Mrs Clifton realising he was going to have to call on her again if he was to gain her full confidence, but now he could put police work aside. He looked casual, but smart in his sage green cords and black sweatshirt. He winked at himself in his mirror, flipped his car keys in the air and ran down the stairs.

"See you later, mum. Be back around ten."

"Do you want me to keep you some dinner?"

"Yes please – not too much – I'll have it as supper."

David Taylor wasn't absolutely certain where he was going or what he was going to do but he found himself heading for the hospital to see how Judy was progressing. He hoped the flower seller would be at her usual pitch. Freesias. He was sure Judy would like Freesias.

Tony glowered at the plate of unappetising food in front of him and the little medicine cup containing his standard medication. He lifted his eyes and watched the faces and actions of the other patients who unquestioningly drank down potions or swallowed capsules doled out by men in white coats.

Even in the relatively short time he'd been incarcerated, he'd become familiar with some of the drugs prescribed. He was aware which were the most dangerous, the ones to avoid. Largactyl – George had said it was illegal, but Tony was sure one of the sedatives used to restrain or more appropriately, lobotomise the young boy in his ward, when the lad had gone beserk, was largactyl or something very similar. Tony had seen an injection transform storming anger into mindless, subdued, unnatural calm. Tony studied the boy now who rocked back-ward and forward as if to some nursery rhyme rhythm that had settled – never to leave – the prison of his mind.

Tony's big day was coming up. He would be meeting with the panel of psychologists that would be assessing him. They would be asking more questions and he would be told the date of his preliminary hearing where they would testify whether or not he was fit to stand trial or if further tests had to be completed.

Tony struggled to suppress the shout that threatened to burst from his lungs. He wanted to cry, he wanted to be held, he *wanted* his mother.

Perhaps if he were to see her...? No, that wouldn't work. Maybe, he could stage manage an outburst and call for her? Or... Maybe, he could play the psychologists at their own game? Maybe, he could call on his inner voices, the other side of him to help? Maybe, he could come to God like Jonah had to and then he would find respite...maybe...maybe.

Tony sat playing a game of chess with himself, adopting the Sicilian Defence and...he thought.

3

DREAMING IN METAPHORS

Holly wretched violently. Her hands clasped at the antique pine toilet seat as she knelt on the floor of the en-suite bathroom.

She wiped the dribbling, yellow spittle from her mouth with the back of her hand. Just as she thought the violent spasms were under control she doubled over once more and her diaphragm contracted involuntarily, forcing out a thin stream of vomit.

She coughed and sat back on her haunches, reached for the soft toilet tissue to clean her mouth, sighed and stood up. Her legs, still shaking, nearly gave way but she steadied herself by holding on to the sink which she filled with fresh, clean, cold water, splashing it over her face. Almost sure that she had finished being ill, she cleaned herself up and reached for the soft, plum towel on the rail and patted herself dry.

She peered at her complexion in the mirror. Her skin looked blotchy. She appeared unwell. Holly tried to quell the queasy sickness bubbling within and steadied herself on the wash basin.

Her head was throbbing. Voices and words came echoing back at her, a rising crescendo that faded and pulsed with the beat in her head.

It happened again. She reeled back as if pushed and sat back on the lavatory pan like a puppet whose limbs and nerves twitched spasmodically as if some greater force was pulling the strings.

She watched with the watcher.

The girl on the corner stood under the glare of the street lamp, inspecting her nails in the gloom. She cast a wary eye out for potential clients and the law.

The wind was starting to gust. It tried to separate the strands of her carefully coiffured, heavily lacquered hair but without success and the rain began to fall.

The girl hastened for the shelter of a doorway. An old sheet of newspaper caught by the wind blew along the road wrapping itself around her fishnet stocking clad legs. She hurriedly picked it off and watched as it scurried and tumbled down the road before catching on a lamp-post where it became too sodden to move and began to disintegrate in the ever increasing rain.

The heavy make up hid a naturally pretty face, the clothes matured a young budding body. This one was ripe. This one had strayed. This one deserved punishment.

A hiss of anger erupted from Holly as she watched the girl run from the shelter of her doorway to a kerb-crawling motorist who had halted, but kept his motor running.

The electric window purred down. She heard the driver ask, "Are you in business?"

The girl acknowledged.

"How much do you charge?"

There ensued a wrangled bartering over a price and what services it bought. The door opened and the child prostitute climbed in, pulled the door shut and the car drove off.

No matter! She'd be back. The car would return her to her pitch. A small wait was in store. That was all.

The time would come for punishment. It was fast approaching. She would reach her nemesis.

The glory of rain, the wonder of the night, cloaking the deeds and activities of retribution in Divine secrecy. No-one to see, no -one to watch – but wait! Eyes *were* watching, eyes were seeing.

Holly shivered and looked around with surrogate eyes – just another call girl, interested in her own tricks. Yes, it was safe. It *was* safe.

Holly fainted and cracked her head on the window sill. The slide into unconsciousness was complete.

Mrs Clifton sang lustily as she gathered a few things together. She was visiting Tony today.

It was an important day for him. His hearing was in the afternoon. She would see clearly the evidence stockpiled against him. She would know what to do.

In her view, Sandra Thornton's evidence would be the most damning but Sandra Thornton had not been accessible; obtaining her address had been relatively easy, not so finding a way through to her, but she was working on it.

Sandra Thornton was the only living person who could identify Tony.

Forensic evidence linked him to the murders but with a little careful planning, doubt could be cast on his guilt.

Mrs Clifton had watched with growing interest the number of cases of miscarriages of justice where innocent people had been imprisoned on manufactured evidence, or freed on a technicality. She had been to the library and had researched her subject well.

She tugged on her church bazaar hat, wrapped her Isadora scarf around her neck, pulled on her drab coat and armed herself with her roomy shopping bag containing all she needed and prepared to leave for town.

It would be quite a walk to the bottom of Hill Street and the bus that would take her to the outskirts of town and Tony.

But first Mrs Clifton went to her hand carved wooden box and took out a tiny scroll. It read,

> 'And then thou shalt be secure, because
> there is hope; yea, thou shalt dig *about*
> *thee* and thou shalt be at thy rest in
> safety.

Job Chapter 11 verse 18.

Feeling righteousness on her side, a triumphant gleam came into her hooded snake eyes. She closed the door with a satisfying clunk and made her way along the dusty street to the bus stop to wait.

She was unswerving in her devotion to Tony, she must at all costs have him back. With this as her greatest motivator, safe from rejection, her main rival for Tony's affections now gone, her single mindedness showed in her unblinking stare. She barely acknowledged the hushed 'good morning' of her neighbours, Harpal Kaur and Lehmber Singh. She avoided conversation with Junior Walters, a member of the Gospel Choir from her church, but her scheming thoughts trapped in the narrow corridors of her mind purposely led her forth like Moses and the children of Israel.

The throaty rumble of the bus assaulted her ears and she climbed aboard the dust warm vehicle that belched out its diesel fumes into the roadside injecting the litter with ghostly life on the graveyard streets.

She sat on a window seat over the wheel feeling comfort in the vibrating hum that travelled up her feet and spread through her body.

She furtively replaced her bus pass in her decrepit purse. Its crocodile jaws clasp, shut with a snap. She patted her bag and settled herself for the journey watching the idiosyncrasies of the people on the pavements going in and out of the shops. A dog weaved its way through the crowds stopping on the sawdust laden step of a butchers before being shooed away. These and other images played before her eyes until the movements became a blur.

Mrs Clifton thought, plotted and planned, and although her face appeared to scan the roads outside, it was as if she was blind, deaf and dumb to all activity surrounding her, on and off the bus.

Julie Flemming found herself being ushered into DCI Allison's office and asked to sit down.

He examined the seemingly old and valuable canvas in front of him and listened carefully while she explained, yet once more, how it had come to be in her possession.

DCI Greg Allison grunted when she had finished,

"So, do you believe the lad? Did he find it as innocently as he pretended or is there more to it?"

"Knowing Ronnie, there's a lot more to it than that. Certainly it didn't *seem* as if he'd opened the package, but he's a fly one, a little bit of an entrepreneur. I'm surprised he's not already known to you."

"He may be. I've sent down to Juvenile for any records. We'll need to talk to him to show us exactly where it was found."

"You'll be lucky. He's never home! His mum drinks and his dad works away. Does something on the rigs – I think – Aberdeen. I've been trying to catch up with Ronnie and get him to school for the best part of a year. He was fine until his brother died – solvents," she explained, "He sniffed Butane gas. The first time too – pressured into it by his peers. He was unlucky – dead on arrival at the hospital. The family haven't got over it."

Allison inclined his head sympathetically

"His mum spiralled into the depths of despair and tried to find solace in the bottom of a bottle. dad couldn't cope with his own grief and took a job away and Ronnie.... Ronnie was very close to his brother, Tim. He just went off the rails. A pity, he's a bright boy."

Allison listened carefully. There were a number of youngsters like that, who through no fault of their own suddenly messed up. He felt sorry for this waif but he knew he had to talk to him..and talk tough.

"When am I most likely to catch him in?"

"He comes home to sleep...some nights. I should imagine you'd have more luck on a Sunday morning.

He knows I don't work Sundays," she added wryly.

Is there anywhere else he's known to frequent?"

"His Gran's...and I've caught him a few times hanging around Auchinleck Square... Also, he has a friend, older than himself, works in the jewellry quarter. I remember him telling me about this chap back in the days when he trusted me and I had his confidence. He doesn't seem to trust anyone anymore... sad little chap. But...." she sighed heavily, "He's a survivor. The

Ronnies of this world will always get by somehow. This one does... lives on his wits."

"Hmm!"

Allison stood up and extended his hand,

"Thank you for giving up your time. You were right in thinking that this painting could be a valuable item. We have your details if we need to contact you again."

Julie Flemming shook his hand warmly and left the office. She still had a couple of home visits to do before her work was done. That and a call to Social Services. It was time Ronnie's name was put forward for a case conference and possible inclusion on the child protection register. His home circumstances were unsatisfactory and maybe a visit from a social worker with offers of family consultancy could help them all come to terms with Tim's death and bring them back together as a unit.

He would have been picked up sooner and counselling would have been initiated for the whole family if there hadn't been a change of personnel at the area office in Birmingham

As soon as Julie Flemming left, Allison picked up the phone.

"Get word to Brand wherever he is – tell him to report ASAP. I think he'll find what I have here interesting – very interesting indeed."

He replaced the receiver, opened his desk drawer and reached for his Mars Bar. Thoughtfully, he removed the wrapper. As he bit into the melting sweetness he picked up a file from his overflowing in-tray and flicked through the notes. A crumb of chocolate escaped his mouth and caught on his chin. He tried hard to retrieve it with his tongue – without success, and resorted to using his fingertips which he licked with relish.

Feeling a sense of peace and satisfaction he was more able to concentrate on the files and notes in hand.

Mark Stringer rapped on the door.

"Enter." Allison looked up at his young sergeant. "Ah Mark-Look at this." He gestured to the crumbling canvas on his desk.

Mark whistled low and hard, "Looks valuable."

"Looks valuable – but is it?"

"Search me," muttered Mark.

"I'm no expert but isn't this the type of painting that is being passed off as genuine? Part of the antique fraud that started in Kidderminster. That Brand is working on?"

"I wouldn't know – Looks real enough to me. "

"Me too – I'm just guessing. P'raps it's not fake. P'raps it's the genuine article. I've left word for Brand to call. Either way, it's his baby. *Either way*, we need to talk to a young lad – name of Ronnie Soper. Juvenile's checking on him now. Name mean anything to you?"

"Soper...Soper?" Mark shook his head thoughtfully. "I've not come across him – But that doesn't mean anything. Rarely have dealings with juveniles. How old is the lad?"

"Fourteen."

"Mmm. No – don't think so. Changing the subject, has anything come through on Dan yet?"

"Not to my knowledge..."

"Want me to check?"

"Give Hurst a ring – Get the reports to me."

"Right."

Allison stared again at the apparently ancient canvas. He just wasn't experienced enough to make any sort of assessment on its worth. All he had was a gut feeling that it was in some way connected to the multi million pound fraud that had been rumbled by the West Midlands Police, but he'd need to have that confirmed.

David Taylor sat opposite Judy in the television lounge adjacent to the ward.

"So... How are you doing?" he asked shyly.

"Fine," came the automatic response. She continued, "Why do we always say that? Even if you're ill – someone asks, 'How are you?' and the immediate answer is – OK." Her green eyed, steady gaze held him, "To tell the truth – I'm scared. I don't know what's going to happen or what to expect."

"Aren't you working with one of the psychologists – to try

and help you remember?"

"A mind doctor?...Yes of sorts. Actually she's quite pleasant – a Dr Mills... Rebecca Mills. She's being very patient with me but if I don't start remembering pretty soon – we're going to try hypnosis – see if that will work."

"TV and press are going to help."

"In what way?"

"Print your photograph – show it on TV. Anybody who knows this woman etc etc...See if that will trigger someone's memory – see if anyone knows you in this part of the world."

"Yes, but what if someone does and it's *not* good news. I'm not sure I want to know. What if I'm not a good person, not who I would like to be and what if my past is something awful?"

"Well if it is, you're not known to us. Your photo has been faxed from county to county and with your permission your fingerprints have been checked. So, if it's any consolation you haven't got a criminal record."

"What's next? Dental records?"

"It's a possibility. I hadn't thought of that."

They both eased into a comfortable silence. David Taylor examined the face before him, the huge green eyes, smattering of freckles, raven dark hair with burnished lights and he liked what he saw.

"How much longer will you be here?"

"Not long at all. Only another day or two. There's no reason to keep me in. I can attend Dr Mills' clinic without remaining here. She's already said that Social Services will help me to find some sort of accommodation – anything will do until I can discover my past." Judy returned David's steady gaze.

"David, I'm frightened."

He reached out and took her hand. A trembling prickle of electricity flowed between them.

PC David Taylor gave a comforting half smile.

"It'll be all right. I'm sure it will. Here.." and he passed her the small bouquet of flowers that he'd purchased before the visit.

"Freesias!" She smelt them appreciatively, "My favourite," then she stopped and laughed, "Don't ask me how I know... It's just one of those things."

David Taylor squeezed her hand.

"Treat it as a voyage of discovery. You know you approve of the name Judy; you've found out that you like freesias. They're just little things but the more you find out, the better picture the psychologist will have and the more likely you are to discover your past."

"I suppose that's true. I've been finding out all sorts of things – some of which are really quite pleasing."

"Like what?"

"I can play the guitar!" she smiled, "Not brilliantly – but I know which finger goes where and I can strum a few tunes. A woman in the end bed had a Suzuki, nylon string, classical guitar – I picked it up and started to play. "

"Suzuki? I thought they made motor bikes! Tell me, do you sing as well?"

"A bit – It seems I must have been a Helen Reddy fan."

"Don't think I know any of hers."

"You must do – *Angie Baby* – it's a classic – *Woman, Delta Dawn* and so on."

"I'll have to listen out for them."

"Do that – she's good."

There was a shy pause before David launched off again.

"Any other talents I should know about?"

"I can draw – at least – it seems I'm quite good with a pencil. Look."

She passed him a little sketch pad that she had been carrying.

David opened the pad and saw a sketch that was an excellent likeness of Rebecca Mills. The pencil shading gave those grey eyes life and knowledge.

"Hey, that really is good." He turned the page and saw a hospital vase filled with daffodils.

Judy tried to stop him before he turned to the third page.

"What's the matter?"

"It's just...." she shrugged and blushed. David turned over to see a startlingly accurate portrait of himself. Judy cast her eyes down. David whispered gently,

"I'm flattered. It's good, really good.'

"I did it from memory – my rescuer – my knight of the road." The words rushed from her in an embarrassed fluster.

David Taylor smiled, "I'm glad you think so – then.... you won't mind me visiting you again?"

"I'd like that, she replied.

"Well, you had better take my phone number." He hastily scribbled it onto a scrap of paper from his notebook and placed it in the back of her pad. "Just in case they move you out... Let me know so I'll know where to find you." PC Taylor stood up and took both her hands, "Take care until I see you again."

He gazed deep into those incredible green eyes before moving out of the lounge, through the corridor and from her sight.

Judy watched him leave with more than a little sadness. She glanced at her pad again. She could do much better than that. She set to with her pencil trying to capture the expression of tenderness, she hoped she had interpreted correctly, that she had seen on David Taylor's face.

4

DON'T CRY

Mrs Clifton sat opposite her son who was fighting to control his emotions. He longed for those pudgy hands dry as parchment to hold him, comfort him and tell him that all would be well. She patted his hand,
"At the beginning of thy supplications
the commandment came forth,and I
am come to shew *thee*; for thou *art*
greatly beloved: therefore understand
the matter, and consider the vision.
Daniel chapter nine
verse twenty three."

She reached into that roomy, canvas bag with her gloved hand and took out a rosary.

"Take it, kiss it and say a prayer with me. Come on." Her thin reedy tones became more fevered as she uttered, "O Lord hear; O Lord forgive; O Lord hearken and do; defer not for thine own sake, but grant us your blessed favour to finish the transgression and make an end to sins. Make reconciliation for iniquity and bring in everlasting righteousness. Bring your chosen one home to me. Amen."

Tony clasped the crucifix and kissed it; a solitary tear splashed on the floor.

"There now, return the cross to mother. I shall light a candle before it when I go home and keep it burning by night and day until our prayers are answered."

Tony meekly dropped the rosary into the bag, where it landed on the soft polythene covering which protected the other necessary items.

51

"Here," she took a small ornament from her pocket. "Remember these?"

He nodded silently, as he recognised the small tabby cat that was one of a pair.

"One for you and one for me, " she went on, "Kiss it and then we'll swap. I'll have yours and you keep mine until we're together again. And we will be." She narrowed her eyes and Tony returned his cat to the bag which she held open. He closeted the cat she gave him, cradling it in his hands.

"Mum, will you be there at the hearing?"

"I'll be there. You don't think I'd let you suffer that alone, do you?"

"Will Amy be there?"

"Amy?" She said more sharply than she intended.

"Yes, she said she'd be there for me. In her last letter, she said she'd be there with you."

"You'd better forget about Amy. She's not for you."

"What do you mean?"

"Oh she's sweet, she cares but is that enough? Does she understand? Can she help you, cleanse you as I can?"

"Mum, Amy has understood me more than anyone."

"More than me?" She rasped jealously.

"No, no that's not what I mean."

"What *do* you mean?" she questioned.

"She's kind, mum. She tries to help. She keeps in touch and has promised to visit."

"But she's not been yet? And I bet she won't"

"I can't believe that."

"I don't think you'll see her again. Mark my words."

"Mum, I wish you wouldn't." His head was starting to pound. Her reedy whine was beginning to penetrate his ears and grate on his nerves. He wanted her to shut up. He wanted to *shut* her up. He was losing control. If he wasn't careful they'd be upon him, restraining him, quietening him, sedating him, stealing his will. He lifted his eyes heavenward and whispered, "Oh God."

"That's right, trust in the Lord. Let Him be your guide and strength," uttered Mrs Clifton fervently.

"Please mum," he begged. " Leave me be."

"I don't know what's the matter with you. What are you rolling your eyes for? " Her voice began to rise becoming more strident. "Tony, you're not listening. *Tony* !" Mrs Clifton's agitation was apparent.

Tony appeared to blank his mother out. He was becoming confused, angry and...dangerous. His chair scraped backwards as he leapt up. His hands clenched tightly at his side. The twist of his mouth showed pain and hatred.

His mother hissed, "Remember St Mark, chapter twelve verse twenty-four." Her tone altered, becoming more reverent as she continued,

"And Jesus answering said unto them, Do you not therefore err, because ye know not the Scriptures, neither the power of God?"

A low rumbling roar began deep in Tony's throat, softly at first, gradually building up to a terrifying howl like a demented demon denied the right to destroy.

A nurse moved quickly to Tony's side, talking slowly, calmly. He nodded at Mrs Clifton,

"I think you'd better go... *Now.*"

Grace Clifton furrowed her beetle black brows and grabbed her bag. She hurriedly pulled her coat around her and muttered disconsolately to the second nurse that was coming across the ward to help.

"I was only saying a prayer for him and he went all strange. I just mentioned the Lord, that's all. It's too much for him, all this. It's too much for my Tony." She reached down and retrieved the small cat ornament that had dropped to the floor when Tony had risen.

The second nurse began ushering her to the end of the ward. She went reluctantly, protesting her concern and called back to her son.

"Don't you go worrying now. Trust in the Lord. Trust in me."

Her voice reciting the Scriptures could be heard as she left the ward and walked down the corridor.

Tony began to sob.

Ronnie Soper looked furtively around him. He had no intention of being collared by Julie Flemming, nor the cops. That was definitely not on his agenda this morning.

Things had been difficult since he'd given her the slip. The fuzz had been round to his house. His mother had become all concerned, wanting to do the right thing. It was becoming increasingly difficult to operate. Ronnie was worried he might have to return to school and he just wasn't ready for that yet.

He decided to pay a call on Fred to have a chat. It would give him something to do. Surely the police wouldn't find him there. He set off in the direction of Hockley taking good care to keep a low profile, ducking in and out of the back streets travelling through back yards, darting in the doorways of the numerous discount clothing outlets until he arrived at Fred's place.

He was about to breeze in when he heard raised angry voices. Ronnie slipped into the shadows and positioned himself quietly where he could hear, but not be seen.

"Come on, Freddy boy. Give. A fancy leather like that, how did you come by it? Tempted were you? What else did you take?" The chilling voice was full of menace.

Ronnie could see a thick set man who had grown stocky with years of weight training and steroids.

Fred was starting to babble. His nose was broken and blood drenched the front of his sweatshirt.

"Look guys.. I told you..ain't nothin' to do with me. "

"Tell us again. I don't think I heard right the first time. And if I don't like what I hear I'll let you know," said a man whose voice, Ronnie thought, resembled that of a rattle snake.

The alarm in Fred was clear for all to see. He started rambling with such bluster and fluster Ronnie thought that he was going to pee his pants.

"I told you. I bought it. I did a kid a favour. Part payment, he gave me this coat cheap."

"How old, this kid?"

"About fourteen."

"Don't pull my pisser!" The rattlesnake voiced man spluttered and he brought his knee up sharply straight into Fred's crotch.

Fred yelped in agony and doubled over.

"I don't like that answer. You telling me a fourteen year old is capable of this sort of caper?"

Fred wretched and started to spew up the contents of his stomach. The other man with an oily, sadistic manner whom Ronnie christened 'Rats', moved hastily out of the way and muttered sneeringly,

"Aw! Did it hurt? Did it hurt then? Diddums. Is Freddy boy uncomfortable now?"

"Uncomfortable?" said Rattlesnake, " He'll be singing in a different key by the time I've finished with him," There was the swish of a stiletto blade as it swiftly left its sheath. Rattlesnake toyed with the sharpness of the blade before pressing it against Fred's throat.

"In fact, if he don't tell us what we want to know he won't just sing a little higher... he may not sing at all."

Ronnie pressed himself back against the alley wall and listened closely.

"Where's the painting, Fred?"

"And the money?"

"What about the numbers?"

Fred coughed, his voice little more than a hoarse whisper, "I don't know what you're talking about, honest. All I did was buy a coat."

"Yeh, yeh. And my name's Charlie Brown and this is a Snoopy movie. Get real. We want the name of this kid. Where he lives. Talk and talk fast."

"I don't know his name. If I did, I'd tell you. I would," he gurgled in desperation.

Rats smiled and pressed the blade a fraction deeper drawing fresh red, blood.

"Look at that! He bleeds. He's mortal after all."

"Yeh! Think he'd be more careful; 'bout his friends I mean," added Rattlesnake.

"Yeh, especially as he won't have them for much longer."

"What do you mean?" asked Fred urgently.

"Well, if you won't tell us, then you leave us no choice. We can't have you blabbing to the police, now. Can we?" Rattlesnake continued.

"I won't tell, I promise. I won't say a word. If the lad comes round, I'll call you. I will."

"Sure, you won't tell. Cos you won't be there," spat Rats.

"No! Please don't do this, please....PLEASE!" Fred's last word was an agonised shriek as the knife slipped into the thin flesh on Fred's neck.There was little resistance.

Ronnie didn't wait to hear anymore.

He fled.

Tony stood meekly in the dock listening to the evidence that was offered against him.

The court stenographer's fingers nimbly transcribed the proceedings, an artist from the national press sketched likenesses of the main players in this drama and reporters rustled note pads as they jotted down words and reactions.

The forensic findings were conclusive – DNA fingerprinting, Flotex fibres, claret shoe polish stains, Amy's statements and the testimony of Sandra Thornton who was prepared to take the witness stand.

Much of what was said floated in and around Tony's brain as he searched the gallery in Birmingham crown court for a glimpse of his beloved Amy. All he saw was his mother listening and watching anxiously, scribbling notes in a little book at intermittent periods.

Counsel for the defence requested that the reports commissioned from eminent psychologists be brought before the court.

The judge settled back to listen to the conflicting views of Colin Brady and Rebecca Mills against those of James Bingham and Jeff Daniels.

The court was left to make up its own mind. The hearing was adjourned to give time to consider the evidence.

Tony was led away amid a flurry of movement from press and the rest of the court.

Mrs Clifton had what she needed. It didn't matter now whether Tony was condemned to stand trial or not.

Tony's mother would risk anything for Tony even her own life.

Allison sat at his desk grimly stirring his tea. It had been one hell of a day.

The local police in Handsworth had pulled in a fifteen year old for the racially motivated stabbing.

What was society coming to?

Juvenile and CID were in interview room three. He had Colin Booth from the press breathing down his neck, parents with solicitors clamouring for the fifteen year old's rights. No-one seemed to be clamouring for the dead man; cut down at the age of twenty-four just because of the colour of his skin.

The PM report had arrived on Dan. There was nothing accidental about his death. He'd been shot.

Allison had just returned from the scene of a crime in the jewellry quarter at Hockley where twenty two year old Fred Wells had been brutally hacked to death and mutilated in a particularly horrible way, the details of which were not to be made public.

The police had been tipped off by a phone call alerting them to a serious assault taking place on Mr Wells' premises. Serious! He was dead when the police arrived. The killer or killers must have escaped only minutes earlier.

Allison had heard the recorded tape of the nine, nine, nine call. The voice was young – could have been a boy or a girl – it was difficult to tell, but it was definitely someone who could help them with their inquiries.

Allison was going to have to appeal for help from the general public. He made the decision that someone must know the voice. The tape would be played on the television, radio, maybe even a phone line.

Greg cursed silently – he was supposed to be going out to dinner tonight with Mary. He was already late. He knew what problems that would cause at home. There was nothing for it. He had to leave all of this behind for his already overloaded staff.

Annoyingly, he still held the canvas. Brand hadn't yet been in to examine it and advise whether or not it was genuine.

Holly had her arms around Paul's neck and was enjoying a tender moment when it hit her.

Her stomach felt as if it had been struck with a baseball bat. She let him go and was flung back with a supernatural force that pushed her to the floor.

Paul instantly picked her up and carried her to the settee.

Holly was winded and dazed but it didn't end there. She *watched* again.

Paul looked on helplessly as he saw her vision cloud over, and clear. Her rapidly moving eyes appeared to be observing some intense scene as if she was looking out of the window of an express train or following the action of a high speed car chase on film.

When Holly was like this there was nothing he could do to help. He could only wait until it was over.

The pretty child prostitute was back at her pitch. The street was almost deserted. She knew she had little competition in this wild and windy weather. There was more rain on the way. She could hardly believe that there was anything left to fall out of the sky. The sea must have dropped at least ten inches! Those were her naive feelings at ten-fifteen that night.

One more trick. Just one more then she'd head home to her seedy little bed-sit in Moseley. But not for long. Jay had promised her. Jay had said that the good times would come. A luxury flat in the best part of Birmingham, glamorous modelling assignments, and even a part in a film, all that was within her reach he had told her.

A single tear, laden with hope travelled down her cheek as the chill wind caught her eye. She brushed away the black streak of mascara before it had chance to stain and form panda eyes.

The gusts stabbed through her like knives, lacerating her hands blue. She shivered in the increasing cold under the street lamp on the corner. The crystal stars iced down from heaven's tarmac. The moon's silver shards wedged through the trees and alleys, pooling the puddles to a glacier mint brittleness and the new leaves on the trees to frosted glass. She almost felt she could hear them tinkle as they brushed together in the ever sharpening cold.

The young girl gazed up, mesmerised by the clarity of the star formations. It would freeze tonight. She sighed heavily and minced her way over to a doorway. No sense in parading around when no punters were about. She would retreat from the needle fingers of wind that tried to prise off her jacket and lift her skirt.

Standing back in the relative shelter from the prodding breezes she caught a movement across the street. Emerging from the shadows was a small squat lump that blobbed onto the road. A woollen tea cosy hat was pulled down over its head, a tired and faded coat worn too tight with buttons ready to burst prowed its way forward like some out dated battleship ready for the fray.

The young girl jumped nervously and then laughed, her giggle taken away on another rush of wind.

It looked like a bag lady. Nothing to be frightened of unless she was a loony. But Anna, the young girl, was frightened. She couldn't explain it. A twisting spiral of fear circled inside her. She tried to suppress it, but the feeling wouldn't go away.

The woman was drawing nearer now and Anna could see

dark eyes that glared out from a ghastly pale complexion that seemed from another world. The child prostitute made up her mind there and then as the figure loomed closer, that the street was not the place for her tonight.

No more tricks for Anna tonight! Never mind what Jay would say. She was off!

Anna started for the pavement. The woman was moving quite swiftly now. There was less of a slithering gait about her and Anna could see thin pale lips that dribbled a trail of spittle which hung on her chin.

"Wait!" shrilled the reedy tones. "Don't go."

Anna hesitated fractionally. It was enough.

"You didn't ought to be out so late on the streets, a pretty girl like you. You never know who's about."

Anna felt compelled to answer, "Oh, I'm all right. Don't worry about me."

"It's not nice, this area. Bad things happen here. I've seen them."

"What do you mean?'

"Things you needn't concern yourself with. All you need know is, it's not safe. Now, get yourself home. Your mum will be worried."

The thoughtful words seemed out of place on those stark lips hiding yellowing teeth. Anna looked harder at the black beetling brows that shaded those slit, snake like eyes. The woman reminded Anna of something, something she had seen on one of those wild life programmes presented by David Attenborough. Anna struggled to think what it was.

The nasal whine grew stronger as the wind began to groan through the alleys sending the pages of yesterday's newspapers racing and tumbling around the corner.

"Hearken unto the words of Micah, chapter two, verse ten. Listen and repent:

Arise ye, and depart; for this is
not your rest: because it is
polluted, it shall destroy you,
even with a sore destruction."

Anna froze as the words of the Scriptures rained upon her ears.

" In Hosea it is said:

Let her therefore put away her
whoredoms out of her sight,
and her adulteries from between
her breasts...And I will not have
mercy upon her children; for they
be the children of whoredoms."

"Shut up you stupid old bat! You're scaring me."

But the voice ranted on,

"For their mother hath played the harlot..."

"I said, **SHUT UP!**" screamed Anna as she tried to pass this loathsome toad of a woman that was blocking her path. That was it! A toad or some other hideous reptilian creature for which Anna still had to find a name.

Mrs Clifton's body was a perfect barrier, eclipsing the light from the lamp, filling the doorway with her grotesqueness. Preventing the girl from leaving.

"Out of my way!" shrieked Anna, praying that someone would deliver her from this evil hob-goblin. It was strange, when Anna had struggled for a comparison there were none that came readily to mind, now a score of comparisons cascaded through her brain in the time it took to snatch a panicked breath.

Holly's eyes focused. She let out an anguished cry of terror as she felt the pain.

The knife appeared from the depths of a pocket and slashed viciously, unrelentingly; ripping, tearing, destroying. Anna slumped to the granite path with its diamond bright sparkles dulled by the blood which flowed, mixed and twined like a coiling serpent with the muddy water of a puddle.

Mrs Clifton forced the girl's face into the paving slabs threw back the lacquered hair and deftly cut a sliver of flesh in the shape of a cross from the nape of Anna's neck saying,

"And now I will cover her lewdness in
the sight of her lovers, and none shall
deliver her out of mine hand."

Anna's chest ceased to rise and fall as the blade twisted and pierced the heart.

Mrs Clifton clasped the dead girl's fingers carefully around the beads of the rosary that had been brought for that purpose making it look as if Anna had wrested it from some assailant.

Mrs Clifton scuttled away into the ever increasing darkness that had befriended all her deeds.

Holly had begun to froth at the mouth and gurgle.

Paul couldn't bear to see her so tormented and pulled her limp form to him. She became rigid and pushed him away before gorging herself on air.

Paul studied her face. These *happenings* as Holly chose to call them were draining her soul. Her eyes were ringed by dark shadows and she was losing weight.

Paul rang Colin Brady.

5

BRING IT ON

"Your hunch was right," confirmed Brand as he sat facing DCI Allison, the canvas on the desk between them. "We're looking for a clever band of fraudsters who are duping innocent people along the way."

He pointed at the picture in front of him. "The canvas would have to be carbon tested in order to get a true reading of its age and that's what this band rely on."

"What do you mean?"

"They rely on dealers and so on, not to test. Mind you the forgeries have to be pretty damn good. They're constantly changing their methods and approach to the market. That's what makes them so difficult to track down."

"So," asked Allison, "Is this genuine or not?"

"Hard to tell, without experts examining it. It could be. If not, then the work has been subjected to *craquelure* or *cracklin* as the English call it."

"What's that?" puzzled Allison in his gruff tones, miffed that he was so ignorant of artistic terms.

"It's that cracked, crazy-paving effect you see on the glaze of china and on the surface of old paintings. Forgers try all sorts of tricks to age pictures." Brand launched into further detail. "They put them near heat to crack the paint, rub the tops with dirt, wipe on turpentine and scrape it over unclean surfaces and varnish it. Very effective to the untrained eye. Certainly, if there is no suspicion of it being a fake then it's not likely to be tested. Carbon testing can sometimes damage the painting."

"So, what's so clever about these fraudsters?"

"For starters, they are obviously using a very accomplished, talented artist or artists who can effectively reproduce the style of some of the great painters, and the equally valuable lesser known talents. The art work is aged. Sometimes in the manner I've described, sometimes by painting over really old canvases that are not worth much, even working on a canvas twice, removing the to layer to reveal, low and behold, a hitherto unseen work by a particular artist!"

Allison gave a low whistle, " So, with the artificial aging on a piece like that, the canvas could possibly be the right sort of age which would make the forgery more difficult to detect."

"Right!" said Brand.

"They must need some fair size studio to do all this?"

"One would think so, but there again maybe not. It doesn't take a lot of room to stack pictures. **But**, if we did find their workshop, we'd be part way there. The trouble is that this network is working both here and abroad. They're a cunning lot."

"They sound it," agreed Allison, somewhat dazed by the intricacies of the organisation.

"Not only that," went on Brand," What is so ingenious is how these items are finding their way on to the market."

"Refresh my memory. I need updating on the details as I've not been handling this case."

"They are constantly changing their approach. Copies have been made of masterpieces and switched, but not often discovered until the artwork is sold or auctioned on the commercial market."

"So, in other words, there could still be undiscovered forgeries in private collections or even galleries?'

"Right! If they do a gallery or museum these buggers are so tidy, the break-in is sometimes not discovered or if it is, it's too late and the trail has gone stone cold."

"But how do they sell the articles on?" asked Allison trying to clarify the details in his own mind.

"There are a number of private collectors both here and abroad who would pay dearly for such treasures, purely for their own pleasure and just deny them from the rest of the world. It's iniquitous!" Brand obviously felt passionately about this case. He had been working on it for nearly a year.

There was a tap on the door and Stringer entered.

"Sorry to interrupt Chief-I've just been talking to Dan's missus. It seems he had a fair bit of cash the last few months. He was cagey about his dealings but had mentioned something to do with art."

Both Brand and Allison raised their eyebrows and looked at each other. Mark continued,

"He was frightened. Running scared, his missus said, since last week. He'd stumbled on to something he shouldn't. Told Alice he'd have to disappear for a while. But what's even more interesting, a brown package with five thousand quid was sent to Alice this morning."

"Alice?" queried Brand.

"Alice Fletcher, Dan's wife." replied Mark, "She wants to know if she can keep it. Reckon it's blood money? asked Stringer.

"You can be sure of that," growled Allison, "Go on."

"Well, I've taken an initial statement, told her to think carefully and *anything* that she remembers to write it down and give us a call."

"Right! Get down to his local, speak to his cronies. See if you can pick up anything. Have a word with the landlord, Ken."

"Sir," Mark acknowledged, "What shall I tell her about the money?"

"No-one has reported it missing or stolen. It wasn't found. It was sent to her." He paused, "She'll need it – now Dan's gone – All we want is the packing envelope. It might give us some sort of clue."

"Already got it!" said Mark triumphantly, "Trouble is, it looks like any other brown paper wrapping."

"See if it matches the one which covered the canvas. I doubt if there'll be any prints. Too many people have handled it – But it's worth checking.'

"Sir." Mark nodded at the Chief and Brand, then left.

"Right. Now, where were we?" asked Allison, "I seem to remember I was having a lesson on artistic terms?"

Brand grinned, "Come on Chief! Don't send me up!"

"I'm not," protested Allison, "Truly, I'm listening. Go on."

"Well, it's the *way* the paintings are coming on to the market. Some are stolen or switched. There are other thefts I'm sure, yet to be discovered. Occasionally, the market offers a new as yet unseen work that has been hidden in a private collection or found beneath another painting or even totally new works created in the same style as a particular artist and produced on an old canvas. Even existing works are built into new ones."

"Surely, when the fraud is spotted it's a relatively simple matter to trace their origins."

"One would think so, but it's just not the case. If and when the forgeries come to light, investigations lead us down blind alleys and come to a full stop. The best break we've had on the case all year is the picture you've had handed in."

"Why is that?"

"Because if it is genuine and known – no-one has yet reported it missing. If it *is* a replica of an original then we may discover who was going to be hit next. We'll have to see."

"What do you think it is?" Allison gestured at the painting.

"It looks like an early Cézanne when he was indulging himself in a violent, sombre and theatrical kind of painting in which his sexual obsessions and distraught dreams figured,"

"Sounds like a day at the nick," interjected Allison. "Sorry," he added seeing Brand's expression.

"It's OK. But you can see what I mean. He painted weird, fantastic scenes with thick impasto, where sickly blues and livid whites slash the gloomy backgrounds."

"Looks a bit of a mess to me."

"That's exactly what Manet said of his work."

Allison's mouth gave a pleasing half twitch at the thought of sharing the opinion of a great artist.

"So, what next?" asked the Chief.

"I'll need to check this out first." He picked up the painting.

"Do some research. The little guy, Ronnie, whatever his name is will have to be pulled in. This picture could be a good lead. I'll take it to Maureen Holland. She knows her art. I'll get back to you."

"Keep me up to date...By the way what is impasto?"

Brand just chuckled and left taking the painting with him.

The blue strobe lights of police cars and an ambulance flickered in the rainy, wind-swept street. Distorted voices on radio reverberated through the night as the area was cordoned off. A camera flashed illuminating further the grisly scene.

Allison watched the eyes empty of life but still retaining their stark look of horror, being closed. The once vibrant body of Anna Sherbourne, slashed and bloodied was placed in a bag, zipped up and loaded onto a stretcher ready to board the waiting ambulance.

Allison stepped forward,

"Wait!"

The paramedics halted at his authoratitive, gravelly voice and replaced the stretcher onto the pavement. The chief lumbered forward. He undid the top of the bag revealing the child prostitute's head and shoulders.

Now that the eyes had been closed, the bloom of death gave praise to her prettiness. The heavy make-up and rouged cheeks seemed natural, almost glowing. It looked as if with one shake she would awake and open her eyes, except for the tell tale blood spots spattered on her face and hair.

Allison turned Anna's head to one side. It lolled easily with no resistance. He lifted her hair. There at the nape of her neck was the unmistakable shape of a cross.

"All right. You can take her away." The bag was re-zipped. The noise buzzed oddly in the haggard night.

As if in slow motion, the doors of the ambulance shut and hurtled off into the rain that had begun to sheet down, bouncing off the pavements with such force that the thickly congealing ocean of blood which had been Anna's bed began to dissolve and run in rivulets before joining the main tributary leading to the pulsing river of red that flowed with dirt, dust and litter from the pavement and into the gutter speeding towards the drain.

Allison carefully placed the crucifix and rosary prised from the dead girl's fingers into a plastic bag and sealed it ready for forensic.

Allison stood there for a moment puzzling. He had strange misgivings about this one. There was something too pat, too complete about this and the Calcutt killing. They were linked. That much was obvious but Allison felt convinced that these were more than the serial killings they appeared to be at first examination. He had a gut feeling that there was a far more devious mind at work than that of an opportunist psychotic or sociopath.

Greg Allison devoured his Mars Bar without his usual fervour and without the trappings of secrecy that he usually enjoyed. He needed to think. He needed time and his own company.

Ronnie Soper was petrified. Fred was dead. Ronnie's call to the cops had been too late to save his mate and he didn't know if Fred had fingered him before he croaked. All he knew was, that someone was looking for him. Not just the EWO and the cops, but two men, whose descriptions sounded remarkably like the two he had dubbed Rats and Rattlesnake. They had been nosing around his district. Ronnie was becoming distraught and was thinking seriously of returning to school. He felt he would have more chance of safety there even if the shit did hit the fan as far as his attendance was concerned.

He felt in his pocket and produced the bundle of notes, all in fifties and counted it. Two thousand. He hadn't been wrong. Not just petty cash. Too much money for him to be able to explain it away with any hope of being believed. Ronnie lifted the rug by his bed and using a screw driver he prised up a loose floor board reached for his biscuit tin of treasures and added the

money to his collection. He turned over the cards in his possession, Dale's Antiques, Morrises Mini Mart, Allure Flower shop
and Timbrels.

The cards meant nothing to him nor the telephone numbers
scribbled on a scrap of file paper. An Edgbaston number he
noted, by the exchange, 454 – 110 something. The last digit was
unclear where the paper had torn. It could have been anything
from a three, five, eight or nine to another zero. Ronnie decided
the best way of finding out would be to ring the various combi-
nations and see if the response shed any light on the mystery.

He replaced his treasure trove, covered his tracks and crept
down the stairs to the hall. His mother was slumped on the
kitchen table, an empty bottle of gin in front of her, her lipstick
smeared on one side of her face. He used to be so proud of her.
She had been really pretty, but now the alcohol was taking its
toll. Red thread veins spidered down her nose and across her
cheeks, her lips had a blue tinge under the artificial shimmer
pink and her skin had lost its healthy glow to be replaced by a
sallow look.

Ronnie's heart went out to her. He wanted her back as she
was, lively, vibrant and fun, not running to fat and half
comatose. Ronnie approached her. He stroked her soft fair hair.
She murmured quietly and turned her face to one side. He
kissed her gently on the cheek and whispered, "I love you
mum. What have we got to do to get through to you?"

She groaned and sleepily opened one eye, "Tim. Tim is that
you?" A faint note of hope crept into the gin raddled
voice,"Tim?" There was more urgency now.

"No, mum. It's Ronnie."

"Oh," she said with a hint of disappointment, "Ronnie." She
fell forward again and closed her eyes.

"Come on mum. Time for bed." Ronnie put his arm around
his mother's waist and placed her arm over his shoulder and
struggled to lift her. It was with difficulty he managed to haul
her up the stairs talking to her as one might a child, counting
each step as they went up. His mother giggled and flopped,

exhausted by her exertions, onto the bed. Ronnie removed her shoes and covered her over and fondly kissed her goodnight.

She opened her eyes and looked at him,

"You're a good boy, Ronnie. Do you know that? A good boy," and she fell into the snoring sleep of inebriates.

Ronnie leaned over and kissed her again.

"Night, mum." He choked hoarsely, a tear escaping from his eye. With a loud sniff he left her room and ran down the stairs to the telephone.

He inserted the code to mask his number, then dialled the number he had found, adding the missing digit. Not knowing what to expect or what to say, if anything. A voice answered. A smooth voice with a metallic bite on the hard consonants, a voice with a slightly sibilant 's' like the menacing hiss of a reptile. Ronnie would know it anywhere, Rattlesnake!

He slammed down the phone in a panic. He needed to think... but there were footsteps approaching his front door. He darted up the stairs to his bedroom and peered out from the unlit room trying to work out who had come calling. He could hear muffled voices and see the top of a head. There were no other clues. He waited trying to catch any whisper, any word, but to no avail.

His patience was eventually rewarded as their knocks were unanswered and the two men sauntered back down the drive and climbed into a parked Jaguar SJ6. It wasn't a police car and Ronnie didn't know the men. He kept quiet and stayed perfectly still.

Ronnie was a very frightened little boy.

Colin Brady sat in a soft easy chair that seemed almost to envelop him in comfort, and played with the rim of his wine glass. Marcelle was perched on the floor between his feet. She made soft mutterings,

"Give my shoulder a rub, Colin. Go on. You've got such strong hands and I'm really aching. You're the only one who can do any good.... Mmm!" She sighed contentedly as he drained his glass and left it on the small table to be replenished before setting to work, manipulating her shoulder with love and care, easing the knots of tension that had solidly risen to aggravate and nag at her.

Paul refilled Colin's glass before attending to his own.

"So what do you think?" Paul asked.

Colin continued to massage Marcelle's left shoulder with one hand and took a sip from his drink.

"It's good. German wine?" he questioned.

" No.. Italian. but that's not what I meant."

"I know." Colin acknowledged.

"Come on Colin, what are we going to do? How can we make them stop?"

"You mean apart from putting me to sleep?" asked Holly as she came in with a tray of nibbles."

"That's not quite what I meant, but since you've asked, it may be a solution."

"What do you mean?" enquired Holly.

"Well, your powers have accelerated since the accident?"

"We've already established that."

"But, you don't pick up on *any* disaster?"

"No. Just those who are close to me, family and friends and now this."

"There's the puzzle," said Colin. He picked up the Birmingham Evening Mail sitting on the coffee table. "Just look at the horror stories in our own local paper." He pointed at the items on the front page and began to read, "Fifteen year old youth arrested for fatal stabbing... Young mother mugged walking five year old to school... Joy riders kill two... " He glanced up from the paper, "None of these or any other violent crime made the psychic connection?"

"No." murmured Holly. "I can see where you're coming from. Why the others and none of these?"

"Exactly. There's plenty here to fuel a sensitive mind. Why then are you being selective?.... Who do you connect with?"

"I'm tuned in to Paul. Good and bad things affecting close friends and family, and these... happenings."

"Nothing else?"

"No."

"You're sure?" reiterated Colin tossing the paper aside.

"Positive. The serial killings... Nothing... now this."

"Let's go through it again. From the beginning."

Holly sighed and with Paul's prompting began to retell her experiences and the facts she had accumulated about the murders.

"Let's face it, the information you've got could only be held by the murderer him or herself. Or from a witness."

"What are you implying?"

"Nothing. I'm only emphasising, what you yourselves have already come to realise. The knowledge Holly has, puts herself as a suspect. That is, she would be if she didn't have such water tight alibis."

"That's ridiculous. If I was involved why would I say anything about the murders at all?"

"I know, I know. Just calm down. The only other thing your experiences do is point the finger of suspicion at someone close to you."

"Don't look at me," said Paul.

"I'm not, but you can see what I mean, can't you?"

"I'm not sure. What are you getting at?"

"Well, Holly only picks up on those close to her; family, friends and blood ties."

"Blood ties...that *is* family... what are you getting at?" queried Paul.

"You agree that it seems strange that with all the violent crime about, that she should tune in to the serial killings and now two more murders that appear to be in some way connected?" Colin stopped and stared hard at the face of his friend and then at Holly whose silence only served to express her own concerns. Finally, Holly spoke,

"Come on, Colin we've known each other long enough. Get to the point."

Colin took a deep breath, "How much do you know about your past?"

"Not a lot. Why?"

"You were adopted at the age of three. Right?"

"Right."

"I see where you're coming from," interrupted Marcelle more alert now that Colin had ceased the massage. "You think Holly is tuning in to real family members."

"That's absurd! I don't know any of them.... I don't remember anything... That must mean I'm related in some way ..to a killer. I don't believe it...I won't believe it."

"Like it or not it's a possibility and one that needs to be explored – if we are to find the truth."

Holly shook her head vehemently, "I've never been interested in my real parents. They didn't want me. They gave me away. My mother and father," she corrected herself, "My *adoptive* parents are the ones that nurtured me and loved me through childhood."

"Weren't you ever curious?" asked Marcelle.

"When I was about fifteen or sixteen, I went through a stage of wondering and then I decided against it after talking it through with my mum. I could see how desperately upset she was and I vowed then never to raise the subject again. That's it! End of subject."

"Don't you want to know?... Once and for all, why this is happening to you?" asked Paul.

"Not if it means delving into my past and upsetting those who love me most... I'll just have to put up with it," she said stubbornly.

"No-one is asking you to upset anyone, " pressured Colin. "All I ask is that you think about it. You don't have to get involved in anything legal. Let me regress you. I'm sure you'll have enough memories locked in your mind to be able to satisfy us as to the truth. What do you say?"

"I don't have to think about it," said Holly firmly. "I'm not prepared to do it. "

"Holly," said Paul pleadingly.

"NO! That's the end of it. NO! I don't want to hear another word." Holly gulped at her drink and went to the CD player and put on a Seal album. Soon the room echoed with the haunting, melodious voice singing 'A Prayer For The Dying'.

Colin looked hopelessly across at Paul, Holly's choice of music was strangely apt.

6

KISS FROM A ROSE

David Taylor couldn't believe what he was hearing.
"Are you sure?"

"There's no mistake. I'm sorry." Judy lowered her eyelashes and stared into her cup of coffee. The light and life had gone out of her eyes.

"I can't believe it," murmured David, obviously stunned by the news.

"It's true. Dr Milman told me...Maybe you'd rather not see me again."

"Don't be silly. It may not mean what you think." said David trying to ease Judy's pain.

"However you look at it, David, I've had a child. The medical evidence is there. Approximately three years ago I had a baby.. What makes it so awful is that I don't know in what circumstances, whether the child is alive or dead. If I conceived in or out of wedlock. I may be married for God's sake."

"I'm sure if you have a husband, we'd know about it. He'd be looking for you.." His tone softened, no-one could have loved you and just forgotten you... no-one."

The silence between them was filled with emotion, of things left unsaid, of yearnings and puzzlement and the tremulous fears of what it could mean.

"I've got no rights," stormed Judy angrily. "I'm not even a proper person. I know nothing about myself. Judy indeed!" she spat. "What frivolous stupidity! I could be a Gladys, a Jean or Penelope and I wouldn't know," she started to cry

David Taylor placed his arm around her and held her shuddering body convulsed with sobs.

"Don't cry, " he soothed, "Please, don't cry. It breaks my heart to see you like this." She turned her salt streaked face to his with those incredible green eyes spilling over with unshed tears and whispered, "Oh David."

He smoothed her hair away from her face with such tenderness that her heart welled with emotion and a lump rose in her throat.

David Taylor couldn't drag his gaze away from her sorrowful look and before he could help himself his lips met hers with a wild passion that had them both clinging together as if their very lives depended on it. Eventually Judy pulled away from him.

"I'm sorry."

"Don't be,"

"I've no right."

"You don't know that."

"No. And until I do I shouldn't get involved with anyone."

"Oh Judy," he sighed.

"Don't call me that." She rose from the settee in the small bedsit where she had been accommodated by the social services. " I think it's best if we don't see each other again."

"You can't mean that?" He said incredulously.

"It's for the best, " she sniffed, "Rebecca has made some headway with me. We've uncovered a lot about my personality. She's tried to regress me with hypnotism but either I'm not a good subject or I'm just not ready to learn the truth about myself yet."

"What are you trying to say?"

"I thought I was making myself quite clear. Until I discover the truth about myself I don't think we should see each other again."

David moved to interrupt her but she stilled him with her hand, "No, please let me finish. Rebecca feels that I come from somewhere in the South West. Don't ask me how she knows. Call it gut instinct or what you will but I think she's right. She's arranging for me to travel to Devon, to stay with friends of hers who run a boarding house. She's taking some time off to join me and I'm going to waitress for these people, visit various places around there in the hope that I might remember something or someone might remember me."

"You can't mean it."

"No matter what I'm feeling now I can't possibly become involved with anyone. All I can promise is to keep in touch and when I know anything, to tell you."

"Then can I believe you do feel something?"

Judy took his face in her hands and gazed at him hard, "What do you think?" she whispered and brushed her fingertips along the line of his jaw.

David Taylor exhaled deeply, "Can I have your address?"

Judy smiled wistfully and nodded, "I promise I'll be in touch... Promise."

David took her hands in his and tried hard to find the right words.

"I'll wait...I feel somehow that this was meant to be... I'll wait. Just keep your word."

Judy nodded and struggled to suppress the fresh tears that were threatening to rise and overflow. David Taylor put his arms around her and held her close until her breathing returned to normal.

"It's time we went in to see Clifton."growled Allison.

"Can you sort it?"

"I'll get right on to it, sir."

"Damn!"

"What?"

"Isn't it his hearing today or was it yesterday? Aren't Pooley and Taylor scheduled to give evidence? We may have to leave it until tomorrow. See what you can do," he ordered curtly.

"Sir," acknowledged Mark.

"Oh and Mark,"

"Sir?"

"Mary asked if you and Debbie were free for dinner Saturday week? Cally's home from university and we're having a bit of a get together. We'd like you both to come, if possible."

"I'm sure that'll be fine. I'll call Jean. See if she can babysit; check with Debs and get back to you. OK?"

Allison pursed his lips and nodded. He watched his young sergeant leave, before taking his Mars Bar from its resting place and opening Brand's reports and case notes on the antique fraud.

Allison read with interest of the deVere family, well respected, and owners of a vast collection of art treasures, who after renovations on their vast property had uncovered a cache of hitherto unseen and notable works of art.

Allison studied the list carefully. in the last eight years no fewer than ten works had been released on to the market, verified by experts. Four of these purported to be paintings that had been documented in the art world as existing, but of which no trace had been found. Three were brand new pieces, two were deemed to be preliminary sketches for recognised masterpieces. The last was a small marble sculpture that had yet to be authenticated, but already had the backing of three notable art experts.

Allison read on. The DeVeres were a wealthy family who appeared above suspicion. However Brand had singled out the daughter, Pamela, for closer investigation.

The Chief let out a long low whistle when he saw what, he felt to be, a simple preliminary sketch by Degas for 'Misfortunes of the City of Orléans', had fetched at auction. The sketch now accompanied another study for the same work and was hanging in the Louvre.

Brand was right. There was big money to be made at this game. Paintings and antiques were big business and clever fraud could go for years without being detected.

He pulled himself out of his chair and paused to survey the familiar scene outside. It was raining, again! The seasons seemed to be shifting and blending all into one. There didn't appear to be the sharp distinctions between winter and spring, and following months, as there had been when he was a child.

The phone rang disturbing the Chief's thoughts. He answered gruffly.

"Woodward here."

"Yes? What have you got?"

"Vencat's back."

"Are you sure?"

"I've seen him myself. He's lost his expensive dental work. No gold tooth at the front now, change of hairstyle but he still looks an evil little weasel. Received a tip off. Caught up with him in Malvern, at the theatre they've got there. He was visiting some actress on tour of a so called pre – West End play. Gave me the slip in Worcester, going past the race course and into the one way system. Thought he may be headed for Brum. If we've got the men, p'raps we could keep an eye out at some of his haunts. I'm on my way in. "

"Can't promise anything, we're short staffed as it is – with the projected cuts, the Super is disinclined to run up any overtime," complained Allison. "But I'll do what I can," he promised.

Allison replaced the receiver. Vencat! He hardly deemed it possible. Yes, there'd been sightings, but the Chief felt sure Vencat would have stayed clear of this country. It must be some fat deal to make him risk his neck by returning so soon. Greg Allison wondered what it was.

He sat for a moment allowing himself the luxury of a moment of reverie before returning to the notes in front of him.

Ronnie Soper sat in his bedroom and thought. Things were getting hot. Two men had been hanging around the neighbourhood watching his house and questions had been asked at his various hangouts. The police had been round and the EWO was on his trail.

One good thing had come from this mess. His mother had become so concerned over the steady flow of enquiries about Ronnie that she seemed to have lessened her drinking. That was good because she was showing concern and a return to her caring nature. It was bad because now he was having to answer questions, and Ronnie didn't have all the answers. Sooner or later he knew he would be hauled in by the cops or the unknown enemy would catch up with him. He didn't know what to do.

The doorbell rang.

Ronnie froze. Who was it this time?

He crept to his bedroom door and opened it just a shade and recognised the voice of Julie Flemming.

"Ah, Mrs Soper. I hope you don't mind...I saw the light in Ronnie's room and thought I may catch him in. Is it possible to have a word?"

He heard the hushed tones of his mother inviting her in and the firm click of the front door shutting out the night.

Decision time. He could either face her and listen to what she had to say... or do a bunk. It wouldn't be the first time he'd escaped through his bedroom window into the branches of the horse chestnut tree on to the wall and into next door's garden.

He listened carefully for any sign of footsteps on the stairs. There were none. He tiptoed on to the landing and strained his ears trying to pick up anything that was being said. The muffled words made little sense to Ronnie so he started to creep down the stairs to enable him to eavesdrop more comfortably.

He heard his mother's hushed tones apologising for her neglect,

"It's all my fault. If I hadn't let things get on top of me we probably wouldn't be in this mess. I've let him run wild, but he's not a bad lad. I know he's not," she said vehemently as if persuading herself of the truth of her own words.

" You've had difficulties Mrs Soper, I think anyone would recognise that. What we need to do now is look out for Ronnie; do what's best for him."

"Yes, yes of course. Whatever you say."

"For what it's worth you're looking a lot better," said Julie encouragingly.

"I've stopped drinking," murmured Mrs Soper gently. "I'm

so ashamed, I let it become completely out of hand. I knew I was doing it but I couldn't seem to do anything about it. Do you understand? I just couldn't help myself."

Julie Flemming made soft noises of reassurance and Ronnie's mum continued. She obviously needed to talk. "I fell apart after Tim died. We all did and then things didn't seem to matter anymore – which was wrong, I realise that now. I only hope I've realised in time... You won't be taking Ronnie away from me will you?"

"I shouldn't think it would come to that," promised Julie, "Especially now that you've started to get yourself together. But Ronnie...Ronnie's the one we need to think about."

"Yes, yes. Of course."

"We need to get him back to school. He's missed a great deal, but he's bright enough. With a concerted effort we should have him back ready to choose his options for his GCSE years. The missing year won't have done too much damage. I hope. He'll need help adjusting, of course. Maybe a stint with family consultancy. If you're willing?"

"This is what the lady from Social Services was talking about. Is it really necessary?"

"I know you feel it's a bit of an intrusion, but I believe it will help...Yes. There are still factors regarding Tim's death that Ronnie needs to come to terms with himself. He needs to relinquish the guilt he's feeling. Professionals can help him do that. They will also be a source of strength for you, should you hit a bad patch."

Ronnie didn't wait to hear anymore. He picked his coat from off the banister and softly made his way to the front door. He eased back the catch and fled out into the chill evening air.

The frost was already shooting its crystal ferns over the windscreens of cars. Ronnie stomped on the brittle ice panes of covered puddles that cracked and bubbled satisfyingly under his weight. He attempted to slide on the diamond bright path and cursed mildly when the rubber on his soles prevented him from from travelling any distance. He leapt up to grab a handful of greenery from the budding trees. He almost lost his balance but a figure came swiftly from a driveway and firmly secured him. Ronnie gasped in surprise which quickly turned to shock when he heard the rasping tones of Rattlesnake.

"Careful now. Don't go falling over. You could hurt yourself. Ronnie yelped loudly. But there was no-one to hear.

A hand was firmly clamped over his mouth and Ronnie found himself being bundled into the back of a Jaguar SJ6. The sound of the engine starting up drowned out any sound that the boy might have made. But there was no-one to see or hear anyway.

Tony Clifton sat uncomfortably, his solicitor at his side, in the small medical room off the main ward next to the nurses' station facing Stringer and Allison. A male nurse leaned against the door. The atmosphere was tense in that cramped room.

"You understand why we've come to see you?"

Tony didn't respond. It didn't suit him to answer – not yet. He was in listening mode but to those assembled he appeared distant and uncommunicative.

His solicitor, Steven Briggs, spoke for him,

"You can address all questions through me," he puffed pompously.

"According to our records you have been confined here, since transferring from the hospital wing at Winson Green prison and have not left this establishment except for the preliminary hearing in order to attest your suitability for trial. Correct?" enquired Stringer.

Allison scrutinised Clifton's face. He really was a handsome man. No wonder so many women had fallen for his charms, but it was hard to believe, from looking at him, that he had killed five women.

Clifton sat, his face impassive. His solicitor spoke,

"That is correct. And what may I ask warrants this intrusion on my client's time?"

Stringer barely contained a snort of derision at Steven Briggs' manner.

"Our murder investigations have brought us here and necessitate us asking a few questions."

"Surely, you have done all the investigating you need? My client cannot afford you any new information on the killings."

"No, not on the serial killings, but on another more recent murder. Tell me, Clifton, have you had many visitors here?"

"If there has been another murder then my client cannot possibly have had anything to do with it. If, however, you have had another murder similar to the ones with which my client is charged then I reserve the right to be informed of all details."

Clifton swivelled his head around slowly and watched Stringer's expression. For that moment, more than any other, he resembled his mother in that chameleon stare.

"If you are unprepared to answer then we can check hospital records. " continued Mark.

Allison's gravelly voice interrupted the hostility between his sergeant and Clifton's man.

"Mr Clifton, Tony...Has Amy Calcutt been in to visit you?"

Tony's eyes blinked and fixed on Allison. At the mention of Amy's name, his face changed as if harried by storm clouds. A muscle twitched spasmodically in his cheek and his mouth took a savage downward twist. He took in a lungful of air and a weak whimper escaped his lips.

Allison paused, then repeated his question. The anguish that filled Tony's heart was plain to see and he stilled his solicitor with a wave of his hand. The small room was filled with his cultured, resonant voice.

"No, she's not been in to see me. Nor was she present at the hearing," The pain in his voice was more noticeable now. "Although, she promised me...." his voice trailed off to little more than a whisper.

"Mr Clifton, " pressed Allison, "Have you any idea why she hasn't visited you?"

Tony's eyes rolled back in his head and he let out a sigh of such deep and utter sorrow that all in the room fixed their gaze on him. The male nurse stood apprehensively, but alert. Tony shook his head, a lock of his blue black hair fell on his forehead, his eyelids trembled with the pressure of resisting the urge to cry. He managed to whisper, "I don't know..I just don't know."

Allison glanced across at Mark who continued,

"Maybe you didn't realise that she was not allowed to visit you. That privilege was only extended to your mother." Tony's hands tightened on the chair arms. The colour drained out of his face. He snatched another gulp of air.

" I'm sure," Mark went on "that Miss Calcutt would have attended the hearing if she'd been able. I don't think she would have let you down."

"Then why did she let me down?" He bit hard into the back of his hand endeavouring to stop the wail that wanted to shriek from him. The blood from his wound dripped off his hand and splashed on the table.

Allison pressed home his advantage,

"She couldn't, Mr Clifton. She was dead. Amy Calcutt has been murdered."

A stunned silence was followed by a terrifying cry that filled the empty void created by those words. A cry so bereft of human feeling, so tortured, that even Allison felt his own spine tingling and was unable to suppress a shiver.

The nurse hastily opened the door to call for assistance as a deep throated roar that seemed to emanate from the pit of Hell itself ripped violently through that small room, finding its way into into the ward and stopping all activity. Even the marathon man who endlessly paced the ward stopped and listened, snuffing the air like a wolf.

Tony brought down his fist and sent the table lamp crashing to the floor. A tidal wave of colour ebbed through the contours of his face replacing the white spectre of shock.

He was flanked on both sides by a nurse and each put a restraining hold on his arms. Tony buckled in abject grief and was helped out of the room and from view.

"I hope you're satisfied with my client's response," muttered Steven Briggs superciliously.

Allison growled at his Sergeant, "I think that's all," he paused fractionally before adding, "For *now*."

Allison and Stringer left the hospital.

The Chief felt as if a rose from the grave, belying the soft bloom of the petals, had thorned his side with a poisoned barb.

Clifton's reaction was telling, very telling. Allison knew he had to look elsewhere for Amy's killer.

7

PEOPLE ASKING WHY

Judy watched the countryside race by as the train ate up the track that took her to the South West.

Nothing seemed familiar. Nothing struck a chord. Still, she was patient enough and she believed Dr Mills. It would take time. "Let's face it, girl," she said to herself, "Time is something you've got plenty of."

Judy allowed her mind to ramble and wander. She ran over the events that had brought her to this as she idly leafed through the pages of a magazine. Hypnosis had been unsuccessful. She had remained in a trance dream like state, mumbling nursery rhymes and Rebecca had been unable to get any sense out of her. Whatever had happened to Judy had caused such deep trauma that she was unwilling to expose herself to the memories. What they had ascertained were her links with rural Devon. Judy was on her way to a small village outside Barnstaple. She was to be met at Tiverton Parkway by Hayley Roberts who ran a small but select hotel and farmhouse accommodation business. The complex was just twenty minutes from the coast and itsounded idyllic. Just what she needed. Judy was to work the season there waitressing, cleaning, pretty much anything that she was asked to do. She would have free board and lodging and one day off a week in rotation with other staff. And Rebbecca would join her in a couple of weeks

Judy cast a desultory eye around her at the motley collection of passengers travelling in the carriage. A fat woman with plump hands and scarlet fingernails caught her eye and smiled. But Judy, not wishing to be drawn into conversation, began instead to read the magazine article in front of her with exaggerated interest.

The noise of the train wheels on the track sounded like whispering demons that taunted her, over and over again. "You'll never find out; you're never to know. You'll never find out; you're never to know." Over and over in her brain the words repeated until she wanted to cry out.

She rummaged in her bag and took out the Walkman that David had bought her as a going away present and didn't see the flutter of a tiny scrap of paper which fell to the floor, holding David's phone number. She put on the headphones, in an attempt to drown out the prophetic clamour of the train, and tuned into the melodious voice of Helen Reddy singing *how nice it was to be insane; that no-one asks you to explain* and closed her eyes. Next stop was Bristol Temple Meads. She hoped by then to have erased the cacophony from her ears and be lulled into a gentler rhythm.

Ronnie awoke in a room ten foot by eight. He paced it out carefully, with one arm outstretched, the other groping along the wall. There was a door...locked, a hard wooden bench with some sort of coarse, cloth blanket, an old pillow, a wooden cask with water and ladle, and a bucket. There was no light switch, but three quarters of the way up the wall by the makeshift bench bed was a small chink of light. Ronnie supposed that it came from a small window that had been effectively covered with some sort of black out material or blind. He strained his eyes struggling to see in the almost perfect blackness. If he could somehow clamber up and remove the curtaining or whatever; he may have an idea of his whereabouts.

He climbed on the bed to think. Standing there, he still couldn't reach the tantalising glint which was creeping in from outside. The upturned bucket gave him no extra height even if upended and placed on the bed. He examined the small water butt. That was marginally larger but he was reluctant to pour away the water incase he was stuck 'in this dungeon' for days.

He didn't want to save the water by putting it in the bucket which he felt had been left for an entirely different purpose and probably wasn't clean. Ronnie jumped down off the bed and thought. If he dragged the bench on its side and rested it against the wall like a ramp, it was possible he could reach the window. It was worth a try.

He tiptoed to the door pressed, his ear to the wood and listened. The blood pulsing in his head roared and rushed. Nothing. All seemed still and silent. Ronnie tugged at the bench. It moved! He had been half afraid that it would be fixed to the floor.

Not wishing to alert the faceless sleepers behind his door he removed the rough blanket and lay it on the floor. He eased the bench out bit by bit, careful not to drag it noisily, although the temptation was there. But, he told himself, care and not speed was of the essence. He inched backwards manoeuvring the board bed until he had it at the right angle. He lifted it onto its side, pulled the foot towards him whilst letting the head rest against the wall. It thudded dully. Ronnie stopped, his heart pounding, terrified that the sound had given him away to his captors.

Nothing happened. No shouts of alarm were heard, no doors unbolted. Nothing.

Now, he had to try and climb up the bench. His palms were slick with sweat. He wiped them on his jeans and tested the ramp with his weight. So far so good. He gripped either side of the bed with his hands and brought his feet up to meet them with a funny little jump that brought the bed away from the wall to thump back with a crack... He waited and held his breath. Nothing. He tried again; one hand, then the other gripped the sides a little further up. Up with his feet and.. crack went the wood on the wall, a chunk of plaster gouged out and skittered to the floor. It sounded deafening in that room of shuttered dark.

Still nothing. Once more he went into this routine. His hands splintered by the rough wood were sore and beginning to bleed.

His ankles were scraped and bruised, his muscles taut and painful. Time seemed to have slowed to a long, metronome beat.

Ronnie took a gulp of air, two more jumps to go. Just two more. He stretched his hands up into position and tried to pull himself up instead of jumping. It was disastrous. Ronnie felt himself falling backwards with the bed crashing on top of him on the cold, stone floor. He felt a sharp pain in the middle of his spine before the back of his head smashed against the floor and red seeped behind his eyes.

Ronnie was helpless and now unconsciousness.

The train lurched forward with an ungainly clank as the signals changed. The passengers' shoulders propelled forward and back as the idling time ended and the locomotive's familiar rhythm began once more. Slowly at first, then gathering momentum to haul itself into the station where it sighed to a halt.

Judy pulled her coat around her, yanked her bag off the wire mesh rack and moved towards the automatic door where the carriages met. There was a hiss and clunk as the electronic door rushed to open. She moved through into the waiting space by the exit from the train. A gentleman waiting to board tugged at the handle leaving the way clear for Judy to step out and onto the platform.

She deposited her bag on the concrete and scoured the faces of the people waiting. There was no-one she knew, no-one she recognised. She picked up her bag and walked to the steps that would take her to the car park and hopefully a taxi. Or maybe someone had come to meet her.

At the first turn on the iron stairway leaned a large lady with a merry face and fine head of burnished tawny hair tied up in a pretty, pastel chiffon scarf. She wore a voluminous black wool cape and resembled an outsized Fairy Godmother.

She stood up and the breeze caught her cape which filled with air and ballooned like a pumpkin. One of the ends of her scarf fluttered across her cheek and caught on her lips, damsoned with colour. She spat the offending material from her mouth and, with a hint of a Manchester accent impinging on some words, addressed Judy.

"Judy? Judy from Birmingham? ...Rebecca Mills ...Yes?" She nodded with Judy as if answering her own question and gushed, "Here, let me help you with that," and whisked away Judy's bag from her as if it was nothing more than an empty paper carrier.

"Follow me. The car's parked down here. I've kept you some supper. Just something simple. There's plenty of hot water if you want to freshen up after your journey." She paused by the black Rover and opened the boot. "I'm Hayley, Hayley Roberts." She extended her hand after closing the boot and shook Judy's vigorously. She chattered constantly as she unlocked and opened the passenger door. Judy eased herself into the luxurious comfort and settled back to enjoy the ride and listened to the gentle, amiable prattle of her hostess and employer. But Judy wasn't fooled. There was more to this woman than met the eye and she didn't mean it facetiously!

Holly sat opposite Colin Brady trying to take on board what she was being told.

"If we are ever to uncover this mystery then you will have to apply for information on your real parents. I could only go so far but unless you either authorise me on your behalf or start your own enquiries then, it's another door closed. "

Paul broke in, "Holly, I know we've been through all this before. I know you want nothing to do with the blood relatives that abandoned you. I know you don't want to hurt your mum and dad..."

"Too right, I don't," she said fiercely the tears starting to spring up behind her eyes. "You're telling me, that behind my back, without my consent you've been ferreting around in my past. Trying to discover what I don't want to know and have never sought to know?"

"Holly, don't take it like that, " said Paul quietly.

" And you..." She turned on him in cold anger, " You've been a party to this... this... ultimate act of betrayal. I will never forgive you." Her eyes glittered like diamonds, brimming with fire and unshed tears. Before she shamed herself into falling apart before them, she swept out of the room. They heard her footsteps running up the stairs and her bedroom door slam.

"I'm sorry, Colin, " Paul sighed. "I know you only want to help. She'll come round in time."

Colin pursed his lips, "Maybe I was wrong to meddle, but I firmly believe the key to these happenings are in her past and if she is to conquer them, then she must be prepared to face the truth... I guess I went about it the wrong way. I've been too impatient – I should have let you talk her round first – not have gone wading in with both feet."

"It's OK Col, you meant well."

"Yes, but what about the damage I've done to your relationship?"

"We'll come through. We have enough love for each other to survive this. She'll come round," Paul murmured, his confidence waning more by the minute.

Colin rose from the settee, "Sorry to leave you like this, I'd better be off." He glanced at his watch, " Marcie's arranging dinner for eight thirty and by the time I get back I'll just have time for a shower. "

"When are you two going to sort yourselves out?" asked Paul, "If ever there was a match made in heaven, it's you two. Why don't you live together and be damned?"

"You'd better ask Marcie that one. She's stubborn. Says she's grown too selfish now to live with anyone else. Likes things the way they are. We joke about it – I tell her she's a professional mistress and she asks when she's going to have a pay rise."

They walked to the hall. Colin reached for his coat from off the stand.

"It's cold this evening, freezing! I wouldn't mind betting that we're in for some snow...The weather man said..."

"The weather man said...." echoed Paul derisively.

He opened the glass door to the porch and turned the latch on the stout, wooden front door. A gust of icy air pinched its way into the warmth and lifted the pages of the telephone pad on the hall stand. Both men looked up and saw thick heavy flakes come spiralling down, softly and silently muffling the iron hard ground in a light wool covering. The grass lawn was being swiftly covered in a lumpy crystal coating. The suicide flakes that brushed the glass of the hall door melted and trickled down the pane and ran off the polyurethine varnished wood. As they watched, the texture of the snow began to change. It became thicker and harder, falling in dizzy swirls of confusion which dazzled down from the starlit night.

Colin pulled up his collar, "It's times like this I wish I wore a hat," he said reflectively, "Marcelle said they make me look like some American gumshoe, so vanity prevails and I freeze."

"I'm beginning to freeze too," Paul grumbled good naturedly, eyeing the weather and rolling down his shirt sleeves.

Colin was just stepping out onto the path when they heard it.

A high pitched caterwauling whine rose from above them and crescendoed into a shrill scream.

The two men looked at each other.

"Holly!" exclaimed Paul, "Holly," he shouted and leapt up the stairs three at a time closely followed by Colin.

The porch and hall doors slammed shut cutting off the chill of the invading night and battalions of snow.

Paul tried to enter the bedroom but the door seemed weighted against him.

"Is it locked?" asked Colin.

"There's no lock on the door," Paul replied.

"Perhaps she's wedged something against it."

Paul leaned hard against the panelled wood...Nothing!

A pitiful sob was heard followed by a whimper of terror. Paul mustered all his strength and shouldered the door like a battering ram. The wood gave way with a splintering crunch and the two men ran in.

Holly was sitting astride her dressing table stool; the mirror in front of her was cracked, shards of glass littered her make up tray. Her slashed left palm was dripping blood which profusely, spotted and swarmed redly on the marble surface of her dresser.

The cologne bottles danced and shimmied over their palais floor; clinking, chinking and vibrating together like whirling dervishes. One tiny, delicate Ystatis phial pirouetted into the air and fragmented spontaneously. Another, heavier bottle of Yves Rocher Chevrefeuille catapulted and whistled past Colin's head, shattering on contact with the wall, staining it in perfumed accusation like a martyr's blood. Small beadlets of glass crunched underfoot. Granules from atomisers like jewelled rodents' eyes embedded themselves in the carpet and under the skirting as if massing for attack.

"What's happening?" yelled Paul.

Colin stood transfixed, unable to answer. He had never witnessed anything like it before.

Holly gave a shudder and collapsed to the floor. Everything was still. The perfume collection ceased rattling, the manicure set halted its ritualistic tribal beat.

The snow continued to swirl past the window.

Paul went at once to minister to Holly.

"Put her on the bed, " ordered Colin. "I'll clear this mess up. Can I use your phone?"

Paul nodded as he lifted her onto the double divan. He smoothed away the glass from her hair, her eyebrows, and her cheeks before taking a flannel from the sink and rinsing it in cold water to apply to her injured hand. He pressed it into her wound then inspected it to see what damage had been done.

"It's OK, " he said jokingly, "You'll live." And in the best traditions of the English cinema he added, "Just a flesh wound, Nurse. No more."

Holly sighed, and turned towards him, "What happened?"

"You tell us, " said Colin armed with a dustpan and brush, ready to begin sweeping up the broken glass that littered the floor.

"But first, let's get that hand seen to – then we'll talk. Downstairs."

Holly sat in fear and trembling while Paul bandaged her hand. He had removed splinters of glass from the wound which was now thoroughly cleaned with TCP, despite the complaining yelps from his girlfriend.

"I'm not sure we shouldn't take you to casualty and have this stitched. "

"Don't fuss Paul, I'll be all right."

"I think you've done a good job," interjected Colin. "It should heal well."

"There you are, you see. Colin and I agree," rejoined Holly.

Her face was drained of all colour. Her dark fringed eyes served to look more haunting and ethereal than ever. She reminded Paul of a wood nymph or water sprite. He wasn't sure which, just that she looked more vulnerable now than he had ever seen her. He stretched out his arms and held her close, brushing his lips through her fragrant hair.

She fell into his arms and gripped him fiercely as he whispered ,

"What happened up there?"

Holly pushed herself away from his tender grasp and studied his face carefully before replying,

"You don't think I'm mad, do you?"

"Good heavens, no! What on earth makes you say that?"

"I don't know," and a large tear freed from her eyes travelled down her cheek and splashed its warmth on Paul's hand.

"It's just... so many things have happened – and now this. I've had enough." She turned to Colin, "OK.. " she said slowly, "You're telling me that if we investigate my past, my blood roots," she couldn't bring herself to say 'family', "That these happenings will end?"

" I can't promise that, Holly, no-one can, but if we can understand *why* you have these experiences, then that puts us in control and possibly, yes, we could end them. Or at least make them easier to bear."

Holly looked from one to the other, earnestly searching their faces for any lie or uncertainty. She saw none and sighed resignedly,

"Very well. I'll give you the authority. See what you can find out. "She turned to Paul, "I hope I'm doing the right thing and I'm not going to regret this."

"You won't regret it, darling. I promise," and he hugged her close.

"Are you going to tell us what happened up there?" enquired Colin.

Her hand went to her lips in an expression of doubt as she studied both men; one her lover, the other a friend. She pushed back a strand of hair before answering,

"You'd better sit down. Both of you. This is going to sound weird."

They sat together in that elegant room while Paul poured them each a drink, and outside in the shadows of the streets, snow fell. Billowing phantoms ghosting together and drifting palely and icily like nights' magicians changing all in its wake.

"I was really angry with you," she frowned at Colin, "Knowing how I felt about everything and you being so insistent, I just lost my rag. I rushed up there and sat at the mirror and started to brush my hair. I needed to feel something, something other than the pain in my head and heart. I was brushing far too hard and I made my scalp bleed. I stopped to inspect the damage and peered at my reflection. The glass had a peculiar effect on me. The more I stared the harder it was to draw my eyes away. The mirror underwent a subtle change." She looked across anxiously at them, trying to see the effects her words were having.

Paul gently encouraged her, "Go on, darling."

Holly cleared her throat nervously, "The surface looked wet, as if I could dip my hand into it, like it was a pool and I could ripple the silver liquid into ever widening circles. I stretched out and the tip of my fingernail seemed to rest on something filmy almost ready to give. Just one little press and my finger would disappear into forbidden depths. I'm not making much sense am I?"

"You're describing what you saw, what you felt – that's good enough for me," said Colin.

"And me," added Paul.

"I felt a strange tingling sensation and was on the verge of pushing my hand right through this.... whatever it was, when it all seemed to gather together like tiny sugar granules. I watched as these crystallised into almost transparent celluloid. Everything was sharp and in focus. I was watching a street. A woman paraded up and down, over powdered, over rouged and she was being watched. She had good legs I remember; her skirt was up to her bum, but they were good legs, long and lean. No cellulite," she added almost jealously.

"I was watching, observing and as I did so a mixture of emotions welled inside me. I felt burned up with hatred and loathing whilst feeling a deep sense of loss. I knew that if I timed the attack just right that I would in some way appease the clamouring, persuasive whisperings in my head. I knew by one action, I would be saving another. It's hard to explain. These weren't *my* thoughts, but they were, if you see what I mean. I was living them through someone else."

" Go on," prodded Colin.

"I was actually beginning to enjoy the hunt, enjoy stalking the prey. I was being careful, well guarded and..."

"Yes? Yes?"

"The watcher *knew* . Knew I could see. And what's more knew it was *me*. My name was shrieked into the night like a salivating monster lurching to rip my flesh from my bones. The name Gillian crashed into the silence left by the wind."

"But your name *isn't* Gillian," said Paul.

"I know. It doesn't make any sense. But somehow I know the watcher knew me and knew me as Gillian." Holly looked across to Colin for explanations, "Another life maybe?" she smiled half-heartedly.

"Don't ask me, " muttered Colin, " I'm not into all that reincarnation stuff. One life's enough for anyone."

" I just freaked then. I wanted it all to go away. I smashed my hand against the mirror to stop its foul predictions. The glass smashed, I gashed my hand. The rest you know."

Holly shivered and took a gulp of her brandy. The warmth burnt her throat pleasantly., "I'm so tired," she added. "I feel as if I could sleep for a week."

"Look," said Colin, "You get upstairs and rest. You're in a state of shock. You need to keep warm. You'll be hit by an attack of shaking soon. It's best you were in bed. I'll give you something to settle you; help you to sleep. OK"

"OK" said Holly, too weak to argue.

"Go on, off you go. We'll sort everything out. I just want you to sign this before you leave. It authorises me on your behalf to find out about your real parents." Colin removed a buff envelope from his inside pocket and took out a document which Holly duly signed.

Colin gave Paul a valium. "Get her to take this once she's undressed. It will help her to relax. I'll leave a few with you in case she needs them." Paul nodded and took Holly upstairs. Colin poured himself another drink and waited for Paul to return.

"She's sound asleep." Paul had answered the unsaid question. "So,what do you think?" Paul continued, as he descended the stairs.

" I've never seen anything like it. I've read about it."

"What is it?"

"Kinetic energy. She was under such acute psychological stress that she employed telekenisis."

"Explain please," said Paul rolling a cigarette, "Although I think I know what it means , I'd rather hear it from you."

"Telekinesis is the ability to move objects or to cause changes within objects solely by using the power of the mind. Thought waves if you like. As I said, it's something I've read about but never witnessed. Incidents of telekinesis has most often and reliably been reported in times of severe stress or crisis situations. For example, there have been cases in America where automobiles have been lifted or rather levitated from injured people, similarly debris removed from people in collapsed buildings and so on. I don't know. But what I think we saw was Holly's subconscious dealing with her 'happenings', trying to prevent herself seeing anymore."

"So what do we do?"

"Wait. Wait until I get back to you and see what I can uncover. Meanwhile, look after her."

"That goes without saying." He shook Colin's hand and Paul watched him go into the snow filled streets. The freak weather had already left a four inch covering and still the flakes came spinning down.

8

NEWBORN FRIEND

Judy was settled in a comfortable, warm, back kitchen on a wooden settle in front of a coal and wood fire that flickered and crackled.

The heavy mahogany kitchen table was covered with a wipe-clean, vinyl tablecloth. The scene reminded her of a story book country grandmother. *Why* did she think that? She struggled to remember a fleeting memory but it was elusive and didn't want to be recalled.

She continued to look around her. The terracotta quarry tiled floor was spotless. The scatter rugs strategically placed to take the chill off the floor. A dog basket rested by the open fire where a snoozing black and white spaniel lay, paws stretched towards the heat, breathing contentedly.

The shelves by the table were overflowing with cookery books, correspondence, magazines and newspapers. The kitchen end was a space saving design with dark oak units. The space was currently filled by Hayley, busying herself with a casserole pot on the hob from which she was filling a large bowl.

"Sit yourself up at the table. We've all had ours. " She gathered a fork and spoon with a table mat and set it down. A steaming bowl of lamb and vegetable stew was placed before Judy. Hayley offered her a basket of homemade bread rolls still warm from the oven.

Judy's mouth watered at the aroma. If it tasted as good as it smelled then she would have no trouble polishing it off.

Hayley sat opposite and poured them both a glass of red wine. She didn't ask, just assumed that everybody enjoyed a drink and would have been surprised at a refusal.

"So..." chirruped Hayley, "What's the story?"

"Don't you know?"

"Only what Rebecca has told me. I'd rather hear it from you."

Judy recounted as best she could the events that she remembered.

All the time she spoke, Hayley's direct gaze never wavered from Judy's face who found this somewhat disconcerting. The more she talked to Hayley the more she realised that this was not only one very astute lady, but one who could drag a confession from a priest. She had a way of making you explain yourself, making you focus and think. Judy came to the conclusion that she would make a brilliant friend in a fight, but an extremely bad enemy.

Hayley didn't let up with her questions,

"So what about this young copper then? Is there anything likely to develop there?"

Judy wanted to tell her to mind her own business, but she didn't. Somehow, she found herself telling her all about David.

There was something about Hayley, something Judy couldn't help warming to – she liked her.

Hayley's directness wasn't anything Judy was used to, but she accepted it. She began to realise that this woman would give her opinion on anything, whether she was asked for it or not, which somewhat amused Judy. Hayley was a plain speaker who didn't mince her words and she enjoyed being privy to secrets.

She reminded Judy of a queen bee. The more they talked, the more physically large Hayley appeared. Judy knew it was just an illusion, but she could easily see how some people could be frightened by her forthright nature.

The phone rang.

"It's for you." said a quizzical Hayley, passing Judy the phone.

"Hello Judy, I just rang to see if you'd arrived safely,"

"Fine thanks. I'm being spoilt at the moment," said Judy,

delighted that David had contacted her.

"Won't be so spoilt tomorrow," chipped in Hayley, cheekily, "You'll be working for a living."

David continued, " There's another reason I rang, I've got some good news."

"What's that?"

Queen Bee arched her eyebrows as she saw the change of expression on Judy's face.

"We've found someone who knows you..." he paused, and felt a change come over Judy as she listened on the other end of the phone.

"Yes?" she said with urgency. " Tell me."

"Our publicity it seems has paid off. A woman has come forward, claims to have gone to school with you, recognised you straight off and knows a lot about you. She lost touch with you after you left school and would love to catch up with you. It seems you were really good friends."

Judy hesitated, "What's her name?"

"Penny. Penelope Hughes,"

The name didn't mean anything to Judy, "So what can you tell me?"

"Heaps! Where do you want me to begin?"

"How about the beginning?"

"Are you sure this isn't going to be too much for you to take?"

"I need to know sometime. Now is as good a time as any."

"It won't be damaging or anything? In your condition?"

"You make it sound as if I'm pregnant," Judy's nerves were stretched to the limits. She tried to quell the shaking that had manifested itself in her hands, her stomach fluttered and churned. She wanted to scream at him, instead she spoke very quietly, "Tell me," and she waited.

"All this has to be verified of course. It will be thoroughly checked but we have no reason to disbelieve her. I'm jumping the gun a bit by telling you. It should be done officially, but

Sergeant Stringer gave me the go ahead after squaring it with the Chief."

Judy was now so highly strung she felt like a spring about to burst from its confines. She managed to sound patient and repeated, "Tell me." Then as an after thought added, "Please."

"Right, I've kept you in suspense long enough. Are you ready for this?"

Judy's answer was to grip the receiver even tighter, her knuckles showing white.

" OK," David launched into details about her life which filled Judy with puzzlement and trepidation. It was as if he were talking about someone else.

" Your real name is Marie Court, you were born in Lordswood Maternity Hospital, Harborne, Birmingham. Such intimate details are known because Penny was born in the next bed. Her mum and your mum were friends! Your birthday's in August, August eighteenth and you're twenty five years old. You're an only child. Am I going too fast for you?"

"I don't know, my head is spinning."

"Look, I've been given permission to drive down, I'm bringing Penny with me. I can only stay overnight, then I have to be back at the station. Can you fix me up with accommodation?"

"Hang on a minute," Judy put her hand over the phone and mouthed at Hayley, "It's David, they've found someone who knows me, can we fix them up with somewhere to stay?"

"No problem, tell them to come,"

"It's OK" said Judy into the telephone, "What time will you arrive?"

"We're leaving here at nine, should be with you by noon. I'll ring if we get delayed. Hear the rest tomorrow. OK?"

"OK," she agreed and replaced the receiver, her heart thumping. Queen Bee sat expectantly waiting to hear all the news.

She wasn't disappointed.

Mrs Clifton carefully signed her letter to the four OAPs with a flourish. Her meticulous research had given her the names of four old age pensioners in Manchester who were prepared to fight miscarriages of justice. Affectionately known as the A team she was convinced that they would be able to help her, in her mission to free Tony. She addressed the envelope to Mr Stephenson.

A second letter was sealed and stamped, addressed to the new court of appeal set up by the government especially to oversee cases of rough justice.

She licked her lips fervently. Her eyes darted about her as she thought, eventually coming to rest on the saintly gaze of Christ, whose hand was raised in blessing over the huge oak dinner table, polished and clean, the fringed cloth folded to one side.

Almost as if this gave her inspiration she opened her mouth and sang lustily from the heart, in her thin reedy voice, a Sankey hymn, an old favourite.

> "Yes, we will gather at the river,
> The beautiful, the beautiful river..."

She stopped suddenly and swiftly paced to her box of prophesies, selecting a tiny scroll.

> "Be ye strong therefore, and let
> not your hands be weak: for your
> work shall be rewarded.
> 2 Chronicles Chapter 15 verse 7."

Mrs Clifton triumphed in religious glee. She felt invincible.

There was just one little problem. Someone was aware of her plans, someone had crept inside her thoughts. Grace Clifton thought she knew who that someone was. And she felt safe that nothing would be done, perhaps never. But if there was just a hint of danger then she would have to seek, find and destroy. Of that she had no doubt. But now there was work to be done. The video recorder was set. She would need to watch the evening's television upon her return.

Now, a phone call; she dialled and waited. Her prayers were answered.

"Hello Junior? It's Grace here. I'm feeling a bit rough tonight. It's the unexpected snow; I think I've caught a chill so I won't be at the meeting tonight. I'm going to wrap up warm, with a glass of warm milk, watch a bit of telly and have an early night."

The choir master protested something and Grace became more insistent,

"No, no. It's all right. I'll be fine. I don't need anything. If I do I'll ring. All right?"

Evidently hearing what she wanted to hear, she said her goodbyes and replaced the receiver.

Her heart filled with joyous excitement. Time enough to return to the pitch. Later, when the inky night would cloak her presence. She had already chosen her victim from the line of harlots that paraded their Jezebel wares.

More importantly now, she had to prepare her case for Tony's appeal. She needed to convince the solicitor that it was worthwhile going ahead. Certainly the spate of new murders was in her favour, as far as implying that the police had manufactured evidence was concerned, but she couldn't use any of that information until the police admitted finding connections between the deaths and Tony. That admission may be a long time coming, but Grace Clifton was certain that she could pose a few taxing questions that might begin the enquiry.

The biggest stumbling block was Sandra Thornton. Her evidence would be crucial. Grace thought carefully about ridding herself of the bar to Tony's freedom. But it would need careful planning as had all her mission work.

Ronnie Soper felt a surge of gentle warmth spread through him.

"Christ!" he thought, "I must have pissed myself."

He hesitated before opening his eyes, but when he did they were shielded by some sort of blindfold, so he couldn't see anything anyway. He tried to lift his hands but they seemed to be bound securely at both wrists and elbow, restricting movement and preventing him from reaching his face and eyes.

A voice at the side of him made him jump. It was Rats,
"Just cleaning up the damage, Ronnie baby. You had a bit
of a fall. I'm not surprised, fancy trying to climb up to the
window," he tutted slowly in sarcasm. "Made quite a mess of
yourself, the bed falling on you an' all."

Ronnie tried to speak but his mouth was tightly gagged. All
that could be heard from him were a few muffled sounds. Panic
started to leap inside him like the flames from a forest fire. For
once in his life, Ronnie was stumped and he didn't know what
to do. His various talents and charm for wriggling out of things
seemed to be all used up.

The oily voice, unnaturally calm started its interrogation.

"Ronnie Soper, isn't it?"

Ronnie had to think quickly. He somehow knew confession
would damn him. If he could make them believe they'd taken
the wrong boy, if he could remember all he said. Lying was the
easy part; remembering the lies, that was the difficulty.

Ronnie's mind was working overtime. If he could tell them
something....

He felt the gag around his mouth being worked loose

"Not speaking then?"

Somehow or another Ronnie managed to find his voice.

"Yes.. Yes. Who did you say?"

"Now, sonny don't come that crap with me. Just answer the
questions."

"Where am I? What's happened? Why can't I see nothin'?
Who are you? What am I doin' here?"

"I said *answer* questions not *ask* them," said the oily voice
with a hint of irritation.

"Sorry," said Ronnie contritely.

"We'll start again. Name?"

" Johnny.."

"Johnny? Johnny who?"

"Johnny Lethaby," came the pat response.

"Who? Who's Johnny Lethaby when he's at home? What do
you know about Ronnie Soper?"

"Ronnie's my cousin. Who are you? What do you want?" He managed to get a feeling of fear into his tone.

"So you're Ronnie's cousin, are you? What are you doing at his house?"

"Came to see him – to visit. Haven't seen him at school for ages, thought something had happened to him. Stopped by my auntie's and had tea, hoping he'd show."

So far so good. Putting himself in his cousin's place, he could tell enough truths to disconcert his captors.

There was a short pause whilst Rats digested this information. A throaty voice with a sibilant 's' hissed at his right ear. Ronnie jumped.

"Don't much like kids do you?"

"Course I do. I go to school with them don't I?"

He received a stinging blow across his cheek.

"Don't get cute with me, Ronnie."

"I told you my name's not Ronnie. It doesn't matter what you do, that's not going to change."

Rats intervened, "Are you sure we've got the right kid? Have you seen him, this Ronnie."

"Course I have," hissed Snake, "And he looks just like *him*," he spat angrily.

"That's cos we all look alike; Ronnie and his brother Tim, me and my brother, all like peas in a pod, mum says."

There was a silence, cold and uncomfortable. Ronnie retreated into a corner of his mind where he built a wall – brick by brick, layer by layer – to protect him from this onslaught of questions to which he had no answers; no answers that would help him. He was glad they couldn't see his eyes. His eyes would tell the truth, and with a bit of luck they never would. Ronnie knew that once he saw their faces, then he wouldn't live long; they wouldn't risk him seeing them, unless they had no use for him.

He felt another crack across his face.

"I don't like stubborn, mulish boys. If you don't want any more of that, then you'd better speak when spoken to.

Kids today...." Snake tutted, "No manners."

"Sorry, " squealed Ronnie. "I didn't hear you."

"There's only us here. Are you deaf? I'll ask again."

Ronnie thought hard, he hadn't heard the question. He was too busy locking himself into his mind, a little safe room where he could hide until it was over. Only it wasn't over. There was no place to hide and he had to have an answer for them or feel more pain.

"What did you do with the picture?"

"What picture?" There was another stinging blow that caught his lip. His teeth dug in to it. He could taste the salty blood and feel his mouth puffing up like after a visit to the dentist.

"I've told you I don't know... I'm not Ronnie."

Rats and Snake dropped their voices to a conspiratorial whisper. Ronnie couldn't catch fully what they were saying. All he heard was the word, "check."

"All right Ronnie boy, we'll just leave you to think a while on what we've said. Rest assured we'll be back."

Snake and Rats were satisfied by a small sob that came from the lad.

Ronnie listened keenly. He heard one set of feet move away from the table he was strapped to, and the door open and close. Was it one set of feet or two? He strained hard for any sound of movement or breathing in that room. He held his breath.... Nothing. He flexed his fingers, stretched and curled them to prevent them from going numb. His hands felt blown up like balloons as if they'd been given a dose of anæsthetic. His feet had gone to sleep and his face hurt, especially his lip.

He murmured weakly expecting a slap.

There was nothing.

He tried to loosen the bonds on his wrists. It always looked so easy on the films. If only he'd been conscious when they bound him he could have tensed his muscles; that way when he relaxed, he'd have had room to manoeuvre.

He tried speaking softly, "Anyone there?"

Silence.

It was difficult to talk; his mouth was dry and the lump on his lip was causing extreme discomfort. Ronnie felt certain he was on his own. He had to do some figuring... and fast.

Judy sat in the wicker rattan chair next to the glass topped cane table in the conservatory. A profusion of plants grew and meshed together up the walls along the door frame while painted ivy inched its way along the raffia blinds. She studied the face of the visitors carefully. David Taylor's face was imprinted on her heart, yet still she looked for identifying marks or scars. She saw none.

She turned her attention to the face of her friend. It was curious she felt nothing, didn't recognise her and felt totally unnerved and disadvantaged. She reached for the cup of Earl Grey that Hayley had served to them all and took a sip.

Penny Hughes was an attractive young woman, slender with natural strawberry blonde hair that fell loosely over her shoulders. She had a slight smattering of freckles over her nose and pale, limpid blue, topaz eyes. Her mouth was full and generous, turned up at the corners. Her voice had a slightly husky quality that sounded as if any moment she would break into giggles.

"Hello you, " she said as if they hadn't been formally introduced. Judy attempted to smile and continued to feel uncomfortable.

Thankfully David Taylor broke the silence that threatened to develop.

"Well, *is* this your school friend?"

"One and the same. I'd know her anywhere. We were friends for far too long." She pulled a face, " Do you really not remember me?"

Judy shook her head.

"It seems impossible, we were so close," she sighed and rolled her pastel eyes. "Where do we go from here?"

"I don't know, Dr Mills said to take it steady, one step at a time. I suppose you just ought to talk, get to know each other.

Penny can answer your questions and fill in the gaps."

"Makes sense," Penny agreed.

Judy wished her inner tremblings would cease. She coughed nervously before speaking, "OK in for a penny..."

"In for a Hughes, as we used to say," interrupted Penny and chuckled.

Judy laughed in spite of herself. "p'raps you can tell me something..."

"Shoot. If I can tell you I will."

"Why do I like the name Judy?"

"That's easy. Your mum's best friend was Judy ...she died quite tragically. You were really fond of her, even called your favourite doll after her – Then, there was your love of *The Wizard of Oz* – You adored Judy Garland. Thought she was terrific. We used to play a game where we pretended to be famous film stars. You were always Judy Garland. Sometimes I'd make out I wanted to be Judy and we'd fight over the name. Maybe that explains it!"

"It certainly tells me why I had an affinity with it," murmured Judy. "I can't warm to the name Marie. It just doesn't seem me, especially now."

"Well, if it's any consolation, you often called yourself by different names. "

"What do you mean?"

"We used to have lots of fun. Let's see, when you were French you were Simone, Swedish it was Britt, American – you favoured Stevie. Do you want me to go on?"

"Heavens no!" exclaimed Judy.

"I'll tell you about some of the scrapes we got into," she eyed David warily, "Or p'raps I'll save it for when we're on our own. I don't see why you shouldn't continue to use Judy. It's second nature to me, anyway. Besides, I know a number of people who prefer to use their second name rather than their first. So it's no problem."

"Hold on a minute. What do you mean second name?"

"Didn't I tell you? Your second name *is* Judy – so why not use it?"

"Thanks. I will," said Judy feeling happier than she had done previously. "What's next?"

"Well, I suggest that Penny and I book into our rooms. Then maybe we can go for a drive somewhere, have lunch -basically to get you two talking. What do you think?" asked David.

"Sounds good to me," affirmed Penny.

"Me too, " said Judy.

"Right then. Let's see your Mrs Roberts and see where she's put us."

"I can tell you that," said Judy. "Penny is in the cottage with me and I believe she's found you a room with one of her friends in Eastacombe."

"Where's that?"

"Not far, only about three miles away. "

"Isn't there room in the cottage?'

"It's only got two bedrooms, but I suppose we could share the twin bedded room and let you have the double, or there's the sofa downstairs."

"Sounds fine to me. It's only for one night. I'll go and square it with Hayley. Then I'll bring the bags across. OK?"

"Right."

David left the moist warmth of the glass conservatory and went to find Hayley, leaving Judy to rediscover her past with her newborn friend.

9

FIRE AND RAIN

Allison chewed dreamily on his Mars Bar, his thoughts a million miles away from the routines of police work. His daughter was coming home. He looked forward to that. He just hoped that he'd have enough time to spend with her.

He hadn't seen her since her half term holiday in November. She'd gone skiing to Avoriaz with a group of friends for Christmas and her February half term she'd spent at her boyfriend, Jake's house.

They had a lot to catch up on, plus all the other silly things they liked to do together. Yes, Callie coming home was definitely the best news he'd had since they caught Clifton.

Allison turned his mind to other things.

The station was buzzing today. The costume and make up lady from the Birmingham Rep was coming in, to age up two WPCs, well versed in self defence techniques. They would be made to look like grannies and individually they would patrol an area of Handsworth which had seen an increase in muggings of elderly ladies. The practice exercise had been successful. Allison hoped that word would get around and then maybe the muggers would think twice. If it meant that the perpetrators would stop targeting the old and frail, then that too, would be something to celebrate.

There was also the launch of the first database in genetic fingerprinting. All known criminals were to have samples taken and recorded on computer file. It was as revolutionary and exciting as the concept of fingerprinting when the idea was first conceived. This was all happening in Birmingham. Brum was to lead the world.

Allison shoved the last bit of chocolate into his mouth. He allowed himself a sigh of reverie and took a moment to think of the advances in police work; the discovery of DNA, computerised identikits, CD identikits, but instead of more staff and more cash to aid progress, they faced staff cuts, a shortfall in budget and increasing mountains of paper work.

Allison groaned, they needed more manpower, bobbies on the street, a system of reporting that helped not hindered. Now, often the paper work for a simple arrest could take over a morning to complete; a copper needed to be a word processor, come secretary, even computer whiz, recording things in triplicate, quadruplet and even quintuplet.

He was feeling depressed and he was getting a headache. It didn't do to dwell on what was and now is. He growled through the intercom to Maddie and asked for a cup of tea, reaching in his desk drawer for the paracetamol to chase away one of these man made headaches, which were becoming more frequent and making him grumpier than usual. Allison put it all down to stress. Too much to do.

He picked up the top file in his in tray and began to study it.

Mrs Clifton forked her last mouthful of egg on toast between those pale, leering lips. She wiped the crumbs that had dropped onto her chin with a crisp, white linen napkin and eagerly read the item in the newspaper. Local news was full of this new data base for DNA, genetic fingerprinting, but what interested Grace Clifton was another article, this time from the nationals and a television news item in which an eminent barrister was interviewed about this miracle. Barrington QC was quoted as saying that genetic fingerprinting was not fool proof, that mismatches could be made and therefore so could miscarriages of justice. She ignored the Home Secretary's statement that Britain was leading the world and with a fervent look in her eye devoured everything that Barrington QC had said and stored it away for future use.

> "In thee O Lord, do I put my trust;
> Let me never be ashamed;
> deliver me in righteousness."

Her thin, nasal whine reverberated around her room; she veiled her head and lit a candle in front of the cat ornament, that had been kissed and held by Tony.

She had two more things to do. The prostitute who shamelessly peddled her wares in that infamous street in Balsall Heath needed seeing to, she had watched her long enough, now was the time for action, part of her plan to discredit forensic evidence. And.... Sandra Thornton.

The time *had* come.

But first a visit to Tony – his needs were foremost in her mind even exceeding her own. She remembered the priest's words, her seducer many years ago. She padded to the heavy sideboard and opened the cupboard door taking out the huge family Bible inherited from her mother before her. She opened it to the book of Isaiah chapter fifty four, verse four and read aloud in her reedy tones,

> "Fear not; for thou shalt not be
> ashamed: neither be thou con -
> founded; for thou shalt not be put
> to shame of thy youth, and shall
> not remember the reproach of thy
> widowhood any more.
> For thy maker is thy husband....

Here she stopped and read the lines again. Had it been so long since she read Isaiah? The lines that followed were not as she remembered, and her memory and talent for recitation were unsurpassed. She read the verses again. No there was no mistake there was no mention of the lines:

Thy redeemer his chosen one;
to minister to spiritual and
bodily needs, in his name; to
cleanse and satisfy and bring
thee to Jehovah.

She slammed the pages shut. Maybe this was a different version.

She went to her book shelves filled with Bibles, prayer and hymn books and took out a copy of the revised version. She flicked through the pages with a frantic desire, until she found the chapter and verse. No... There was no mention there.

One by one she deftly searched the pages of her various Bibles but the words changed little.

Grace Clifton let out a small wail of sorrow that grew into a fierce keening. She clutched at her heart as if witnessing the betrayal of Christ.

Confusion mushroom clouded through her mind. Her fervid rantings, wild at first, subdued into grim resignation followed by a long exhalation where she tried to calm her innermost spirit. She drew back those thin, pale lips and spoke, hoarsely at first, but growing more passionate, with each word.

"So be it! I will not deny my Lord. I will not accept my life has been a sham. If motherhood be esteemed and Holy, then by almighty God, I shall prove it so now."

Grace Clifton could almost hear the choirs of exalted angels singing, praising and glorifying *her*. She put on her gloves, ran to the dresser and took what she needed.

The video recorder was set to record, the curtains drawn, the lights left on low. Tony's visit would wait. As soon as darkness fell, she could leave.

A triumphant, yet demonic howl left her lips, a howl that the Singhs next door would remember.

Tony Clifton was distraught. His dreams had been troubled. Resurgence of his crimes, those he remembered, billowed wildly before his eyes, intermingling with his mother's image and

114

the faceless victims of the dead. His dear, sweet Amy was no more. Her precious life stolen from him in a wanton act of vandalism and destruction. She was the first woman, the only one who had tried to understand and help him.

He took out her last letter, read a thousand times, now grubby and tear stained and, as he read the poetry of her words, the fire in his heart melted the ice behind his eyes and he started to weep.

Too long have you suffered the torture
In your mind, too long.
Too long have you endured the guilt
Of your father, too long.
Yet from dark corners
And hidden recesses,
From the secret depths of your soul
I see a purity, a goodness,
A light so bright
That when touched by love,
The damnation that you felt was yours
Seeps away.
I am waiting, to see you through,
I know this cataclysm will abate,
There is a life for us both
Hot tears of passion will wash away
All that is woeful.
Take my strength, take my love
Too long we have waited
Too long.
Our time is to come
And will, you'll see.
I love you.

Amy.

"I say are you all right?" asked George Harper, the old man on the ward who had become not only his chess partner but his friend.

Tony looked up from Amy's letter. There was a look of disillusion, dark melancholy and pain in those brilliant blue eyes.

"I still can't believe it..."

"What son?" asked George, kindly.

"When the police came, I didn't tell you, I thought it was" he corrected himself, "*hoped* it was a trick. That there'd be another letter, a visit. She didn't come to the hearing because death broke her promise... I didn't want to believe it... didn't want to face it. Now there's nothing. Nothing to get myself well for."

Old George didn't want to interrupt but Tony wasn't making a lot of sense. "Are you talking about Amy? What's happened? Is she dead?"

Tony nodded mutely.

"But how? How did it happen?"

"Murdered."

"What?... But who would want to... Was it revenge?"

"The worst thing is, they think I did it. ME! ... It's absurd, I loved her..."

"You couldn't have done it. You were in here... I don't understand..." George was lost for words.

"Now I know why my mother said to forget her. She knew, but she couldn't tell me."

During their conversation the Shuffler had shambled alongside their table and appeared to be eavesdropping on their conversation with great interest. He clapped his hands together in glee and then began to rub his palm down his crotch, kneading and manipulating his penis through his trousers. His hand movements became more frantic and his eyelids began to flutter. He unzipped himself and took out his huge, engorged member and teased the foreskin back, it stood out at an angle of twenty degrees from his body. His hand was moving faster now, his eyes firmly closed, he started to lean backwards while

with his other hand he caressed his testicles. Hot semen volca-
noed out. He groaned softly. His sperm had flown out and left
little blobs of grey jelly, surrounded by milky white opales-
cence, on the chess board and a drop had landed on Amy's
letter.

George Harper had turned away; he had seen this happen
before. He felt disgusted and degraded by the Shuffler's
actions. Tony appeared transfixed by this aberrant behaviour.
He was stunned into silence but when Amy's letter was conta-
minated, a terrible rage grew inside him and his foot delivered
a short sharp kick, bringing groans of agony where there had
just been pleasure.

The Shuffler doubled over, fell to his knees and then lay on
his side clutching his testicles. He coughed in pain, and brought
his knees up into the foetal position and gently rocked from side
to side to soothe the agony.

Tony was filled with extreme loathing and complete distaste
for the man. He moved across the ward and drew up a chair in
front of the television, his eyes aimlessly watching a cartoon of
Elmer Fudd and Bugs Bunny.

None of the nurses were aware of what had happened. One
came out from the nurses' station and hurried across to help
George who was trying to lift the Shuffler to his feet.

"What happened?"

George glanced at Tony who had his back to them and
replied,

"Up to his old tricks, " he thumbed at the Shuffler, " 'e was
getting off so 'igh, with 'is eyes shut an all, lost 'is footin' an' fell.
Caught 'imself on the corner of the table. Nasty."

"Well, it was bound to happen sooner or later. Help me get
him to his bed. Who knows, it may teach him a lesson."

George pulled the Shuffler's arm around his shoulders and
the two men half dragged and half carried the acute schizophrenic to his bed.

George ambled over to Tony and drew up a chair next to him.
They watched the inane antics of the rabbit racing round the TV

screen, with Elmer Fudd in his deerstalker, shouldering his gun calling out,"O wabbit where wah you?" and Bugsy elevating up from a hole munching a carrot, delivering the immortal lines, "Eerr what's up Doc?" before depositing a black fizzing bomb at the hunter's feet, darting behind a tree and stuffing his rabbit fingers into his ears.

"You mustn't mind 'im; 'e can't 'elp it. It's one of the reasons why 'e's in 'ere. 'e used to be at it all the time. Nurses 'ad to sew up 'is pockets. Used to 'ave to give 'im lots to do, occupational therapy, to keep 'is 'ands busy. 'E ain't done that in a long while."

The fire in Tony's eyes masked by the rain of his tears left George rambling to himself.

Tony thought... He wanted revenge.

Mrs Clifton had timed it just right. The lighter evenings since putting the clock forward an hour meant she had to wait until fairly late before she could safely move onto the streets.

But as luck would have it, there were few people braving the unexpected cold snap. She returned to watch the street in Balsall Heath famed as a red light zone. Two teenagers stood on the corner, underneath the street lamp, obviously working as a pair. The seemingly senseless death of one of their kind had made them cautious. The older long legged woman with her Jezebel looks was not so rattled by the recent stabbing. She was experienced enough, or so she imagined, to assess her clients. She trusted her regulars, but as she had commented many times in the past, the risks came with the job.

An old D reg blue Vauxhall Cavalier cruised up to the two girls. Words were exchanged, money changed hands and the two girls climbed into the car, giggling and laughing.

"D reg was right," thought Mrs Clifton with her warped humour, "D reg for the *dregs* of humanity, the girls and the driver." She secretly hoped they'd catch something.

Grace Clifton turned her attention to the older prostitute

who had thwarted her plans the other evening by telephoning a mini cab, going home and not returning to her pitch.

Grace knew that 'the whore' would not escape this time. This time it would be right. This time she had it all worked out. This time, the prostitute would be caught unawares.

Grace slithered out of the doorway where she had remained hidden. She lumped onto the pavement and approached the painted lady.

"Excuse me, " she said, thinly.

"Yeah? What do you want?" replied the well spoken, yet abrasive tones of the hooker.

"I don't quite know how to say this. I've never done it before and Lord knows I'm ashamed, but it has to be done."

The call girl was intrigued, "Spit it out, lady. What is it?"

"Oh dear. I'm so embarrassed. You see I've never, how do you say it? I suppose the word for it is procure. I've never procured before."

"What are you talking about?"

"Well, it's like this. I have a son and he has physical needs like any man. It was fine before his accident, but now he can't get a woman to look at him. He's so frustrated and screwed up inside, I think he may do something silly."

"What's wrong with him? Is he ugly?"

Mrs Clifton rambled on as if she hadn't heard. "It's his anniversary today, the anniversary of his accident *and* his birthday. He had the car crash after he'd been out celebrating with his friends. Straight through the windscreen he went and under the wheels of an oncoming car."

The prostitute inclined her head sympathetically. "So what do you want from me?"

"Oh dear. How can I say this? It's been a year now. His face was badly smashed. He lost an arm and a leg. It's terrible when I think of what he was. Would you.....Could you do anything for him? You can come to the house. It's not far. I've got money I can pay. Look." She removed a roll of notes from her battered bag.

The call girl's eyes glimmered greedily. "What do you want? How bad is he? I'll need to know so I can keep my face impassive. How long do you want and how much will you pay?"

Mrs Clifton drew back her pale lips and attempted a smile, the hooker was hooked!

"His face isn't pretty, and he's self conscious about his body. I want you to sleep with him. Do whatever you can. Give him a night to remember. Stay all night."

"All night? That'll cost!" exclaimed the woman.

"All night." Grace affirmed. "Two hundred and fifty enough?"

"Make it three hundred and you've got yourself a deal."

"Three hundred it is, " leered Tony's mother.

"Well then, where to?" asked the woman secretly pleased at cutting such a good deal on a night when business had been slack. It was already ten forty and she didn't suppose she'd turn more than one trick tonight. She repeated her question, "Well, where are we off then?"

"Follow me. I'll take you there. It's not far. I know a short cut. It'll only take about ten minutes."

"OK. Can we exchange money now?"

"Can't it wait until we arrive? You can have it then."

"Money always changes hands first. That's the deal."

"I've only got two fifty here, the rest is at home."

"That'll do."

"And what's to stop you running off?" whined Mrs Clifton craftily.

"I've got more honour than that." replied the woman "But I suppose you're not to know ..." She paused and noticed the pained expression on Mrs Clifton's face. " OK I'll make an exception. You pay me what you have outside your front door, I'm hardly likely to run off then. You can pay me the other fifty when we're indoors."

Mrs Clifton grinned, "It's this way," and she scuttled off into the dark.

The call girl's long legs stepped out with a characteristic click clack of steel tips on concrete and she hurried after Grace Clifton.

Tony's mother hastened down the dimly lit street, turned left down an alley, and onto a deserted building plot, where the ghost like, skeleton scaffolding revealed the shell of a future residence.

The prostitute struggled to keep her footing. She swore as she scraped her shoes on the rubble and caught her fine ten denier stockings.

"Here, where are you taking me?" she called anxiously.

"It's not far. This is the short cut I told you about. Just five minutes more," came the thin, reedy whine.

"Not so fast" called the woman with the hint of a tremor in her voice.

Mrs Clifton smiled, the whore was afraid. Good. She had need to be. Grace Clifton turned around the side of the building and slipped into the gloom of an intended doorway.

"Don't go so fast, I can't keep up," called the woman.

" As I said it's not much further, just across this site and we're home," called Grace Clifton from the shadows.

"I can't see you. Where are you."

The woman turned the building block wall, passed the gloom of the doorway. She hesitated fractionally. There was a sudden movement, a glint of silver.

Holly screamed.

She began flailing her arms around, reversing across the room until her back was against the wall. She attempted to cover her body as if she was escaping a rain of blows. She slumped to the floor and began to weep.

Mrs Clifton looked up from her grisly task at the moon whose light ribboned through the scaffolding. A smoky, grey cloud drifted over the glowing map face, of earth's satellite. Half of Mrs Clifton's face appeared eclipsed. The other revealed her moonstruck nature.

Grace felt the hidden eyes, she felt another presence, and she knew the name. Grace Clifton turned her unblinking, lizard eyes towards the birch-bark light of the moon. A thin, wispy strand of grey hair caught in the stirrings of the wind and Tony's mother let out a simian cry which surged from within her. The pupils of her eyes dilated, sucking in the sparse beams that reflected back like tiny rays and her lips formed the word, "Gillian", which echoed in whispers and tormented Holly's ears. The malevolent, insinuating, oh so soft tones culminated in a terrifying, humourless laugh that menaced Holly, leaving her shivering in horror.

Holly bit her lip so hard that she drew blood. She mustered up her energy and shrieked into the night,

"Let me be!"

But there was no Paul to rush to her aid, no Colin to explain things away. She was on her own with the happenings and this time Holly was positive the watcher knew of her existence. What Holly was less sure of, was the significance of the small cat ornament clutched in the dying prostitute's hand.

"Dying!" exclaimed Holly, "not dead."

There was a chance, a slim chance. If she could identify the area, phone the police.... but the chance was ripped from her as the sharp knife sliced through the woman's throat. That last opportunity to save a life seeped away with the prostitute's blood.

Judy was learning more and more about herself. She had a name, a background and a friend, more than *one* friend. She believed luck was with her after all.

David had returned to Birmingham. Penny had stayed on a couple of days and Hayley had somehow roped Judy in to help with the village's spring fete. All in all, she was feeling pretty good about herself.

Now the police had a name, it was just a formality to find out whether or not she was married, the whereabouts of her child and a number of other questions that she felt were yet to be answered. It wouldn't be long. David said he would be in touch and somehow Judy knew she was more than just a case to him. She hoped that at the end of the day they would be able to know each other better without any guilt or worries.

"Are you ready?" came Hayley's strong assertive voice as she climbed down the wooden stairs by the back kitchen. "The meeting starts in fifteen minutes."

"Are you sure you want me there?"

"Of course! If you're going to become involved in village life, then involved you will be." Hayley's tone didn't brook dissension. "You'll meet everyone on the committee. We'll all pool our ideas, as I said, I think your idea of sketching portraits is brilliant. Besides we need to take you out and about and let as many people see you as possible."

"That's not so important now, surely?"

"Don't let's rest on our laurels, and as my mother would say..." here Judy noticed a slight hint of a Manchester accent impinging on her hostess's words, "You never know!"

Hayley grabbed a soft, warm, black, woollen wrap which she threw around her with gusto, covering a striking zebra print suit. "Will you be warm enough in that?" she fussed.

"I'll be fine. It's much milder here than the Midlands. Birmingham was freezing. It really feels like spring here."

"It's milder true, but it's often wetter. I'm sure that's why we've such a large green welly brigade! Talking of which, have you got any wellies? You'll need them, I'm sure."

Judy shook her head.

"No matter. We'll kit you out. If there aren't any to fit you round here, we'll pay a visit to Mole Valley Farmers. They've got the lot....Right, come on then let's get going."

Judy found herself being ushered out of the door and felt rather like one of mother hen's chicks from the farmyard.

Ronnie felt he was doing rather well. He was bruised and in some pain but he didn't believe that they were entirely convinced of his story, but neither did they reject it out of hand.

They were checking. He was sure of that. Had he told enough of the truth for them to doubt his identity? Ronnie had to look on the bright side. He'd answered all their questions as if he really was his cousin, Johnny Lethaby, and they *were* alike. He might just get away with it.!

He was uncomfortable. No longer strapped to a bed but bound sitting up in some sort of hard wooden chair. He still couldn't see and his eyes were sore and puffy. He wondered if anyone missed him. It was unlikely. He skipped off so often no-one kept tabs on him anymore.

Ronnie's feet had gone to sleep. He wondered if he dared try to move them. He couldn't tell yet whether or not he was alone.

The numbness was excruciating. He listened carefully for the sound of breathing, anything...He tried flexing the fingers of his hands tied behind his back and pressing into the ladder back chair. It hurt almost as much to move them as to keep them still. He waited ... nothing.

He gently eased his foot forward but as he did so...

"Ah Ronnie baby. You're awake. Now, where were we?"

Ronnie's heart took a dive. He was not alone. Rats was with him. Now, what could he do? "Remember!" he told himself fiercely, "Up here for thinking, down there for dancing." He feigned a groan as if not fully conscious. But Rats was not to be fooled. Ronnie received a sharp blow on the side of his face.

"Why do you keep calling me that? My name's Johnny... Johnny Lethaby.." Ronnie persisted stubbornly.

"We'll see" Rats breathed heavily into his face. Ronnie grimaced, the breath was unpleasant, fetid. It made him want to wretch. Somehow he managed to suppress his revulsion and turned it into a cough.

"Could I have a drink please? I'm really dry, my throat is so sore."

"You can have a drink when you tell us what we want to know."

"I've told you, I don't know what you're talking about."

Fire and Rain

A door to Ronnie's left opened with a slight creak. Someone came into the room.

"We've got the wrong lad," hissed Rattlesnake.

"What?" snarled Rats in astonishment.

"Everything he says checks out. Ronnie and his cousins are like peas in a pod. Short of making things awkward for us I asked as many questions as I dared. Seems to pan out. We've got the wrong kid."

"Now what do we do? We can't let him go. He knows too much."

"But, he hasn't seen our faces."

"Immaterial, he's got to go."

"Now, look here," complained Rattlesnake, "I'm not in to killing kids."

"What did you think we were going to do with him. Send him on safari?"

"I just didn't reckon on killing a child."

"There's a lot at stake here. "

"Yes, but how much does he know? ...He knows we're after his cousin. He doesn't know why. Can't we just dump him somewhere?'

And have him alerting all and sundry to what's happened and that we're after Ronnie?"

"I won't say anything. I promise," burst in Ronnie growing more alarmed with what he was hearing, "I don't know who you are. I won't say, I swear."

"Too right you won't. You won't have the chance."

"Please," screamed Ronnie with real terror creeping into his voice.

"Shut the brat up, I can't think," yelled Rattlesnake.

Ronnie felt a hard weight clout him on the back of his head and he remembered no more.

10

WHIRLPOOL

Allison stuffed his hands in his pockets and surveyed the scene to which he'd arrived. The area around the building site was cordoned off with tape. Car radios blared with distortion.The fleet of coppers and Forensic were making a detailed search of the surrounding area.

He sighed philosophically, this was becoming an all too familiar sight.

He shivered, not with cold although it was bitter, but with the knowledge that this could be anyone's daughter, could even have been Cally, only he thanked God it wasn't. This young woman's life had come to an abrupt end. The paramedics had tried everything they could to revive her but the small flame in her psyche had been snuffed out. She was beyond recall. At the nape of her neck a small sliver of flesh had been removed, in the shape of a cross.

"Somebody *must* have seen something," growled the DCI almost to himself.

"No-one on the streets, sir," answered Mark believing he'd been addressed.

Allison turned abruptly, screwing his eyes up against the blasts of fiercely chill air.

"Anything else to report?"

"She was clutching a little cat ornament. Where it came from I don't know, unless it belonged to the killer."

"Handle it carefully, give it to Forensic."

"Already done. Sir, how did you know there had been another murder? In normal circumstances the body wouldn't have been discovered until morning when the builders arrived for work. It's fairly tucked out of the way here."

"Colin Brady," replied Allison as if that explained it all.

"Sir?" questioned Mark.

"That weird friend of his who tapped into the other murders. Had another happening as she called it, rang Colin and he rang me. I telephoned the incident room. It wasn't difficult to pinpoint the place from her description. It's a well known red light area, a few more minor details and it was easy enough to find. It just doesn't make any sense. I'm not one for this supernatural stuff, but she's been right every time."

"Has she an alibi?"

"Oh there's no question of her being involved. I just find something like this difficult to accept, that's all. Too many years in the force with crimes solved by hard work. I can't quite accept it."

Mark Stringer nodded. There was nothing he could say. He wasn't used to seeing his Chief like this, in a defeated frame of mind.

"Well, sir what now?"

"I'm going back home. I can't think straight here. I'll leave you to sort it, file the report."

"Sir."

Allison turned briskly and retreated to his car, leaving Mark in charge.

The young sergeant puzzled for a moment. There was something wrong with his boss, something not quite right. Perhaps Mary would know. He'd get Debs to ring her in the morning for a chat. Something was definitely worrying Greg Allison and Mark didn't think it was anything to do with work.

Holly bravely faced Colin Brady

"Well Colin, what have you found?"

"Not as much as I would like. I'm still working on it. According to the adoption agency your mother was extremely unwilling to give you up, she loved you very much and although her marriage had failed, she wanted you desperately. She kept you for two and a half years but she was in financial difficulties, suffering from depression and not looking after you as she should. You were taken into care and when that happened she took her own life."

"What about my father? Grand parents?"

"Your mother registered you in her maiden name of Fisher. There must be documentation with your father's name. The agency is looking for it. It was a long time ago."

"And the rest of the family?"

"I'm coming to that. Your grandmother was widowed, the shock of losing their daughter was too much for your grandfather and he died. His pension died with him. Your grandmother didn't feel as if she could bring you up alone in such dire circumstances with little or no money to her name. It's a decision she's always regretted."

"You've spoken to her?"

"Only on the phone" Colin cleared his throat, "She wants to meet you if you're willing."

"I've told you, no. I have my family. I don't need another." Holly's mind was spinning. She was in turmoil. "What else did she say?"

"She talked a lot about you and how she had tried to find you after the adoption, but met with blank walls... I think you should see her, hear what she has to say."

"I wish you'd never started this. I don't know what to do."

"She won't tell us what we need to know unless you see her."

"That's blackmail."

"I know... but you must remember this is a woman who lost all hope of ever finding you. She would do anything to have another chance."

Holly sat silently, staring into space. She was confused, angry and hurt. All these conflicting emotions served to make her sullen and still.

Colin rose and spoke to Paul who had been sitting quietly at her side.

"Let her think about it... Talk to her. Help her to sort her feelings out. I'll be home if you want me."

Paul nodded.

"It's OK I'll see myself out. You stay with Holly. I think she'll need you."

Colin left quietly and Paul sat with Holly, taking her hand in his, wondering what to say.

Allison took a bite from his Mars Bar and thought about the call he'd received from Brand. The picture had been examined and X-rayed. It was found to have two pictures underneath the Cézanne, that looked both interesting and genuine.

Brand had explained the extent to which these fraudsters were prepared to go in order to have a work authenticated. They mimicked the Venetian's art of making colours, grinding down lapis lazuli to obtain that unmistakable bright blue paint pigment favoured by the great artists, along with developing colours in a similar way from other precious gemstones. This is what made the forgeries expensive to produce but also difficult to detect. The rewards from this type operation were phenomenal.

Allison sighed, he needed to talk to Ronnie Soper, but the boy was elusive and now his mother had informed them that he'd gone missing.

Allison rubbed his forehead. Another one of his blasted headaches was beginning. He was getting them more and more and couldn't understand it. He'd never suffered with headaches before. He reached in his drawer. The aspirin bottle was empty.

Allison switched on his intercom.

"Maddie," he growled, "have we got any paracetamol in this place?"

Maddie came in with a glass of water and two tablets. She looked concerned.

"Are you all right, sir?"

"Yes, why shouldn't I be?" He snapped. "I've got a headache that's all. Too much to do!"

"Sorry sir, only it's the third time you've asked me this week. You're not coming down with something are you?"

"Well if I am, you'll be the first to know," he said sarcastically and then noticing her hurt expression added, "Sorry Maddie, I didn't mean to be rude. Things are getting on top of me, that's all," and he gave a half hearted smile. Maddie nodded and left his office, shutting the door quietly after her.

Allison lumbered out of his seat and paced to the window to watch the scene outside. That usually calmed him, there was always someone worse off than yourself. But even the activities at the General Hospital had little interest for him now. He groaned and returned to his seat.

The phone rang.

"Yes?" he answered gruffly.

"Greg?"

"Oh, it's you Mary. What do you want?"

"There's no need to bite my head off."

"Sorry, Mary. It's this blasted headache."

"Not another one?"

"Never mind that. Why did you call?"

"Have you forgotten? We have a dinner party tonight. You're cutting it fine."

"Sorry love. I'm leaving now."

"You know Greg, if these heads of yours keep persisting, I think you should see the doctor."

"I'm fine, really. See you in a while."

Greg replaced the receiver but made no move to leave. He had forgotten the dinner date completely.

DCI Allison finally scraped back his chair took his hat and coat and left the office.

"Well Judy, what did you think?" asked Hayley as they bustled in from their second committee meeting.

"There were a lot of people there that I hadn't met before. Some good ideas too."

"Good. Well, we'll set your stand up near the beer tent, you should get a lot of customers that way. I also think it's a good idea of yours to have the children's painting competition judged by someone in the art world. Maybe we could ask the de Veres. They're quite well up and don't live too far from here. I'll give them a call. It's all in a good cause."

"Hayley, is there *anyone* you don't know?" asked Judy.

"What and who I don't know, I make up. Pretend to call in a few favours. Cheek and the luck of the devil! That's me." She winked broadly at Judy, "Put the kettle on, I'll get the phone."

Judy began to prepare the coffee while Hayley started dialling.

"Oh hello Valerie, Hayley here... Fine thanks and you?... Oh good. What I'm really looking for is Hazel deVere's number. I had it in my old address book and can't find it anywhere... It's to do with the fete. Can you help?... Brilliant! Hold on while I write that down... Thanks. Bye."

"Hayley! You are a shocker. You don't *know* Hazel deVere."

"No, but she doesn't know that! Here goes," and she tapped out the number she'd been given and crossed her fingers."

"Hello? Hazel? It's me, Hayley. I've been meaning to give you a call for some time now, What? Hayley, Hayley Roberts we met at Valerie Perrin's party. Remember? We had so much in common and you did say if there was anything you could do to help the village. Surely you... I can't believe you'd forget... I know we all had a lot to drink that night but... yes, Hayley. Of course!"

Judy raised her eyes heavenward as she listened to her hostess convince the woman on the other end of the phone that they had not only met, but that she actually owed her a favour. Before Hayley finished the call she had made arrangements for two of the deVeres to judge the art competition, donate something for the raffle and pose for one of Holly's portraits then to be auctioned.

Hayley sipped her coffee.

"Not a bad evening's work, what?"

Judy laughed and shook her head in disbelief.

"I wouldn't like to cross you," she said honestly.

"I must say, I make a better friend than an enemy!" agreed Hayley with a smile. "Now, how about a night cap?"

"Thanks, but no thanks – not tonight. I've drunk enough coffee to keep me up half the night without running to the loo every hour."

"Fair enough. I'll see you in the morning. Seven sharp. You have breakfast to serve! Night."

"Night," replied Judy and made her way to the cottage across the yard and her welcoming bed.

She had just snuggled under the duvet when the internal phone jangled for attention.

"Hello?" she said sleepily.

"You've got a call," said Hayley. "I didn't think you'd want to miss it. It sounds like your young man."

Judy pushed herself up on her elbow and switched on her bedside light.

"Putting you through," said Hayley.

"Hi! It's me David,"

Judy felt a warm glow spread through her.

"Hello. I'd just gone to bed."

"Sorry, I didn't mean to wake you."

"It's OK. I wasn't asleep. How are you?"

"Fine. I thought I'd give you an update. Are you ready for this?"

"As ready as I'll ever be, shoot."

"Well, you were married to a guy called Gary Kruger, ring any bells?"

"No."

"The marriage was dissolved two years ago after only eighteen months. You were married in Reading where you had studied Art at Bulmershe College after A levels and lived in a place called Shinfield before moving to the West Country. You had a baby boy, Luke delivered at the maternity unit in Reading. Luke died at seven months. Cot death. I should imagine that's what must have contributed to your break up. So you see, nothing sinister. But I reckon when you do remember, you'll need some form of counselling. What do you think?"

"It's a lot to take in... but at least I know something of my past... and that I'm not married," she added carefully.

"It's only part of the picture I know, but it's a start. This information all came from official records. Once we had a name, it was fairly straight forward. But you've a long way to go to fill in all the blanks." There was a pause and then David continued,"I've got some leave due to me, coming up. Would it be all right if I came down to see you for a little while? Do you think you could fix it up?"

"I'd like that, when were you thinking of coming?"

"Would the weekend be OK?"

"Sounds fine. Let me see what I can do. Can you call me back tomorrow? After eight? My mind is like a whirlpool at present. There's a lot to take in."

"Will do. I'll let you rest now. Until tomorrow. Night Judy. Bye."

"Night." Judy thoughtfully replaced the receiver. Her mind was indeed a whirlpool. She wondered if it would ever settle, but before long she was sound asleep.

11

FACE IN THE CROWD

"A boy has been found, barely clinging to life. Could be the missing lad, Ronnie Soper."

"Where are you?"

"On my way back to the station, thought you'd want to know."

"I'll be there as soon as I can. You can fill me in on the details when I arrive"

Allison swung his legs out of bed and groaned,

"Sorry Mary, I didn't mean to wake you."

"That's all right... Greg, what's wrong?"

"Mark rang. He thinks they've found the lad Ronnie Soper, barely alive he says."

"I don't mean the phone call, I'm talking about you. You're not yourself. Don't tell me it's pressure of work, you've been in the force thirty four years and you've never been as pre occupied as this."

"We'll talk about it later," grunted Allison hunting for his socks.

"Don't shut me out, Greg. You've always talked to me before."

"Leave it, Mary. I haven't time for this now. I'll see you when I get back."

Greg Allison lumbered out of their bedroom and shut the door softly behind him. Mary lay awake in the half light, the timid tick of the clock pounded uncharacteristically like a hammer in her head. She turned over and faced the window, listened for the sound of the car engine which she heard shortly pulling away and sighed heavily. There would be no more sleep for her tonight. Well, she thought philosophically, that would make two of them.

Allison rubbed his stubbly chin and listened grimly to Mark.

"It was a sheer fluke he was found. Two keen divers from the Birmingham sub aqua club had got their second class exam coming up and decided to practise for their night dive. They had permission from their instructor who agreed to go along with them and they made their way to Dostil."

"Dostil? Where's that?"

"It's a flooded quarry in Staffordshire used by the club to practise their outside dives."

"I see, what then?"

"They kitted up and their instructor waited at the side. There's a sort of shingle beach. When a torch was flashed across the surface they saw the body of a young lad half in and half out of the water. They hauled him out, tried to resuscitate him while the instructor called for an ambulance."

"What's the boy's story?"

"I don't know. He hasn't regained consciousness yet. We've got a man waiting at the hospital."

"Let me know the minute you hear anything."

"Sir." Mark hesitated, "Greg?"

Greg Allison raised an eyebrow at being addressed by his Christian name. It was something Mark hardly ever did at work.

"Is everything all right?"

"What do you mean?"

"Are you OK? There's nothing wrong is there?"

"Dammit!" growled Allison, "I'm fine. Why does everyone keep asking me if I'm all right? I'm just tired that's all, too much to do and not enough time to do it all in," he stopped when he saw the expression on Mark's face, "Sorry, I didn't mean to bite! I'm tired that's all," he repeated.

Mark could see that his chief was in no mood for discussion, so he made his apologies and left.

"Sorry, sir. I'll get over to the hospital, see if there's any change."

Allison sat at his desk. He needed to think. He needed time and time was a luxury he didn't have.

Pressure was mounting every moment. The publication of the league tables of policing performance didn't help, especially with Nottingham doing so well, that rankled with his superintendent. Allison viciously dragged open his desk drawer and searched for a Mars Bar, something to give him some energy and uplift him, while he waited for news from Mark before he attacked some of the growing mountain of paperwork.

He greedily demolished his chocolate in a few bites, but the comfort he derived from his secret vice began to wane with the onset of yet another headache.

The Chief burrowed his hand into his coat pocket on the stand until he felt the new box of headache tablets he'd purchased the previous day. Allison knew there was something wrong and promised himself that he would make an appointment to see his doctor. There was no use burying his head in the sand, he had to keep his feet on the ground and sort it. He'd ring his quack to arrange a visit as soon as he went home.

Sandra Thornton stepped lightly down the path that led from her house and walked towards the bus stop where she would catch the bus that would take her to the town, the shops and her dojo. She was leaving early enough to give herself time to hunt for a decent present for her mum's birthday and still arrive on time for her martial arts class.

She breathed in the air of the fresh, crisp afternoon. The sun was out and its arrival in the sky heralded the death of the winter. Spring was well and truly on its way and she was looking forward to summer.

She sighed – the seasons seemed to be shifting, melting into one another but she smiled brightly. It was good to be alive!

A lot had happened to Sandra. She knew full well that she was lucky to have a second chance with her family and to have survived Tony Clifton's attack. Thank heavens those two men had seen her when that lunatic was upon her.

Sandra broke into a run as she saw the familiar Ribble bus approach the stop. She had to hurry if she was to catch it and not waste half an hour waiting for the next.

She swung her bag with her karate gi, onto her shoulder, and started to sprint. As she began to run she noticed an old woman hobbling across the street towards her, wearing a pom pom hat and faded coat that was too tight.

Something flickered in Sandra's memory about the old lady. Something she couldn't quite recall but in her haste to catch the bus she pushed it from her mind.

She boarded the bus and moved to the long seat at the back and peered out of the grimy window. The old woman's face registered again. The creature was standing on the corner by the traffic lights staring at the bus as if searching for something. Her eyes met Sandra's for one brief instant, her lips twitched triumphantly upwards and Sandra shivered involuntarily.

The moment was brief. The faces of the people on the street became a blur and Sandra wiped the image from her mind.

Hayley was walking around the fete site with the other members of the committee, checking that everything was in order, in readiness for the opening the following day.

Judy went to see that her pitch was not too close to the litter bins at the entrance of the beer tent. She didn't want the corner to be so swamped with people that her stand would be swallowed up in the crowds.

She adjusted the board advertising her work ensuring that the polythene cover was fully protecting the notice, keeping it dry in case it rained over night. As she stooped to pick up her bag she heard a faint rustling coming from behind the beer tent.

Something made her unnaturally alert and tense. She stood up, stiffened and listened... Nothing. She bent over again.

As she did so she heard a sudden rush of sound and felt a cutting blow to her crown that sent her reeling. A menacing voice rasped in her ear,

"Say one word and you're dead."

She felt another crack, fell forward on the grass, grazing her temple on the tent peg. Her eyes blinked helplessly as she sunk into oblivion.

A figure shaded by the increasing darkness watched for a moment and before retreating, dropped a lighted match on to the bales of straw stacked inside the tent ready to be used as seating the following day.

The dry straw began to smoulder and smoke before bursting into life. The flames greedily licked the bales; the tongues of fire lapped, crackled and leaped, engulfing the straw in its hungry haste and feverishly danced the frenzied jig of a demon. The searing heat blazed out, scorching the sides of the tent until that too burst into flame.

Judy lay still – dangerously close to the tent flaps which began to burn crazily in the dusk with the florid glow of an enforced sunset, and no one saw.

Mrs Clifton sat in the café at the coach station., She needed to plan carefully. She now had a rough idea of some of Sandra Thornton's movements; the days she attended classes at the dojo, her regular weekly counselling appointment, and twice weekly shopping trips. The rest of the week was variable but she usually walked the family dog, sometimes with her dad before he went to work, but always in the evening alone. Tony's mother had to decide which strategy to adopt, and work everything out to the last detail. She would do that at home.

Tony's mother missed the ritual cleansing of her son. She yearned to hold him in her arms, to feel that power, that maleness that she controlled.

Her eyes darted swiftly around her and she licked her lips lasciviously in anticipation of their reunion.

"Hold on, Grace!" she thought to herself, "Don't you get carried away and get careless... Careful planning, that's what is needed."

"I'm sorry, are you talking to me?" interjected a perspiring, fat man with a bald head.

"Sorry," she muttered in her vinegary voice, "I didn't realise I was speaking aloud."

"Oh, I beg your pardon," puffed the man "...I sometimes do that."

"What?"

"Talk to myself. Don't mean to...I just do. It can be embarrassing at times."

"Yes, yes." agreed Mrs Clifton who turned away. She didn't want to become involved in conversation with anyone. That wouldn't do... that wouldn't do at all. She must keep her head down – disguise – yes that was it! When she returned for Sandra she would disguise herself. Her leering lips began to twitch upward. She took a sidelong look at the fat man. Yes, she'd be safe. He wouldn't remember her.

But she was wrong.

Ronnie Soper's mother stayed at the hospital, day and night. She slept in the mother's room on the ward. His hold on life was tenuous and the doctors were doing everything in their power to help him cling on and recover.

Whatever disaster had beset Ronnie, it had an immediately sobering effect on Mrs Soper who had been shocked into sensibility.

She sat by his bed holding his hand, "I promise you Ronnie, things will be different. I know I've been wasting my life and neglected you. It will never happen again... It seems that when Tim died, I blamed everyone more than myself, including you. I'm so sorry... so very, very sorry."

The tears welled up in her eyes, "Please let me put things right – make amends. All I'm asking for is another chance from you and God. I promise I will make it work. I *promise*...You've just *got* to get better."

She lay her head on his hand and wept.

Greg Allison looked stern faced at the young copper in front of him. "Getting emotionally involved with a victim of crime is neither wise nor permitted."

"Sir."

"I realise that Ms Court is now out of our jurisdiction and residing temporarily in Devon, but your continued interest in her, when the circumstances surrounding her attack are still under investigation, is not suitable behaviour for a member of this force particularly one anxious to leave the uniformed branch and who has only recently begun a trial period with the CID."

"Sir."

I realise that you do have some leave owing you and how you spend it is your own business but it would be foolish in the extreme to visit Ms Court."

Allison paused, "in view of your involvement with the young lady concerned, which has only today come to my attention, I am removing you from this investigation. Sergeant Pooley will work with PC Parkhouse and I am assigning you to work with the team dealing with the Calcutt killing. I want you to check these dates with all of Clifton's associates, including his mother," Allison handed Taylor a list.

"Sir..." Taylor hesitated.

"Well?" barked Allison. "Spit it out – What do you want?"

"Can I still book my weekend leave?"

Allison sighed, "Book it, but before you go I want you to visit Clifton's mother again. Check her exact whereabouts with each of the dates and times on the list."

"Sir."

"And Taylor..."

"Sir?"

"Use your loaf, stay away from the Court girl."

As if on cue the telephone sprang into life, jangling for attention which the curt Allison answered before dismissing Taylor with a nod of his head. He listened, put his hand over the mouthpiece and growled, "Wait," to the retreating copper.

"Thank you for letting me know. We'll send someone down."

Allison scratched his chin thoughtfully and stared at young David Taylor.

"How serious is it between you and Ms Court?"

"It's not... We're just friends," blushed Taylor.

"But you'd like it to be something more?"

"I feel it's a strong possibility," answered Taylor truthfully.

"That was the Devon and Cornwall police. It seems Ms Court was the victim of another attack last night."

Taylor's face dropped, his concern was apparent.

"Look, your personal life is none of my business – Your police life is... I've promised to send a man down. We can't spare the staff – so..."

Allison took a deep breath weighing up the consequences of what he was about to say.

"I'm not back tracking on what I have just said – I want you to continue with your reassignment but..." his measured tones continued, "Have the weekend off. Go to Devon and see Ms Court but remember what I've said."

"Yes, sir. Thank you, sir. Is Judy... Is she all right?"

"You must understand that you have to complete your work here first." said Allison ignoring the question. "Visit Mrs Clifton first, then on Friday take yourself off to Devon." He raised a hand as Taylor was about to interrupt. "She's in hospital in Barnstaple, Fortescue ward, suffering from smoke inhalation and a fractured skull. I'll expect you back for duty, with your reports, Tuesday nine o'clock sharp."

"Yes, sir. Thank you, sir. I'll get onto this right away."

The words tumbled from him.

"And Taylor...."

"Sir?"

"Curb your enthusiasm, keep a level head."

"Sir," he stopped at the doorway, "thank you."

Greg Allison watched the door close quietly. He was getting soft in his old age. Mellowing Mary called it. Still at least he could justify his reasons. It made more sense to send Taylor who understood the case. It saved briefing someone else and saved another officer overtime and expenses. He half smiled, "Love," he muttered aloud and tugged open his drawer for his Mars Bar. He needed one now to uplift his spirits.

Mrs Clifton took out a crisp sheet of white cartridge paper from the art notebook she had purchased. She drew up a plan of Sandra Thornton's house – the roads and streets surrounding it and a time-table outlining Sandra's activities for the week.

Grace Clifton was meticulous. The drawing was as accurate as an unqualified person could make it. Sketched with precision, carefully labelled – as were her proposed victim's usual route to the shops and preferred walk with the family dog.

Tony's mother studied the map carefully; Sandra Thornton walked the dog every day between seven and eight in the evening on Tuesday, Thursday, Saturday and Sunday. On Monday and Wednesday she would take the dog out after she arrived home from her Karate class, usually a shorter walk between ten thirty and eleven. On Friday, the routine exercise was earlier between six and six thirty.

One Saturday in the month Sandra attended a special kumite and kata class and Sandra's mother and father would take the dog out themselves. So, it had to be a Monday or Wednesday – that much was certain. And then there was the dog... although not a large dog it was big enough to be a problem and big enough to cause injury.

Grace knew she would have to deal with the dog before she dealt with Sandra. That could be tricky. She'd prepared a batch of apple muffins and injected them with laudanum from a bottle that had belonged to her grandmother which had been sitting in her bathroom cabinet for many years, she hoped that it had not lost its potency. What she needed was something to try it out on. Next door's cat was a possibility but to Grace's mind, a remote one, as she believed that the cat wouldn't be tempted to eat apple muffins. Meat! Meat would be a much better proposition but there again her apple muffins would undoubtedly be relished by a dog. Surely it would work? But how much should she feed it? And *how* could she do it?

Tony's mother padded to her box of scrolls, she needed inspiration. She needed the Lord's advice before proceeding any further. She needed His help in the task.

Divine help was indeed at hand. Grace prayed silently for guidance and carefully selected a tiny scroll. Her hand was shaking as she took it from the box. It read,

> Let my adversaries be clothed with shame,
> and let them cover themselves with their
> own confusion, as with a mantle.
> Psalms 109 verse 29.

She opened her Bible, selected a page at random and began to read avidly. She read of David's desires for Bathsheba. Her thoughts drifted from the text to her son.

The pricklings of desire flickered in her thighs. She needed him. She wanted him. She needed cleansing, but the priest that had performed that ritual deed was no longer around. Excommunicated for his abuse of the ideals belonging to the cloth he wore and besides, his dessicated flesh would not satisfy, she needed and yearned for a young, firm body.

PC Taylor rang the bell.

12

SHADES OF PAIN

Judy was sitting up in bed feeling brighter and more cheerful. Hayley had just arrived and sat at her side.

"You took a nasty crack on the head, what happened?"

"I don't know – one minute I was stooping to get my bag – I heard a noise and the next thing I know, a voice in my ear is telling me that if I spoke I'd be dead. I felt a bang on my head... The rest you know."

"What about your memory? Has that come back?"

Judy shook her head slowly.

"No... But I had some strange dreams. I thought a blow to the head could restore a lost memory but nothing like that has happened for me."

"Well, I've some good news for you. David phoned."

"David? David Taylor?"

"Yes. He is travelling down on Friday... It seems more than professional interest."

"God I look awful!"

"So it *is* more that professional interest." Hayley noted that Judy neither confirmed or refuted the statement and so continued. "I think Rebecca may be coming down too, to see how you are coming on. But, first things first. Get yourself fit and well. I need your help at the hotel. I've also put your name down for a stand at the flower show at the local school. You can do what you were supposed to do at the fete, if that's OK?"

Judy sighed, it was difficult to say no to Hayley – that much she'd learnt. It was far easier to say yes. Besides, whoever had cracked her on the head might be tempted to have another go but this time she'd be prepared.

Judy let her mind wander off on a track of its own. Her face appeared to be alert and listening. She would put in an 'ah' or 'yes' or 'mmm' in appropriate places but what she was really looking forward to was David's arrival on Friday. She would try and make herself look better for his visit. She didn't know it then, but David wouldn't arrive.

Mrs Clifton unfastened the door a crack. When she saw young David Taylor she opened it wide and welcomed him in with a leering smile that resembled that of a smug frog about to gulp an unsuspecting fly.

The sickly smell of incense drifted out onto the step and PC Taylor took his last mouthful of untainted air before being swallowed up into the house in Golden Hillock road.

The fairy lights around the cross above the door in the hall blinked crazily. David found himself once more in that room of religious icons and dead saints.

"It's lovely to see you," said the vinegary voice as her hooded eyes roamed over the contours of his body. "I'll just pop the kettle on. You *are* having a cup? You sit there, make yourself comfortable," she droned.

PC Taylor sat himself in the Queen Anne chair and even though he had been in that room before, his eyes still roamed over the Biblical pictures and words from the Scriptures adorning the walls.

He shivered with revulsion and in disbelief. He had never been in a room like it. He gazed at Christ's benign face with hand raised as if blessing him and felt unsettled almost disturbed. He thought that if the room were part of a set for film or television, ordinary cinema goers would criticise the designer for having gone too far. 'But,' he sighed, 'in reality truth *was* far stranger than fiction.'

Mrs Clifton's eyes gleamed as she chatted about inconsequentials such as the weather. She laid out the tea-tray and glanced at the apple muffins. It was than that the idea occurred to her.

"Been busy have you?" she asked.

"Relatively."

"How's that young girl of yours?"

"Young girl?"

"The one that lost her memory."

"Judy? It's a long story. I'll tell you over tea... I have some leave owing, so this weekend I'm going to Devon to see her."

"She's in Devon is she?"

"Yes... it seems likely she has links there."

"When are you leaving?"

"After I've seen you. I'm supposed to travel tomorrow, Friday – but I've decided to leave as soon as possible. It will give me an extra night. My report doesn't have to be in until Tuesday morning."

This was better and better. Grace Clifton was sure that God was guiding her hand. Why waste time trying her cakes out on next door's cat when she could try them out on David Taylor.

"It's official then? Why you're here?"

"Just a few questions, some loose ends to tie up, cross checking that sort of thing."

Grace didn't think it sounded serious. She was becoming careless. She wasn't thinking things through. Yes, she felt sure she could bluff her way out of trouble, if he succumbed to her muffins and fell asleep. Besides, he might not even be aware of anything wrong. Grace thought she had been given the perfect opportunity, but she hadn't reckoned on the feelings that would stir within her when she had David Taylor in her power.

The words tripped out so easily to the unsuspecting copper.

Would you like some apple muffins? I've just made a fresh batch with a hint of mint. I've got plenty of cream."

"Lovely," replied David,"The last ones I had here were delicious."

"Muffins it is then, with lots of cinnamon," quavered Mrs Clifton and she resolved to pour extra cream over them in case there was any lingering after taste.

Mark Stringer reported to the copper on duty at the hospital, where Ronnie Soper was being looked after.

"Relief is on the way. Any news?"

"His mother has been with him all night...Otherwise nothing. The doctor seems to think that if he's going to pull through, we should have signs fairly soon."

"I just hope for his sake that he does. So young..." and Mark shook his head sympathetically. "I'll just pop in and have a look."

Mark drew back the curtain by the bed as softly as he could. Mrs Soper didn't move. She was fast asleep with exhaustion. Mark looked at the young, impish face, the wires from machines that were attached which blipped and hummed. Ronnie gave a deep sigh and tried to turn onto his side. Mark was instantly alert. Comatose patients didn't turn themselves they had to *be* turned.

Mark swiftly left the small room and alerted the copper who was exchanging a few words with his relief.

"Quick, get a doctor. I think the boy is recovering."

The policeman dashed for the desk and spoke to the nurse who went to Ronnie's bed to see for herself. Mark quickly explained what he had seen. The nurse alerted the doctor by having him paged. Mrs Soper was now awake and adding to the confusion with her own bewilderment.

Mark hastily repeated what he had told the nurse and the implications of what he had seen. Mrs Soper's eyes filled with tears as she grabbed Mark's hands.

"If what you say is true then there is a God and he has heard me. "

She turned back to Ronnie and sat at his side, talking excitedly to him, informing him of plans she had made, things they would do together and other words personal to her and Ronnie. Mark listened for a moment as her words tumbled forth. He retreated discretely to wait for the doctor and his prognosis. But he felt that Mrs Soper's prayers had indeed been answered.

Greg Allison groaned. He didn't like it. He didn't understand it. The Calcutt killing and that of the two prostitutes showed evidence of Tony Clifton having been at the scene of the crime but that was impossible! Nevertheless, he had a perfect print on a coffee cup, a rosary with traces of saliva which matched Clifton's DNA and a small cat ornament bearing a smudged print that looked remarkably like Clifton's.

Allison slammed his fist on his desk, all this just at the time when a newspaper report had come out casting doubt on the validity of DNA testing. This together with a batch of letters subscribing to the belief of Clifton's innocence and demands for an inquiry. There was also a terse note from the Chief Constable demanding Allison's full cooperation with Clifton's lawyer over investigations into the case that Allison had considered closed.

He grabbed his Mars Bar from his desk drawer which he shut with a slam and took comfort in the satisfying rip of paper before sinking his teeth into the chocolate bar.

The serenity that this temporarily brought him soon vanished with the onset of yet another blinding headache this time accompanied by the most awful impression of flashing lights that whirled around his mind with more ferocity than a waltzer at the fair.

The light hurt his eyes. The Chief managed to draw the window blinds before he sat down and slumped forward in his chair. He felt as if his mind was about to explode and the end of the world had come.

There he stayed.

The phone rang. The noise was excrutiating. Waves of pain tornadoed through his ears, but he couldn't answer it. He couldn't bring himself to move. Every small gesture was agony.

The intercom buzzed. It added to the cacophony of drilling sounds that bored through his head. Allison could do nothing.

He was like this when Maddie found him.

Grace Clifton watched with relish as David Taylor scooped up the last piece of muffin with cream.

"Would you like some more?" She whined.

PC Taylor patted his stomach to indicate his fullness,

"I couldn't eat another morsel," he protested.

Grace Clifton watched him eagerly. Her hooded eyes did not blink. Her thin mouth almost drooled as she licked away the spittle that formed droplets on her lower lip.

David Taylor felt disconcerted, like an insect that had unwittingly become ensnared in the web of a red backed spider whose eight eyes were focused on him, prior to devouring him by sucking out his life force.

The young policeman shook his head to clear the muzziness that enveloped him. The spider image became more distinct and as Mrs Clifton leaned forward, he saw her mouth move and imagined tiny spinnerets and mandibles twitching rhythmically in each corner of that grinning, gaping, rimless opening. He heard echoed words that pulsed in and out of his consciousness first in a crescendo and then diminishing. Her lips seemed out of sync with words that made no sense. He had the feeling that he was floating, leaving his body and watching the whole scene from a great height. He appeared to be losing control of his limbs and his mind. He couldn't feel his extremities or his tongue which lolled awkwardly out of his mouth. The feeling of numbness spread through him.

David Taylor gasped for air and slipped off his seat and fell forward in to the carpet. At the same time he let go of all his bodily functions.

Mrs Clifton smiled.

13

TRUTH IS PARAMOUNT

Holly sat opposite her maternal grandmother. Paul was at her side. Colin stood by the window facing the garden of tangled weeds that was a haven for butterflies and bugs.

"Isn't it peaceful? I keep the front cultivated for the sake of the neighbours, but most of the back garden with its high walls, from the rockery to the back fence, I have resolved shall be a sanctuary to nature. I am rewarded by the wildlife that visit. Do you know I even have a fox that comes to feed?"

Her conversation wasn't directed at anyone in particular but Holly nodded in understanding. She felt strangely drawn to this woman who bore so many of her own characteristics. The same shade of luxuriant hair although liberally peppered with grey was obviously a family trait. She had large dark eyes like Holly, although Mrs Fisher's eyes were aged with fine character lines that creased out in profusion like the shooting fronds of a fern that had woven an ambush across her face and netted on her forehead.

"I wish you had come to me earlier. There is little left for me now and I have reached the evening of my life. To have known you would have filled the void I have endured since my husband and daughter's deaths."

"It's not exactly like that," snapped Holly crisply.

"I understand that," Mrs Fisher replied graciously, "And I admire your principles, agree with your sentiment, but selfishly I suppose I regret your decision. I feel we could have given much to each other."

Holly was about to respond with a suitably barbed comment but Colin forestalled her.

"I'm sure Holly appreciates your words, but time has marched on. If any future relationship is to develop then that is for you and Holly to discuss, but as I explained we are here as a matter of some urgency. We need information on Holly's father and family and some personal details of her family background... if that's all right?" he added cautiously.

Mrs Fisher's gracious face darkened. There seemed to be a momentous pause before she answered.

"Of course, I'll do what I can to help. What do you need to know?"

Colin had plainly taken over the questioning so Paul placed a protective arm around Holly. They all waited anxiously for Mrs Fisher's replies.

"Holly's father...can you remember him?"

"I remember him," she said coolly. "A dark man with brooding passions. Ellie was sixteen when she first brought him home. She was absolutely besotted with him."

Holly was desperate to know her father's name but a warning look from Colin silenced her. Colin believed it was best to let Hilda Fisher talk. She had much to say.

"He seemed a very personable young man, charming and talented. He nearly had me won over except for one thing. I can't quite explain it even now, it was just a feeling, a feeling of dread that seemed to surround me after he'd gone."

Colin made an encouraging little grunt and she continued.

"They were both very young and believe it or not both virgins. It was his first time as well as hers, at least that is what they told me. It's always the good girls that get caught, isn't that what they say?"

"They do indeed," chipped in Paul, who was rewarded with a fierce look from Colin which immediately shut him up.

"He wanted to do the right thing and asked her to marry him. A school boy who was just completing his fifth year at grammar school! She knew he didn't love her enough, but for the sake of the baby, you... she said yes. The first three months they were with me. That's when I saw the other side of him, his terrible mood swings and temper. He could change temperament any minute. His religious fervour - that too, became too much to bear, coupled with his odd moods that Ellie would never detail. She just said that he sometimes acted weirdly in bed. I assumed she meant some sort of perversion or mental aberration, but I could never be sure because she refused to tell me."

Mrs Fisher sighed and stroked her long tapering fingers down her neck. It was obvious to them all that it was still painful to talk of her daughter even now after all these years. Holly said sympathetically,

"You don't have to talk if you don't want to, we'll understand," and she shot Colin her own warning look which yelled 'Back off'.

"No, please. I want to talk. I need to talk. I haven't been able to speak of her you see. Most people avoided the subject after her death believing it best to say nothing, my husband wouldn't speak of her.That was part of the problem, in order to heal the grief you must talk. Oh, how I wanted to, but I've not had the chance until now."

Holly relented, "Then please do...please continue."

"You don't realise what a shock it is seeing you. Here," and she went to her sideboard drawer and took out a black and white portrait photograph.

"This is your mother."

Holly gasped. The face she gazed at, so closely resembled her own, it could have been her in another time and place or, have been her sister.

"Now you can understand why I am so disconcerted."

She retrieved the photograph but instead of replacing it in the drawer she put it on top of the television for all the world to see.

"Too long I have denied my daughter. Now, I must come to terms with her death."

"Please go on," urged Holly, " You were telling us about my father."

"Yes, well.." Mrs Fisher appeared to recover her composure. "Things started to get better. They took a little flat in Handsworth and appeared to be managing quite well until his father died. He committed suicide. Tony took it very hard."

"Tony? Was that his name?" interrupted Holly. This was followed by a glare from Colin.

"Yes..." she muttered almost as if she was remembering his name for the first time in years. "Tony," she repeated. "He had a complete mental breakdown - after that, Ellie left him and came home. She had you at home. It was frowned on then but old Dr Campbell didn't mind. He delivered you. She refused even to have Tony's name on your birth certificate, she registered you in our name. Fisher, Gillian Fisher."

"Gillian," said Holly softly, "So that's my real name."

"Shortly after you were born Tony's mother came to see us. She was a peculiar woman. Black beetling brows and an aura of....I don't quite know how to say it, suffocatingly sweet and kind, but to me she was the total embodiment of evil. I'm probably doing the old dear wrong. I expect she was harmless enough. She was just looking after the interests of her son, but I felt there was something inherent in her personality, something ungodly, although no one professed to love the Lord more than her. She finally persuaded Ellie to try again with Tony, and against my and her father's wishes Ellie went back to him. It was the worst thing she ever did. They came for tea sometimes, when you were a toddler. 'Pobble Daddy, pobble!' You'd cry and you played a game of rubbing noses together which would send you into fits of laughter. Then one Saturday afternoon you didn't come to visit as you always had. Something had happened. I didn't see Ellie again. She didn't talk to us or trust us for reasons that I've never understood. The next thing we know is that Tony has returned to his mother leaving Ellie barely fit to cope and suffering from acute depression. She struggled on alone, too proud to accept help and unwilling to admit she was wrong to place her trust in Tony. You were taken away from her. We knew nothing about it until Ellie's body was found. She left a note...it said that she had no life without you. She loved you very much. The rest you know. The shock of Ellie's death killed my husband which left me in no position to care for you. I lost my home and I was destitute. How could I bring up a little girl when I had nothing to offer."

"I would have had love," murmured Holly, quietly.

"If I'd have known then what I know now, don't you think I'd have done it differently?"

There was an uncomfortable silence while Mrs Fisher regained her composure. Holly cast her eyes down and waited for her grandmother to continue.

"Shortly after the adoption I was lucky enough to find a job, build a career and home, all this that you see now. I worked hard for it, but it all came too late."

"What was Holly's father's full name?" asked Colin.

"His full name was Anthony Francis Clifton."

There was a hush in the room while each person weighed up the implications of that information.

Grace Clifton muttered to herself as she struggled to pull the young copper back on to his seat. He was a dead weight and he wasn't easy to lift. She sniffed imperiously. He had messed his trousers she would have to clean him up and wash him but first where would she put him? If she kept him downstairs there was always the chance a neighbour might see him. The safest bet was up stairs but how could she move him? She was strong, she knew, but strong enough to carry him? She doubted it.

Mrs Clifton scurried out to the garden shed singing stridently as she hunted for some rope, bicycle chain and Tony's sled that he had as a child.

Clattering and banging could be heard until she emerged victorious with a length of brown twined rope, some chain, the sled and a battered skateboard. She disappeared back into the house quoting Exodus chapter fifteen verse two,

'The Lord is my strength and song, and he is become my salvation.....'

Curious eyes peeped from behind net curtains at their neighbour's scurrying. Grace Clifton carried on unaware that eyes were watching.

Mrs Clifton struggled to lift the policeman's limp form on to the sled. She managed to pull up the top half of him and shove the sled under his shoulder blades. She secured him to the sled with a length cut from the rope and then lifted his legs putting his feet and lower legs on to the skate board and tying them to it. The remains of the rope was threaded through the arm bars on the top of the sled and she cleared the furniture to the sides of the room. This done she placed the rope over her shoulder and started to drag the sled across the carpet. Although it was hard going the sled did move, albeit slowly. So far so good. The problem arose when she came to the tiled hallway. There was a sickening scratching as the metal on the under side of the runners met with the uneven tiles. Grace Clifton scuttled to the passage way and lifted the long carpet runner. She placed it over the tiles and lifted the front of the sled on to the mat and tugged. Success! It was bumpy but it moved. Mrs Clifton manoeuvred David's transport to the foot of the stairs. She looked at the flight stretching, it seemed, endlessly before her. This was no good. She mustn't be defeated now.

The words of a hymn threaded into her mind and she began the task, singing lustily as she moved.

She propped the prow of the sled and the tips of the runners on to the first step. She heaved the rope over her shoulder and mustering all her strength pulled hard to drag her cargo up the stairs.

The skateboard was proving to be a hindrance and Mrs Clifton had to fasten the rope through the banisters while she released his feet from the board. She watched as it careered down the stairs across the hall and clattered into the small mahogany table and umbrella stand.

"Let it lie Grace, let it lie," she muttered to herself before resuming her struggle on the stairs. She tugged, twisted and pulled David Taylor's frame. His feet dragged over every stair and his head collided with every step. His scalp bumped and scraped erratically on the wooden lips. She chuckled to herself. He would have a mammoth headache when he came to. Well, she would just have to ease his pain, make him well, kiss him better. The thought of what was in store compelled her to burst into song.

Her reedy tones pervaded the walls as she sang of conquest and love. The Singhs next door smiled. It had been some time since they had heard her sing quite so joyously. They wondered at the reason and resolved to pop round at some point during the weekend.

Grace Clifton finally reached the top landing. She tugged the young man across the floor towards Tony's room and there she undid the ropes that tied him to the sled. With pertinacity that she felt sure came from the Lord himself, she hauled him up by his shoulders and dragged him on to Tony's bed where she confined his wrists with the ropes to the brass bed-head. The rope encircled David's body fixing him securely and his feet were fastened to the end of the bed in a similar fashion.

Mrs Clifton took the jug from the basin and went to fill it with hot water from the bathroom. She returned with soap, flannel and a large towel, larger than she had ever had at home when Tony had lived with her.

She poured the warm water into the bowl on the chest of drawers and turned her attention to the young policeman. She undid the buckle of his belt and released the clip at the top of his trousers. Slowly she slid down the nylon zip, pulled open his flies revealing his Marks and Spencers red, scant pants underneath and although they were wet she couldn't resist running her fingers over the cloth, along his sleeping, uncircumcised penis.

Awakened by the electric pin pricks of desire that trembled inside her thighs, she licked her lips lasciviously as she pulled at his trousers drawing them down to his ankles where they stuck at his heels. Grace Clifton carefully removed the young copper's shoes and placed them neatly together at the side of the bed, next came his socks. They were rolled up one inside the other and deposited in his shoes. With trembling fingers she teased down his under-pants and tossed them into the washing basket by the door.

She turned slowly and stared. Her hooded eyes widened as she viewed his nakedness.

Grace padded towards the bed and slipped the towel under David Taylor's slim hips, leaving enough draped at the side to cover him. What if he were to awake, before she had finished? Grace decided to still those velvet soft lips before they complained.

She disappeared from the room reappearing minutes later with an assortment of items. A length of wide, stout, parcel tape was torn from the roll and wound around PC Taylor's mouth and the back of his head which was bound underneath his jaw to the crown of his head with a bandage. Both the tape and bandage were then secured with strips of surgical adhesive tape. Tony's mother was taking no chances. As long as he didn't gag or choke, he should be perfectly safe.

She removed a blue tube of gel from the bedside table and lubricated herself inside her knickers.

Grace Clifton began her cleansing ritual. She rinsed her hands in the basin of warm water emptied from the ewer. She lifted up her hands to the vaults of heaven letting the water run down her arms and praised the Lord. She begged that he bless her and recited her own adaptation of Leviticus, chapter seventeen, verses twenty four to thirty one that she had misused for her own purposes so many times before, as the old priest had misused it before her.

"And I shall wash thy flesh with water in the holy place."

She immersed the flannel into the bowl.

"And put on fresh garments and come forth and offer my offering and thy offering and make an atonement for myself and thee."

She squeezed out the excess water.

"And the fat of the sin offering shall I give upon this bed."

Mrs Clifton vigorously rubbed soap into the flannel which foamed as if in the height of religious fervour.

"And he that let go the goat for the scapegoat shall wash his clothes and bathe his flesh in water, and afterward come."

She shuddered and sighed as she rolled her eyes and began to wash and massage the limp flesh. As the flannel found every orifice and the water rinsed through his pubic hair, the kneading hands found life beginning to stir.

"Thy body and mine for the sin offering, our coupling to make atonement in the holy place. Our skins, our bodies, our fluids shall mingle together. Our melding together will be an offering of the highest love and gift of God."

David Taylor's penis engorged with blood and the foreskin neatly peeled back. It stood hard against his stomach and Mrs Clifton made a moaning sound.

"She that joins shall wash his clothes and bathe his flesh in water and afterward they shall come together at the camp."

She feverishly pulled up her tight plaid skirt and hurriedly removed her under garments.

"And this shall be a statute forever unto you. The priest shall make an atonement for you, to cleanse you, that ye may be clean from all your sins before the Lord."

Mrs Clifton stroked the moistening glans, teasing the foreskin back and fore with one hand whilst manipulating herself with the other.

She eased herself over the young policeman and guided his penis into her wet vagina, a cry of ecstasy escaping her as she felt his full size inside her. She moved rapidly up and down, squatting over him. It had been so long. She let out a long cry of joy as her inner muscles began to pulse.

David Taylor opened his eyes.

14

WITHOUT ANY DOUBT

Paul gripped Holly by the shoulder,
"You have to accept, Tony Clifton is your father."
"Yes Paul, but he's a murderer! A serial killer – my own flesh and blood. That's not easy to come to terms with."

"You have to realise, you're not going to pick up on bizarre killings any time, any where. Unless you come from a family of weirdos. It just won't happen."

It's already happening. Tony Clifton is inside isn't he? But I'm still having premonitions. What's more, who ever it is, knows me. Someone shrieked my name. 'Gillian' was shouted."

"Yes, that's what I can't work out," interrupted Colin. "Either there's someone else in your family, or the police have got the wrong man."

"How can that be?"

"I can't believe we've made a mistake. The forensic evidence was, to my mind, irrefutable. My studies of Clifton revealed a very dangerous personality. My colleagues and I even considered multiple personality syndrome. I *know* he's our man," said Colin as if convincing himself as well as the others.

"Either way you're telling us, that Clifton is extremely dangerous," said Paul.

"Lethal and unpredictable. I can't believe we *all* got it wrong. But these new murders are certain to throw the whole case into question."

"Could they be revenge killings or copycat?" questioned Holly.

"Please no more copy cat crimes," muttered Colin raising his eyes heavenward. "We had enough with Arthur Crabtree...* No, I don't know. We'll have to wait and see."

"And meanwhile I have to live with the knowledge that my biological father is a murderer. That puts a blight on my whole life. What if his personality disorder, whatever fancy name it has, is hereditary? What then? I can't plan my life, I can't have kids, nothing!" and Holly broke down, sobbing in Paul's arms.

Ronnie Soper was doing well. He had resisted death. His tenuous hold on life became stronger. It seemed his mother's prayers were answered.

Ronnie sat up in bed and chatted to the policeman.

"You're not so bad , you know, " he breathed. "not at all what I expected a copper to be like."

"Well, I should imagine your contact with the police has always been confrontational. This time you're in a position to help us and yourself," smiled PC Parkhouse.

"I can see that, I've got nothing to lose now, nothing."

"It's funny, you know, I've always been a bit of a believer in fate. Maybe this wasn't such a disaster after all. Maybe this was just what was needed to turn your thinking around. Make you appreciate what life has to offer. You're a bright boy by all accounts. Don't let it go to waste."

"A year ago I'd have told you to piss off. Now..."

"Now?"

"Now, I think there might be something in what you say... I've had a chat with Julie Flemming, I'm going to try and make up the school work in the summer with a home tutor. If that doesn't pan out I'm prepared to repeat my year."

"That'll be tough."

"True. But I think I can cope."

"Somehow, I think you will."

"Somehow I do too," grinned Ronnie. "Well, what's next?"

"We've taken a full statement, as soon as the hospital allows you out, we'll expect you down at the station to do a computer

*see *Killing me Softly*

fit on the characters you've dubbed Rats and Rattlesnake. See if we can get a lead – also, we'll need the scraps of paper and cards you found with the coat. You can't remember the registration number of the car?"

"I've tried, but I can't think. I know it was a red BMW, seven series, three litre fuel injection and it was always parked in the same place at the same time – at least while I was watching it. I'm not going to get into trouble for that am I?"

"I think you can count on that. No theft has been reported, so as far as we're concerned, no crime has been committed. I think that points the finger of guilt at our car owner, don't you?"

Ronnie was relieved. His safety, he felt, lay in full co-operation with the police. And that is just what he proposed to do. Cooperate.

David Taylor questioned his own eyesight. He simply could not believe what he was seeing. His head was still muzzy from the effects of the drugged muffins. He could still taste the mintiness that lingered from the laudanum.

Images growing from his mind merged with his surroundings and distorted.The room seemed to be zooming in and out of focus as if he was viewing his environment through the aperture of a camera lens which was constantly being opened and closed. There was a loud rushing in his ears as if the blood was forcing a passage through to his brain. He felt strange. Aroused. As if he had awoken from some erotic dream.

He looked down at himself and saw the squat Mrs Clifton astride him. Her movements gradually subsided until she came to a final shuddering halt.

PC Taylor seemed to know that he was half naked. He tried to move but his restraining bonds held him fast.

His eyes blinked dully as Grace Clifton clambered off him. His thinking, still marred by the drug in his system, could not convince him that this was actually happening. He was sure his imagination was playing tricks or that he was in the grip of some terrible nightmare. His mind was fuddled and drowsy but he determined to pull himself out of this unpleasant dream that had irrevocably taken hold.

He looked up once more. Grace Clifton was gone. The door clicked softly. He allowed his eyes to explore the room. He took in the pallid eyes of the Virgin Mary holding the Christ child, smiling benevolently at her infant son. His eyes paraded around the walls with its insipid colours of lilac flowered wallpaper and heather border. The cream paint on the woodwork had blistered. The light filtered through the amber curtains illuminating the stout beaded wooden cross that faced the bed.

David Taylor had to be in some twilight zone between sleep and consciousness. A surreal existence that made liars of truth.

The last thing he remembered was having a cup of tea with Grace Clifton. He could still taste the gummy residue of the muffins that hadn't tasted or had quite the same texture as before, but were nevertheless, not unpleasant.

His feet had pins and needles. He needed to stamp them to increase the circulation. He flexed his numb fingers and struggled to yawn, but his mouth and jaw would not move.

Slowly the realisation dawned that he was not dreaming. He was becoming more alert and resigned himself to the knowledge that he was well and truly a prisoner of this reptilian old woman.

Allison sat across the desk from his doctor who was peering at him over half spectacles that gave him an erudite, professor quality.

"Come, come Greg. We've known each other too many years to beat about the bush now. What's the problem?"

"Truth is Richard, I don't know."

"Tell me again, what are the symptoms?"

"You know me Richard, hardly ever ill. Then all cf a sudden I'm suffering the most blinding headaches, flashing lights, pressure, nausea... and no reason for it. I've been through more bottles of paracetamol than is wise."

"Mmm. Tell me is there any pattern?"

"Pattern?"

"Come on, you're the detective. Do they occur at a specific time of day? After any particular food? Or activity?"

"Not that I can think of. It seems to be no respecter of time... I can be at home, on the phone, driving - anything, and the blasted thing will strike. As for food, my diet's pretty varied. I really can't think of any correlation between my eats and the headaches."

"Well, that doesn't help me much. There has to be a common factor. These migraines, because that is what you're describing, usually have a trigger... Look, what I suggest you do - is this," Richard Carpenter removed his glasses and rubbed the bridge of his nose, "I want you to keep a diary. Write down everything you do, from walking the dog to close work at the desk. Make a note of everything you eat, and I mean everything, even to a splash of vinegar on your chips."

Allison groaned,

"I have enough paper work without this extra..."

Dr Carpenter cut him short,

"Look Greg, you have a problem, a severe problem. Now, I'm not suggesting you've got a tumour or anything as alarmist as that, but all avenues have to be explored. Migraines usually have a flash point. This could be anything from over work, stress, an allergic reaction or sensitivity to a particular food, drink or substance. So you need to keep a diary. Write everything down that may be a factor. It's a process of elimination. Meanwhile when you feel the onset of a headache take one of these."

Dr Carpenter placed a prescription in the computer printer on his desk and typed out his recommendation.

"Only take one when you feel it beginning. This will stop it stone dead. On no account take one to prevent the migraine manifesting itself. And I want to see you and your completed diary two weeks from now. Is that understood?"

"Affirmative!"

Greg Allison rose from his consultation seat and left clutching his prescription. He would start his diary tomorrow after a good night's sleep, but now... now he needed his Mars Bar.

Judy was worried, David had told her that he would arrive late afternoon. It was now ten past eight and there was no sign of him, no message, nothing.

"Stop panicking," consoled Hayley. "There must be a simple explanation. Either he's held up in traffic and can't get to a phone or maybe he's had to remain on duty. For heaven's sake, he's a policeman. There could be any number of explanations."

"I know, I know... I just have a gut feeling that something is wrong. I'm sure he's not that thoughtless. He'd let me know if there was a change of plan."

"Look, wait until tomorrow. If he's not here by the afternoon, ring him at home."

"I haven't got his number," murmured Judy quietly.

"I don't believe this. You mean to say that this man who you've set your sights on hasn't given you his home number and you haven't asked for it?"

Judy looked crestfallen.

"I know exactly what to do. Just leave things to me," bossed Hayley and looked enquiringly at her.

Judy already knew it was wiser not to argue with Hayley once she had made up her mind. Much better to go with the flow, besides she really would like to have David's number.

Judy sighed disconsolately, "Whatever you say Hayley."

"Good, then that's settled. Now, where does he live?"

"I'm not sure but I think he said he came from Selly Oak."

Hayley marched to the hall and picked up the phone and dialled directory inquiries.

Allison put down the telephone, frowned and rubbed his chin thoughtfully. He switched the intercom,

"Maddie", he growled. "Get Mark in here."

"Sir."

A moment later Mark knocked on the chief's door.

"You wanted me?"

"Yes, something strange... Mrs Taylor has been on the phone. Young David was to have set off for Devon last night. She's just had a call from the guest house where he was to stay. He never arrived."

"What?"

"Mm. He had a brief from me to question the Court girl after he'd finished his assignments here."

"So, where is he? David's pretty reliable. He's not one to go walk about."

"My feelings exactly. Check his files, then get over to Mrs Taylor's. See what you can learn. I've a hunch we're going to learn something very surprising."

"Chief."

Mark abruptly turned and left the office. Allison's hand went to his top drawer and took out a Mars bar from his hidden store. He reached for his notebook, glanced at his watch and made an entry.

"Saturday, 11.15 am Mars Bar."

He paused before tearing off the wrapper and flicked through his diary. He stopped and made a more studied examination. Allison ran his finger over three of his entries for Mars bars each one was followed by another; that of a blinding headache minutes later. He tossed the confectionery back in his drawer and slammed it shut, flicked on the intercom and asked Maddie to bring him through tea and biscuits. Not quite the same, but if his suspicions were right then he wouldn't be suffering a bumper headache shortly afterwards. He'd have to avoid his treat for a while, to make certain.

Maddie knocked courteously and entered with a cuppa and two plain digestives. Allison looked at them unappetisingly. They somehow didn't hold the same appeal. What if he was wrong? 'To hell with it', he thought as he pushed aside the digestives and groped in his drawer for the Mars bar. At least he would know. He ripped off the wrapping and sunk his teeth into that blissfully ecstatic, chocolate delight. Pleasure seeped through him. But moments later he was punished by a tortuous flashing of lights and pains in his head. He searched his jacket for his tablets and cursed when he realised he'd left them in his other coat. Allison mumbled something to Maddie and left for home.

Stringer left Mrs Taylor's. He'd waded through the young copper's files and notes, had a chat with Parkhouse, and David's mother confirmed that he had an interview and report to write before leaving for Devon that night. Something was definitely wrong. He needed a word with the Chief to find out who it was that Allison had sent him to interview. *That* wasn't on file. Why hadn't he informed him of the facts. Whatever it was that was worrying the Chief, it was also affecting his work.

Grace Clifton took out her plans of Sandra Thornton's house and the timetable she'd made of her movements. She hissed in annoyance. It had to be this week end. But what about David Taylor?

Her eyes narrowed and she waddled to her box of wisdom and selected a scroll.

> 'For these be the days of vengeance,
> that all things which are written
> may be fulfilled.'
> St Luke Chap 21, verse 22

Grace Clifton tilted back her head and shrilled in her reedy tones part of the Magnificat. Divine right was on her side.

David Taylor struggled uncomfortably against his bonds. He was secured to the bed, manacled with bicycle chains. He froze as the handle of the bedroom door began to turn.

Grace Clifton eased open the door and waddled into the room with a large tray which she placed on the wash stand. She moved to the bedside.

"Not to worry, David," she droned. "I won't be leaving you for long."

She retrieved the tray with its metal hinged arm and fitted it to the bed. It carried an array of food. A tubed water bottle was attached to the bedstead which the young policeman could access by turning his head to the side. Next, the bonds on one hand were eased allowing him, with difficulty, to reach the food. With a mammoth effort, by lifting his trunk and head he would just be able to to bring the food to his mouth, but not have enough reach to release himself from his chains. In this new position the manacles were re-secured.

Mrs Clifton was in full control. She removed the surgical tape holding the tough crepe bandage which held his jaw closed. Then, the bandage itself.

She took no pleasure in his wince of pain as she ripped the stout parcel tape from his lips, tearing the delicate skin and pulling strands of his hair out by the roots.

"As you can see, you're equipped with water and I've left you a variety of fruit, some cheese, cold meats, scones, bread and a few cakes. I'm sure you can reach....yes, you'll cope beautifully. There's a bottle for, you know... and a pot if you need it. Although that might be a bit more difficult to manage. But, don't worry. I'll clean you up when I get home."

David Taylor moaned softly before futiley struggling against his bondage.

"I shouldn't do that if I were you. You'll knock things over and then you *will* be in a mess."

The copper's thrashings subsided when he saw the glint of madness in her eyes. He tried to speak, but his mouth was dry of saliva. Mrs Clifton grinned in satisfaction.

" Don't worry about making a noise....No-one will hear. You're in Tony's room. It's right at the back of the house. There's no one living next door - and the Singhs on the other side, their bedroom is adjacent to the other terraced house. Besides, this room is more or less sound proof. Tony used to do his recording in here."

Her lizard eyes flicked upwards indicating the ceiling. David noticed that it was covered with egg boxes. He'd first thought it was some kind of artexing or rough plaster work, but now he could see they were egg boxes, a cheap but fairly efficient form of sound proofing. His spirits sank.

"I'll be back before you know it. You'll see." Her thin rimless lips drew back exposing those teeth in an attempt to smile. "I must pack now." She scuttled through the door, locking it firmly behind her. David heard the key rattle and a bolt drawn across.

What now? Without any doubt he was trapped in the spider's web. He must try to think clearly and search for a way out, before he became cocooned in her poisoned silk casing and sucked dry of all life. There must be a way. There had to be.

15

DEEP WATER

Stringer was perplexed. The Chief hadn't arrived home. Now Greg's wife, Mary was worried. He tried to reassure her,

"It's OK Mary. You know what he's like, he's probably following some lead of his own."

Mary shook her head vehemently, "He's not been himself recently - you know that. He told Maddie he was coming home. Something must have happened."

"I'll check back at the station, see if he's called in. I'll be in touch."

Mary nodded, biting her lip nervously. She saw Mark to the door and gave a worried sigh when she closed it behind her.

Mark moved briskly to his car and settled in his seat, contacting base before he moved off. There'd been no word from the chief.

Grace Clifton alighted from the train and squinted around her. She needed somewhere to stay, somewhere she wouldn't be recognised, somewhere she could come and go as she pleased. She padded out from the station keeping her head low and began to walk down the dusty littered street until she saw what she was looking for, but first she needed to get into her disguise. Across the road from the station was an old crumbling red brick public convenience splattered with spray paint and graffiti. Grace swivelled her chameleon eyes across the road and down the street and feeling secure that she was not observed made her way into the ladies lavatories.

She found one cubicle which locked, she hung her bag on the hook and began to undress out of her clothes. Ten minutes later an elderly, portly, old man with spectacles, a toothbrush moustache, worn corduroy trousers, mackintosh and flat cap scurried out of the toilets - much to the amusement of two young girls on their way in. One called out,

"What's the matter grandad? Lost your reading glasses?" They giggled loudly, "Pervert!" and disappeared into the dilapidated building.

Grace Clifton lengthened her stride and walked into the shabby motel further along the street.

She was shown to a chalet at the back of the complex, perfect for her use. The bovine, bored, blond, young receptionist barely gave her a second glance. She was used to all sorts in this establishment. The Ritz it wasn't.

Grace drew the curtains after the young girl left and opened her bag, laying out the contents on the melamine coffee table. A particularly wicked looking knife was placed predominantly in the centre. Grace smiled and stifled the desire to sing.

"Dad? What are you doing out here all alone?"questioned Callie.

Greg Allison was sitting in his workshop, in the garden, in the comforting security of the dark. He lifted his red rimmed eyes heavy with the pain of a subsiding migraine.

"Don't switch on the light, " his gravelly voice ordered. "I just came here for a bit of peace and quiet - to think."

Callie's hand fell back from the light switch. She bent down by her father's side."Come on dad, it can't be that bad. Everyone's worried about you. There's messages flying around all over the place."

Allison sighed and managed a smile for his daughter, "I'll be out in a minute. My headache's nearly gone."

"Do we know what's causing it?"

"My vice," answered Allison bluntly.

"Pooh! you haven't got any!....That is except your fondness for Mars Bars."

"How do you know about that?" Asked Allison filled with surprise.

"Surely, you didn't think it was a secret? We've always known... any knotty problem, out comes a Mars Bar and lo and behold the problem doesn't seem as bad or it gets solved."

"Well, I'll be damned!"

"So, what's up? Are they the cause of your headaches?"

Allison grunted an acknowledgement and Callie began to giggle.

"Poor old Daddy! His favourite crutch has been taken away from him....It's not the end of the world, you know."

"Maybe not for you,"said Allison petulantly., "They help me think, help me digest the facts of a case and now I haven't got that comfort. I can't even think straight if I eat one, I'm plagued with a vicious assault on my senses."

"Ah!" murmured Callie sagely, "But there are alternatives."

"What do you mean?"

"Well, for one thing food allergies are not always permanent. There may come a time when you can scoff your beloved Mars Bars again. In the meantime..."

"In the meantime?"

"Try a healthy substitute."

"There's no substitute for chocolate!"

"Yes, there is. Until the time comes when you get the all clear, eat carob bars instead."

"What's that?"

"Carob bars. Looks and tastes like chocolate, not as rich of course, but you can buy all sorts of varieties in a health food shop. Meanwhile, go to a homeopath and have some treatment to desensitise you." She paused waiting for a response and then continued. "Look - don't let's stay out here. Mother's worried to death about you. Mark has been looking for you. Come back up to the house and we'll talk some more... A fine homecoming this has turned out to be!"

Callie stood up and extended her hand to her father which he grasped to help him from the confines of the garden chair. Together they went up the path to the house.

Judy sat unobtrusively in the corner of the bar at the Hunter's Inn. She placed herself out of sight of the main bar behind the chiming one armed bandit while Hayley bustled to the counter to get them both a drink.

"No good moping about on a Saturday night," she brisked, "Change of scenery will do you good," she called over her shoulder and ordered two dry white wines. The bar was filling up quickly, with young farmers and locals. A few tourists had stopped by hoping for a bar snack or meal.

Judy gazed around the bar, taking in the pictures on display, for sale, by local artists. The clamour of voices increased as the bar steadily filled and Judy watched and observed. She was becoming quite a student of human behaviour. Judy smiled to herself as she eavesdropped on the romantic banter between a young couple standing to the left of her table. She looked beyond them to the far corner of the bar where a lean faced man was focused on his pint of beer in between looking at his watch."Obviously waiting for someone," she thought.

Hayley bulldozed her way through the growing throng and gratefully flopped into the seat opposite Judy.

"The next drink, *you* can get," she bossed. "It's murder at the bar."

Judy smiled and indulged in polite chit chat in an attempt to take her mind off David Taylor. She lifted her drink to her lips and paused, when a movement caught her eye. The man at the bar, she had noticed earlier, had risen off his stool to greet someone and had thrust out his hand to the visitor. As he did this, he nervously ran the fingers of his other hand through his hair in a peculiar washing movement. Judy gave a sharp intake of breath. There was something familiar about that movement. Something frighteningly familiar.

Judy stared harder at the man who before had only warranted a cursory glance, and studied him with interest.

He was tall – about six feet one, of strong build. He had obviously done some weight training. His clothes were expensive, possibly an Armani suit and Gucci shoes. She returned her gaze to his lean face as if to absorb his features.

"And you haven't been listening to a word I've been saying," complained Hayley.

"Sorry?"

"I said... what is it? Have you seen someone you recognise?" queried Hayley peering over shoulder at the busy bar. "You have haven't you?" she probed.

"I'm not sure... There was something, so fleeting I must have been mistaken..."

She broke off as the object of her scrutiny felt her eyes on him and uncomfortably looked around. His eyes engaged with hers and a guilty flush flooded his face. He glanced away hurriedly, picked up his pint and downed it in one. Again, with his other hand he nervously ran his fingers through his hair with an odd washing motion.

Judy replaced her drink on the table. She was feeling uncomfortably hot. The noise in the bar echoed inside her head and the room seemed to rock crazily before her. She had a memory, a vision of a baby crying, that hand running through hair, that hand raised against her, that hand forcing her..... She blinked hard, and said simply, "I remember."

Holly picked up the phone. She hesitated before dialling Colin's number. Paul urged her on.

"Go on. It may be important."

"But, if not, I'm just wasting his time." She bit her lip, and took the receiver away from her ear as if to replace it.

"He won't mind. It's not wasting his time. Come on...He'd want you to ring."

Holly placed the ear piece back against her ear and waited for a reply.

"454 4649," answered Marcie.

"Marcie? It's Holly. Is Colin there?"

"Sorry, he's at a committee meeting. Can I help?"

"Could you tell him I called? If it's not too late, ask him to ring me back when he gets in."

"How late?"

"Eleven?"

"Fine. Anything I can do?... Need to talk?"

"No, it"s OK. I've just had a weird experience. I'll speak to him later. If not, get him to call me first thing tomorrow."

"Sure thing. Bye!" And she hung up.

Paul lumbered over to his girlfriend and put his huge arms around her holding her close.

"Don't worry! Everything will be OK. You'll see."

Holly hoped that he was right.

"Well, what did she say?" asked Paul.

"Not a lot! She'll get him to ring when he gets in."

"Then you can tell him."

Tony studied the chess board carefully, if he wasn't careful he could lose his queen. He had to protect it or sacrifice his knight and that idea didn't appeal. It didn't appeal at all. He must concentrate!

But, there was much to distract him. Firstly, the college girl, Babs who had come to entertain the ward, had been very appealing and had allowed him to join in some of the songs. In fact they had done a 'number' together in close harmony which worked really well. There was something about her. Something which reminded him of Amy. He couldn't quite put his finger on it. Something....Tony thought it was her smile. And then there was the news, big news! In the light of fresh murders, terrifying the streets of Birmingham, murders which bore 'his' hall mark; his lawyer had been granted an appeal and investigations had been reopened. His mother's pleas to the committee who fought for injustice to be routed out of the legal system had listened. The case against him was no longer as water tight

as it had been. Grace Clifton had seen to that. Tony calmly swept away the bishop threatening his queen and announced,
"Check mate."

"Holly, tell the chief inspector what you told me," pressed Colin gently.

Holly sighed and rolled her eyes. She flicked a strand of hair out of her face and took a deep breath.

Allison leaned forward encouragingly and Holly began.

"At first, I didn't know what to make of it...happenings, premonitions, forewarnings, call it what you will, much as I don't like them I'm getting used to them, but this...this is something else."

"Go on" urged Allison.

"After experiencing the first spate of murders, everything seemed to come to a halt after..."she hesitated as if she had difficulty repeating the killer's name, "...Clifton's arrest. Then as suddenly as they stopped they began again. But this time they were different..."

"How? In what way?"

"It's hard to explain, but they didn't seem the same, more calculated killings... than on impulse.Then on one occasion a voice shrieked 'Gillian!' After that, it was as if an invisible link had been made between myself and whoever screamed. Chief Inspector Allison... I'm like a huge radio antennae. I can tune in to the killer's mind and what's more that person knows...I am on the hit list."

"Next?"

"No, not next," she considered carefully, "But soon."

"I think we should share *all* the information with the Inspector."Colin continued.

Holly shot him a glance as if to say, "please not everything." Colin reached across and took Holly's hand and smoothed it.

"Everything," he affirmed.

Holly swallowed hard, this was going to be difficult for her,
"Inspector.... I am Clifton's daughter."

"What?"

Colin moved forward in his seat. "It's true. Holly was adopted as a child, we've tracked back and her real father was... Tony Clifton. We couldn't understand how her powers seem to have accelerated when she had only been sensitive to happenings of those who were close to her, people she regards as family. When it started happening on a grand scale but was nevertheless selective, that set me wondering. Finally, we discovered the truth. But that's not all... go on Holly."

"As I said, I seem to have found the ability to link in to the killer's mind. To begin with, I witnessed events as they happened. But, now...now I seem to see things before they happen. I believe I can tell you what the killer is going to do next."

Colin leaned forward triumphantly, "It's as if discovering her past has opened new territories for her... She can help you, Greg."

Holly pursed her lips. If these happenings can be stopped I feel I will be released. I feel I won't experience such terrors again."

Allison rubbed his bull dog jaw and pondered on Holly's words.

"All right. Let's suppose you can do all this. Help me now. I've got the Super on my back. Agencies are agitating for Clifton's release. Reckon it's a miscarriage of justice. An enquiry has been set in motion and it doesn't look good, not with these other murders clouding the issue."

Colin frowned, "I can't believe people are that stupid. Of course Clifton's guilty...Who else?"

"Ah indeed! Who else? Maybe Holly will enlighten us..."

Holly knew she was being put to the test. She closed her eyes and focused her thoughts and energy. Several times she drew a sharp intake of breath. Allison watched sceptically but Colin was fascinated, mesmerised, silently willing her on as if his focused energy would aid her.

Abruptly her china blue eyes blinked open. They were moving rapidly as if a passenger on a bus or train were surveying the passing scenery. The colour drained from her cheeks and her skin tightened like parchment across her face. She blinked rapidly, and shuddered.

"A room... a bedroom with a television, table and chair. Moss green counterpane and matching curtains....strange...not homely. One picture - a seascape above the bed." Holly moaned softly and closed her eyes which were still fluttering, travelling, moving around the room. "A mirror... he's looking in a mirror, putting on a check flat cap, those eyes...hooded....evil," she shivered.

"Who...? Who is it? "questioned Colin.

"He's turned away. I can't see him anymore. He's closing a door from the room... I think it's a bathroom... more like an en suite...Now, he's moving to the bed," she gasped again, "Uh! The knife." Holly stopped, dropped her head, but her body remained bolt upright. She made a small mewling sound and a tear squeezed out of each corner of her eyes, and she began to cry.

"What happened what did you see?" probed Colin

Holly opened her eyes, "I don't understand... I thought I knew who it was, but I don't. Maybe, I am going out of my mind."

"Why not let us be the judge of that?" offered Allison gently, "Come on, Holly. What did you see?"

Holly lifted her tear streaked face to them both. " I really thought I knew... but this person...this person was a fat, little man, with a toothbrush moustache. He was wearing faded brown, worn corduroy trousers, a crumpled off white mackintosh and a flat check cap... but there was something familiar about those eyes, and I have a feeling he wasn't at home."

"What do you mean? Someone else's house?...."

"Yes.. no.. more like..."

"A hotel?"

"Yes, but not up market... motel, travel lodge standard... that sort of thing."

There was a soft knock at the door and Mark Stringer entered. "Sorry to interrupt, Chief. I've been trying to contact you. I left a message with Mary."

"Yes, she did say something about it. I was about to have you paged when I became involved," he indicated Colin Brady and Holly with a flick of his head. "So, how can I help?"

"I need to know who you sent Taylor to interview before he was to leave for Devon. It's not on file. His mother seemed to think he had a job for you to do.."

"Hell and damnation! It almost slipped my mind, damn these blasted headaches...Clifton."

"What? Tony Clifton?"

"No, his mother Grace."

"I'll get over there now and report back."

"Wait, I'll come with you. Sorry, Colin.. Holly. We'll have to leave this till later."

"If you don't mind Inspector, " Holly coolly broke in, "I'd like to come with you. We'll follow in Colin's car."

Colin raised his eyebrows but said nothing and to Stringer's surprise the Chief merely grunted.

They left for Golden Hillock Road together.

16

CRAZY

The Singhs peered out through their net curtains at the arrival of two cars. Allison pulled at the waist of his trousers, lifting it up over his spreading paunch and adjusted his jacket while he waited for Mark to lock the vehicle. They gazed up at the house with its net curtains, swept path and gleaming brass letter box.

Holly's vision was disturbed. Her sense of balance seemed to have vanished and she couldn't leave the vehicle. She whispered hoarsely to Colin, finding difficulty breathing. "It's here... a house of evil..." She swallowed hard before continuing, "My Grandmother lives here."

Allison and Stringer walked up the path and rang the bell. Nothing. Mark lifted the letter box flap and called out,

"Hello...Mrs Clifton?"

From the confines of Tony's room David Taylor heard the bell and a muffled voice calling. He shouted as loudly as he could, thrashing on the bed trying desperately to think of something to attract the attention of the caller or callers.

The Clifton's neighbour, Lehmber Singh opened his front door and peered at the officers,

"So sorry, Mrs Clifton is not home."

"Do you know when she'll be back?"

"I have no idea, she left earlier today. She was carrying a small bag. Probably gone away for the weekend."

"Does she often go away?" asked Allison.

"No. It's most unusual. In all the years we have lived next door she has only been away twice. The last time was only a few months ago."

179

"Lehmber!" reproached his wife, Harpal, arriving on the step. "You shouldn't gossip. You don't know who they are."

Mark Stringer took out his identification, "It's OK madam, we only want to help."

"Oh, is it about Tony? Such a shame that... She has such a lot to live down. But we would never hold that against her."

The conversation stopped as the passenger door on Colin's car opened and Holly vomited violently into the gutter.

"Dear, dear," worried Lehmber Singh, "Is the young lady all right? Is she with you?"

Stringer hesitated, but Allison ploughed on. "Yes, a relative of the Cliftons. She doesn't seem too well. I wonder if we might trouble you for some water and perhaps you could help us with a few questions.

Lehmber Singh looked concerned and turned to his wife for approval, "I..don't know.. Harpal?"

Harpal Kaur answered by walking down her path to the car and helping Holly out. Colin joined her side.

"Come in, come in. Whatever are you thinking of Lehmber... Ask them in."

Lehmber, spurred into action by his wife, ushered the foursome into their living room while Harpal shooed her children Harjinder and Mohinder out to the kitchen instructing them to make some tea.

David Taylor heard no more. He was sure whoever it was hadn't left. He heard no cars starting up. But what could he do? If he could only manage to attract the caller's attention... but how?

Allison and Stringer heard much about Grace Clifton, her son and her obsessive religious fervour; her flights into song, the clearing of the garden shed and removal of the sled. They also heard about her neighbourliness and gifts to the family.

Holly listened in silence, sipping her tea slowly. Abruptly, the cup slipped from her fingers and fell to the carpet spilling its dregs at her feet. Colin apologised profusely, sprang to mop up the mess and then caught sight of Holly's face contorted with horror. She gasped and wheezed noisily, saliva frothed at the corner of her lips and her eyes gazed dully in front of her.

"What's wrong? What's the matter with her? Is she having a fit?" asked Harpal.

"I don't know," Colin responded. "I think it's another happening."

"What?"cried a fearful Harpal.

"Not to worry," soothed Allison. " The lady just needs some space. Would you mind leaving us a moment?"

The Singhs needed no second bidding and hastily left the room.

"Shall I call a doctor?" Called Lehmber.

"That won't be necessary," replied Colin, "Just give us a moment."

The door closed softly and Colin fell to his knees, "Holly! Holly can you hear me?"

"Pain, terrible pain. He can't reach..."

"Who? What are you talking about?

"The room, everywhere... Christ watches. But he's stuck, a prisoner, such sadness and despair. He fears he'll never see her again."

"Who, Holly? Who are you talking about?"

"J..J..Judy, He'll never know her."

Allison grabbed Stringer by the arm, "It's Taylor. God dammit! She's picked up on Taylor. "

"At Mrs Cliftons!" agreed Mark.

The two coppers were on their feet and heading for the front door.

"Look after Holly,"shouted Allison, "We'll be back in a minute. Mark radio for help. We need to break in."

Allison bounded down the path and back up to Mrs Clifton's front door. He yelled through the letter -box. "Hold on Taylor! We're coming." He ran back to his vehicle as Colin came out from the Singhs his face ashen.

"It's Holly, she's unconscious...get an ambulance." as his

words died away a muffled crash and tinkling of glass was heard. Lehmber Singh emerged,

"It's next door," he confirmed, "There's somebody next door."

David Taylor sighed with relief as he heard the front door splinter open, and feet thundering up the stairs to the landing. He called out feebly,

"In here..."

Mark Stringer shouldered the door, staggered in, slipping on the mess of glass and water on the floor, hardly believing his eyes when he saw the chained constable on the bed.

There was a shout from downstairs and Mark left the back up team to free young Taylor while he went to answer Allison's call.

"Look at this," gestured Allison, pointing to the detailed drawings, map and notes left spread on the table. The two coppers looked at each other and uttered in unison,

"Sandra Thornton!"

Grace Clifton was prepared. She had her bag. She had her knife and she had her muffins. Her disguise was complete. She doubted even Tony would recognise her with the spirit gummed moustache and old men's clothes. She recited softly to herself as she lay in wait for Sandra who should be turning the corner with her dog at any moment now.

> "for all flesh *is* as grass, and all the glory
> of man as the flower of grass. The grass
> withereth, and the flower there-of faileth away:
> But the word of the Lord endureth forever..."

The excitement within her mounted, rising with her fevered delivery of the words of St Peter as she saw young Sandra Thornton enter the road where Nemesis was waiting in the shadows by the post box.

Sandra's dog paused to raise his leg by a lamp post. He routed out the smells and added to them, before pausing and snuffing the air softly. He whined uncertainly in the back of his throat, as if sensing the evil waiting for them. Grace reached in her bag and extracted a muffin in readiness to give to the dog. But the dog was not willing to move. It remained by the lamp post, a growling rumbling in the back of his throat. No matter how hard Sandra coaxed him, he would not move. Frustrated by his stubborness she yanked on his lead, dragging him on his bottom away from the lamp post, but relented when she saw the fear in his eyes.

"Come on you mutt! What's wrong? There's nothing here to harm you."

The dog merely whined and licked her hand in reply.

"Oh very well, have it your own way. A shortened walk for you. Or am I going to have to carry you?"

But the animal was quite prepared to retrace its steps and happily trotted back towards the corner.

Grace scowled blackly, "This wouldn't do...This wouldn't do at all. She hadn't expected this turn of events. Now what?"

She moved off after the retreating figure of Sandra and her dog.

Judy heaved a huge sigh of relief, "That was David," she said with love and joy as she replaced the receiver. "He's all right. He's travelling down tomorrow after he's written his report and made a full statement to the police." Judy couldn't stop the smile of pleasure that rose to her face.

"And what about you?" demanded Hayley. "Did you tell him you remembered?"

"No. I think that's enough excitement for one day. I'll tell him tomorrow with Rebecca. She's coming down with him. Then we'll know what to do." She winked at Hayley.

"You just keep out of trouble. Stay here, no wandering around the village or town. We don't want you taking anymore risks. Remember he is still off guard. He thinks that you still have amnesia."

"And it's going to be so nice when he discovers I haven't!"

"Do you remember everything?"

"Most of it... Rebecca can help me to fill in the blanks, and then ...Bingo!"

She laughed brightly, things were going to turn out well after all. She just had this feeling.

The Nottingham police car sped its way through the busy streets. Its sirens wailing. It turned away from the town and to the leafy suburbs where Sandra Thornton resided.

Grace Clifton searched her mind for a suitable verse or phrase to comfort her in her distress, as she tubbily padded after Sandra and her dog, but none would come. She reached into her inside pocket for one of the tiny scrolls she'd selected from her box, to take with her on her mission.

"Wherefore gird up the loins of your mind,
be sober, and hope to the end for the grace that is to be
brought unto you at the revelation of Jesus Christ
1 Peter Chapter One Verse 13."

She swivelled her cobra hooded eyes heavenward and her sparse, thin, eyelashes fluttered in ecstacy at the joy which was to be hers. The padding steps turned into a defiant, determined, stride as she pursued her prey.

Sandra had turned the corner when she heard the police sirens approaching. She froze in amazement as she saw two police cars, lights flashing, skid to a halt outside her house. Two coppers ran up the drive and rang the bell.

Sandra jerked out of her somnambulist state and began to run to her home.

Grace Clifton hissed to herself and retraced her steps to make her way back to where she was staying.

Once inside the safety of her room, she pulled the curtains across the window and removed her itching moustache and disguise. She flicked on the television set and went to run herself a bath. The early evening news was on TV and she was surprised to see a picture of her Tony smiling across the screen.

She sat down to watch, forgetting the running water.

The reporter made it clear that there was sufficient fresh evidence to cast doubt on Tony's guilt. The case was to be looked at again and appeals from various groups who fought for justice for those wrongly accused were making their protests felt. Mrs Clifton lifted her eyes to heaven and prayed her thanks. Her burbling praise stopped abruptly as the final item on the report was announced which appealed for witnesses to come forward who could testify to the whereabouts of Mrs Grace Clifton, Tony Clifton's mother. There was a clip of film footage which featured her walking into the courts for one of Tony's hearings. She sunk deeper into the seat, her mind racing. Her eyes darted swiftly this way and that as if searching for some visual focus to calm her senses.

Grace tumbled out of her seat and onto the floor. She tore at her clothes as did the Pharisees in Biblical times and stretched her arms up to heaven pleading with God.

"These be the days of vengeance, that all things which are written may be fulfilled. Help me, O Lord, to overcome mine enemies in this persecution that I may come closer to thee."

Grace rose from floor, her eyes gleaming with heightened fervour as she sat to reassess her situation and draw her plans for the future.

The water spilling over the side of the bath forced her to abandon her schemes as she tended to the small flood in the bathroom, and decided to cleanse herself of all impurities to prepare herself for what was to come.

Larry Birtle picked up the phone and dialled the number printed on the TV screen. The bald, portly little man recognised Grace Clifton and remembered his encounter with her a few weeks before. His call was answered and he started to detail events at the coach station as he remembered them. He was extremely observant.

Ronnie Soper sat opposite Brand in a big swivel chair on which he delighted in spinning around. His mother reprimanded him, "Ronnie! Pay attention to Detective Brand. Please!"

"Sorry, mum." He stopped his fidgeting and listened.

Mrs Soper, now, looked vastly different. She had smartened herself up, lost a few pounds and the puffiness around her eyes had gone.

Brand couldn't believe there could be such a transformation in such a short time, but the near death of her son had brought her fully to her senses. The excellent support they were receiving from family consultancy had aided them through the crisis.

"Now, Ronnie - those men out there believe they have killed the wrong lad. They will still be looking for you. That is why your mum put it about that you'd gone away on a family holiday with your dad and that she was joining you."

Ronnie nodded solemnly

"We have to keep you safe, you see. You're a valuable witness."

"But, I didn't see their faces or anything."

"No, but you heard their voices and that's good enough. The last digit you put on the Edgbaston telephone number - do you remember it?"

"Yep," said Ronnie confidently, "It was nine!"

Brand turned to the copper at the door. "Get on to Telecom. Check the address."

The PC nodded and left the room.

"Next we have to look at these cards. " Brand turned them over in his hands, "Timbrels, Dale's Antiques, Morrises Mini Mart, Allure Flower Shop. Do they mean anything to you? Did they get mentioned?"

Ronnie shook his head vigorously, " No, I'd remember if they did. "

"OK. We've been doing a little checking ourselves and we wondered if you recognise anyone in these photographs?"

Brand handed Ronnie a wad of pictures which the young lad

duly leafed through. He stopped at one of a young man in a smart leather coat.

"This is the geezer with the BMW. The one I pinched the CD cassette player from."

"Are you sure?"

"Positive. I've been watching him for weeks."

"That's the guy from Morrises Mini Mart." Brand nodded to the detective who had just returned, "Write in the report that Ronnie picked out Michael Cooper, Manager of the Mini Mart."

The copper scribbled something down in his notebook.

Ronnie studied the other pictures but couldn't admit to knowing any of them.

"Sorry Detective Brand, the others, well, they don't look familiar to me."

"Never mind. You've spotted one - that's a start."

"Is that all for now, detective?" asked Mrs Soper.

"For the time being. We plan on bringing a couple of our suspects in for questioning. When we do, we want Ronnie to view them from behind a screen and listen to their voices. Who knows we just might strike lucky and pick up Rats and Rattlesnake. Now, I suggest you go up to the canteen for a while until we've established your safe house and escort you there."

Mrs Soper rose and nodded to her son,

"Come on Ronnie, I know I'm dying for a cuppa."

They left Brand's office and headed upstairs. Brand watched them thoughtfully. He gestured to the officer to write up the report and called through the door,

"Woodward! Get in here a minute."

Woodward shambled in, hugging his too full coffee mug, which slopped its contents onto his hands and the floor.

"What's up?" He questioned as he perched on Brand's desk.

"We've got a fix on the guy with the leather. Ronnie picked him out."

"Michael Cooper? The guy from Morrises Mini Mart?"

"The same. I reckon he's the middle man, keeps things in

store until they're needed. We're going to need a reason to check out his premises. Any misdemeanor, even a burnt out tail light, anything we can pull him in on, to give us a bit of a break. He'll need to be watched. Can you organise two DC's?"

"Leave it with me. What about the others?"

"I'm pretty sure Dales' Antiques is one of their outlets. For the smaller pieces, statuettes and so on. They probably recommend where bigger items should be sent. It's run by someone called Guy Trevitt. No form, but on the periphery of some of the shadier characters we know about. Neither of these seem to house Rats or Rattlesnake."

"What about the others?"

"I'm coming to that. Timbrels - the big paint place. Now that has a huge workshop, *and* storage space. Enough to run an operation like this. They could easily mask off part of the building for their own use and no-one would know a thing about it. I believe that's where we would find Rats and Rattlesnake."

"And Allure Florists?"

"That's a mystery! Can't see any link there, seems respectable enough, run by two sisters Dolores Lever and Ruth deVere. Possibly, the guy genuinely bought flowers there."

"But, we'll still need to check."

"Of course. I'll see to that. Meanwhile, can you deal with Ronnie and Mrs Soper? Details are here. Lucky the Vencat trail has gone cold. I need all the help I can get on this one."

"Well make the most of it, from what I know of Vencat he won't be off the scene for that long."

"Who knows? Once we get this lot sorted, maybe I can get together with you on that drug baron. But For now....." Brand took a large brown envelope from his pocket and handed it to Woodward. "The fewer people who know about it the better."

Woodward acknowledged Brand with one of his grim smiles and made for the stairs.

"And now Brand boy, let's get some voices on tape." He picked up his dictaphone and positioned it in his pocket, grabbed his coat and left.

Judy relaxed in the reclining chair while Rebecca spoke to her soothingly, but firmly and with authority. David sat anxiously in the chair opposite, listening carefully.

"We're nearly there now Judy, nearly there. Think back. You've traced your childhood, your memories, and art school".

"I don't need to think back anymore. I know exactly what happened. I was so stupid, so blind. Being groomed. Isn't that what they call it? Groomed for whatever they have in mind. Well, he groomed me all right. Swept me off my feet, made me feel special right at the time I was most vulnerable..." Judy's voice cracked with emotion. The silence was filled with the pain of her tortured memories. Rebecca waited then gently encouraged her to go on.

Judy lifted up her head and blinked hard at David, her eyes almost spilling over with unshed tears. David looked at Rebecca asking for permission to go to Judy. Rebecca inclined her head and David went to Judy's side. He took out his handkerchief and gently dabbed at her eyes, mopping up the stray tears then took her hand tenderly in his. His voice was choked with emotion,

"Go on Jude, don't stop now. As Rebecca says,we're almost there."

She swallowed hard and continued, "Mum and dad died when I was in my first year at college. dad developed cancer of the liver. It was discovered too late and his end was very quick. I remember how helpless I felt leaving mum alone to deal with her grief. She insisted, after the funeral that I go back to college and resume my life. It's what dad would have wished....I didn't know then...I didn't realise... simply didn't realise that... that would be the last time I saw her. The doctors couldn't understand it. Two weeks later mum was dead. She died of a broken heart." Judy struggled to keep her voice level. "It was rough.

I had no-one. I was completely alone and..... then there was Gary. Gary was every woman's dream. He was handsome and compassionate and older than me, of course he was an artist, down from the West Country. He came to some of our exhibitions and singled me out for special attention. I was so proud.... so completely sucked in by him. When he began teaching me about the styles of the old masters, I was an eager pupil, quick and hungry to learn. What I didn't realise, was why this was so important to him....not until it was too late.

Naturally, when he asked me to marry him, I accepted. After all there was no one else in my life. He was such a strength to me." Judy looked deeply into David's eyes as she went on, " I don't think I ever loved him but I admired and respected him. I just thought he'd always be there for me." ... Judy stopped to gather herself once more. " He was fine to begin with. I had no idea the copies and portraits I was producing for him were for any criminal purpose. Things were great and then I became pregnant. That's when I discovered what he was really like... he hated me getting fat, losing my figure, not concentrating on the work that was to be prepared for a special exhibition, to fool the art world and critics, to expose the stupidity of some of the highest earners. We were going to play the biggest hoax of all time and enhance our reputations as a result....Such seemingly high ideals.....all a sham.....what a fool I've been." She burst out bitterly.

Gradually, Judy's story began to unfold. The assembled listeners were hardly breathing, afraid of interrupting her flow.

"By then, of course I wasn't enough for him. He'd begun to groom another talented student... the same game all over again."

David's knuckles became white with anger as he struggled to control his feelings when he heard how Judy had been abused, almost imprisoned and forced into virtual slavery to do Gary's bidding.

"The worst time was when Luke would cry. Gary forbade me to pick him up and cuddle him. But I did... when he wasn't there – and then he'd accuse me of not working hard or quickly enough. I disobeyed sometimes, when he was there, and all that would get me was a slapping for not listening to him."

"The man is a monster," exclaimed David involuntarily. "Sorry", he muttered when he saw Rebecca's warning look.

Judy turned and took David's other hand and held them both tight. "Monster... even monster is too good to describe what he did.... He killed my son. Oh, he was clever," she rushed on. "He made it look like an accident like he died in his sleep – a cot death. But he *murdered* him. He took a pillow, when Luke was crying and suffocated him in his cot. When I came in it was too late. His little angel face was blue, his body still and lifeless. I was hysterical. He passed that off to the investigating officers as post natal depression... he was so matter of fact. I was suffering from post natal depression and frequently became hysterical. Naturally, they believed him; he had such standing in the community. Everyone was told I'd gone away to recover but in reality I was transported away to some huge warehouse in the Midlands, where the divorce was set in motion. I was forced to work and when I refused, I was beaten senseless. It was then I lost my memory. The horror of everything that had happened, had forced me to deal with it in the only way I could. I couldn't remember... After that they beat me again and left me for dead in the streets of Birmingham with no clues to my identity, feeling safe in believing that I wouldn't survive to tell my story. The rest you know."

There was a silence while everyone paused to digest what Judy had said. Finally, David put both his arms around her a. Judy melted into him and sobbed onto his chest.

Allison put down the phone and stared across the desk at his sergeant, and Brand.

"Well that solves the mystery of Dan," he growled. "That was young Taylor on the phone. This antique fraud case of yours," he nodded at Brand, "is more complex than any of us realised."

The two detectives waited while Allison gathered himself. He enjoyed holding all the trump cards. "It seems our young amnesiac was a victim in this enterprise. When she was installed at the warehouse, which sounds like Timbrels from the description, one of the warehouse men was an old boy who took pity on the girl. He tried to help her, wanted to get her away. For that, he was shot and dumped in the canal."

"But why then was that money sent to Dan's missus?" asked Mark.

"I'm coming to that. Seems our Mr Cooper in his BMW had a conscience. Knew the old boy, and his situation, had some respect for him... When he discovered what had happened he sent the money to Dan's missus. I think we can use that to do a deal, get him to testify. Not only that, we've got enough now, to walk into Timbrels and see what's what. Well Brand? What are you waiting for?"

"Don't need to be told twice! On my way!" Brand moved to the door then turned back. "I've been waiting two years for this."

David Taylor smiled to himself as the train rattled along the lines taking him back to Birmingham. 'It had been worth it', he thought. All the pain, suffering and stress. He was now sure that his life had been leading to this moment. He had Judy's statement firmly in his briefcase, and what's more he had Judy's heart. This he knew. The experiences they had both been through had somehow cemented their relationship. He was confident they were both firmly fixed on the road to happiness and love's destiny. Even the thought of Grace Clifton popping into his brain didn't have the same shuddering effect it had previously. He was stronger. And he was stronger because of Judy.

Gary Kruger, alias Steve Winson alias Giles deVere.... was soon going to receive the shock of his life. David glanced at his watch. It was now nine thirty. In fact the Devon and Cornwall police would be at deVere's door right about... now. He smiled in satisfaction.

17

HOLDING THE VISION

Tony Clifton sat with old George Harper watching the evening news on television, a strange smile on his face. In front of him on screen Tony's lawyer was being faced with a barrage of questions by the press. The report progressed, and finally concluded. George stared aghast at Tony.

" 'ere, is what they're sayin' true? Are you the last great miscarriage of justice? What new evidence have they turned up then?"

Tony stretched that odd smile even further, "It seems the forensic evidence isn't sound. It looks like something of a frame up."

"But what about that girl? The one in the papers who was left alive. Thought 'er evidence was indisputable?"

"Well, it seems they're not too sure now. Too many other things have happened. These latest killings - as you know-they're nothing to do with me, I've been stuck inside so, unless I can walk through walls it looks like someone else is responsible. The girl's injuries may have affected her memory. You heard the experts, she could be wrong. The evidence is a fix! You'll see, the Lord will protect his own. It's as mother said,

"They shall lay their hands on you, and
persecute you, delivering you up to
the synagogues and into prisons for...
my name's sake...
I will give you mouth and wisdom,
which all your adversaries will not
be able to gainsay nor resist.

Don't you see George? It's my destiny to be free. And free I will be .... one way or another."

Ronnie Soper stood behind the two way mirror in the interview room. He had heard two men being interviewed but nothing in their voices suggested Rats or Rattlesnake. He turned to Brand,

"I'm sorry sir, neither of the two sound anything like the men that took me. Brand nodded picked up the phone and dialled. The copper in the interview room answered the call and nodded. The man opposite him at the desk was taken out.

"Don't worry Ronnie, we've a way to go yet. I think you may find the next one interesting." As Brand finished speaking the interview room door opened.

A short, stocky man entered the interview room. He was thick set with years of weight training and steroids. He had dark hair that was thinning on top. His gait reminded Ronnie of a jungle ape. His arms seemed too long for his body. His coat was stretched tight, as if he couldn't buy one in a size to fit his huge frame.

A gasp caught in the back of Ronnie's throat when the man turned around and sat. There was something familiar about the back of him; the way the fabric of his jacket pulled across his back; the thinning patch of hair on the back of his head; the angle of his face and line of his jaw. Ronnie had a fleeting, but sudden flash of memory, like an explosive video clip, of the man at the wheel of the car which had driven him away from his home after he'd been abducted, before the bag had been put over his head.

"You're wasting your time with me, I've done nothing," spoke the man with the smooth tones. His consonants had a metallic bite, his 's' was sibilant , Ronnie gulped.

"Rattle snake!" he identified.

Brand's usually stern expression crept into a half smile.

"You're sure?"

"Positive. I'd know that voice anywhere. It gives me the creeps. It's so smooth but then those 's' sounds hiss through, like a ... rasp, a rattlesnake."

Brand's half smile stretched into a full satisfied grin. "Got him!"

Mrs Clifton sat in her motel room and stared at her reflection in the dressing table mirror. She hardly recognised the face that gazed back at her. Somewhere in her mind she had a picture of a younger face, with younger skin, not this one harrowed by the wrinkles of time's little mice and so obviously shadowed by despair. She allowed herself a moment, a minute to remember.

Once, she was young. Once, she was attractive. Grace saw beyond the mirror, saw the past as she remembered it, with her husband Frank; heard his melodic voice singing softly to her in the gentle light of their bedroom, in their house; a house like any other, in any other street. She thought of times with their baby son, their pride; her initiation into the church and Father Barrett.

There was something wet on her cheek. Her dry parchment hands dabbed it. Grace stared at the tears which were glistening on her fingers and examined them in wonder. These came from feelings long entombed, too dangerous to remember. Yet, she indulged herself and let herself think.

Father Barrett. Did Father Barrett really cleanse her soul? Did he really teach her truth and bring her to salvation? Or did he, as Frank had always said, deceive and confuse her; steal her innocence in the name of religion?

Grace Clifton howled. It was an odd sound, a lament of longing for all things lost. She forced her face away from the screaming truth of the looking glass and angrily stilled the voices of discontent whispering inside her. The white ghosts of truth that shaped and stretched in her mind were being quickly suffocated by the emergence of a growing, swirling black mass of vagaries proclaimed as absolute; half truths which had multiplied in their treachery, and purged the light, the honest memories and replaced them with something that for her own sanity she had to accept. It was not her place to doubt now, or was it?"

Grace chased off the intruding thoughts that threatened her

whole meaning of existence. She squeezed and wrung and kneaded those ideas out of her mind.

When she glanced back at the mirror, blood trickled down her lips and chin where she had stifled her words with her teeth.

The salty, coppery taste of her warm blood revived her. She drew her hand across her lips and smeared the fresh blood marking her cheeks like a warrior brave on his first raiding party and smiled. Logic and sense had returned once more.

Grace was in a quandary. She couldn't go home. The police were looking for her. Sandra Thornton had not yet been dealt with and moreover someone was tracking her movements. Mentally, she knew she was being watched and the watcher was Gillian.

Grace Clifton gave a leering grin. So, Gillian had the gift. The gift which she herself had turned her back on for all those years. A gift which she now intended to use for her own purpose.

Allison enjoyed this time with a case, when all the loose ends were being tidied up. He was happy for Brand who had lived and breathed the antiques' fraud for two years and was soon to close the book on it. Brand would be assigned to something new, perhaps work with Woodward, if Vencat raised his head again... But, he was less happy with the Calcutt killing and subsequent slayings.

The Nottingham police were scouring the district for Mrs Clifton. Mr. Birtle's phone call had helpfully given the police an idea of where they should pinpoint their search. That search was under way.

'And Sandra Thornton had been forewarned,' thought Allison grimly. "Nothing is going to happen to that little lady, " he said aloud.

"Pardon, sir?" enquired Stringer.

"Sorry," muttered Allison. "I was thinking of the Thornton girl."

"She's safe enough. There's a watch on her house and an

escort wherever she wants to go. At least for the time being until we've flushed out Grace Clifton."

"What do you think about that, Mark?"

"Who? The Clifton business?"

"Mm."

"Hard to say. I'm convinced we had the right man from the start. But then these other killings... makes you think doesn't it... was it her all the time?"

"Was it? Or is that what she wants us to think? What's that famous quote? ...Greater love hath no man but that he lay down his life for his friend. Or something similar. In this case, the mother for the son."

There was a brief silence whilst both men considered the impact of those words. Maddie interrupted them.

"Chief, your wife's on the line. Something about tonight?"

"Damn, yes, I'd nearly forgotten. " Allison turned to Mark. "You and Debbie are all right for this evening? Callie's welcome home meal?"

"Wouldn't miss it. We'll be there."

Allison picked up the phone and began to talk to Mary.

The shadows under Holly's eyes had lengthened and darkened. She sat on the huge leather sofa, her feet tucked under her, a glass of wine in her hand.

"This tastes good," she said as she sipped, "Nothing like it in hospital."

"Nor this," said Paul as he selected a CD. A copy of the seventies song, *In memory of Elizabeth Reed* by the Alman Brothers filled the room.

"Now you're showing your age," smiled Holly.

"Music to make love by, you always said, when I first played it," mocked Paul.

"Maybe. I've changed my mind since".

"Oh, what is it now?"

"Music to forget your troubles by."

Paul smiled and sat next to her on the settee, "So my little waif, what happens next?"

"I don't know. Let's see what Colin says when he and Marcie arrive."

"That shouldn't be too long."

"Then I'd better check in the kitchen - see if everything's OK."

"You checked five minutes ago. You've only just sat down."

"So, I'll check again," she said stubbornly.

Holly untucked her feet and stepped lightly out to the kitchen, taking her wine with her. She placed it on the marble chopping board where the parsley lay ready for garnishing the tiger prawn starter which was just waiting to be heated up. A small breeze stirred the finely chopped leaves and the wind chime by the back door tinkled daintily. Holly moved to the stove and stirred the thickening sauce that was simmering contentedly. She picked up the pestle and mortar and poured some black and green peppercorns into the bowl and started crushing them together. The sound and movement of the corns cracking and grinding together was richly satisfying. The net curtain trembled by the window, shuddered and then fell limp.

Holly returned to her wine and took a sip. The wind chimes jangled again, this time more deliberately as if an unseen finger had deliberately swung them together. The net curtain fluttered and fell. Holly glanced across at them, then the door bell rang. She drained her glass, left it on the marble top intending to return to the sitting room so that she and Paul could greet their guests together.

She had her fingertips placed on the kitchen door handle when the first wave hit her.

The vinegary tones of a woman hissed the name, "Gillian!"

The sound had an effect as physical as a punch to the stomach. Holly doubled over, sprawled back on the floor and slid backwards on her bottom towards the oven door as if giant hands propelled her on ice.

Clearly and distinctly the voice demanded,

"Where are you?"

Holly hesitated and was rewarded with another blow, this time across her cheek. Her face stung.

"Where?"

Holly rubbed at her reddening face and tried to stand. Unseen arms with bony hands clamped her back and fingered her shoulders forcing her against the oven door. The heat seared through her silk blouse and singed her skin. Holly yelped, then cried fiercely as she struggled away from the burning enamel cooker door,

"Damn you! Who are you?"

Grating, metallic, laughter sourly, jack knifed through her brain. Holly put her hands to head and began to sob.

She was whimpering like a wounded animal when Paul opened the kitchen door.

Grace Clifton knew what she had to do. The Thornton girl was inaccessible now. She felt that, too well protected. She would have to be dealt with another time when the threat to herself had been lessened or when she could harness her powers to the full... she was out of practice.

But Gillian... Gillian was a different matter. Gillian was a link with the police, an informant. Her recent encounter with Gillian had just proved that she retained these same abilities, but how far could she go? Leaving her grand daughter sobbing on the kitchen floor was one thing but if she could take Gillian out – then no one could possibly trace her or know her plans and her guilt. There again Gillian was her own flesh and blood. Blood tells. Could she destroy one of her own? What did the Bible say? What had happened to Cain? What did it say about family? These and many more questions rankled and plagued her mind.

Grace went to her beloved testament and opened it. The opening words of Hebrews Chapter Six made up her mind as she read:

"Therefore leaving the principles of the
doctrine of Christ, let us go on to
perfection; not laying again the
repentance from dead works, and of
faith towards God."

Grace Clifton drew back her thin lips and made her plans. She packed her bag, put her disguise in order and checked out of the seedy motel.

The evening was going well. Allison was able to relax and enjoy his meal at home with Callie and the Stringers.

"I can't believe it, dad," giggled Callie, "Two whole hours and no shop! It must be a record."

"Surprisingly enough young lady, I do have a brain which can accommodate more than police work. In spite of everything you and your mother say. Now what's for dessert? I know you've been busy in the kitchen, Mary and there have been some delicious aromas tantalising my taste buds."

"And some of them can stay there," warned Mary with a wry smile. "Death by chocolate is one you won't be having."

"And what pray, am I allowed?"

"Don't worry, you've still got plenty of choice, dad. How about sherry trifle? Or lemon mousse?"

There was a grunt of satisfaction.

"If I know you, Greg Allison, these are the decisions you love making. Spoilt that's what you are. Spoilt for choice too!" With that Mary rose from her seat and returned to the kitchen for the sweets, while Callie fetched the bowls.

Greg gazed with a passionate longing at his bowl containing an ample helping of each of the desserts on offer. He ladled on some double cream and paused, spoon in hand, delaying the moment of ecstasy when the first mouthful would hit his taste-buds. The phone rang.

"Damn and blast!," he grumbled.

"Don't worry dear," smiled Mary, "I'll get it."

Mary Allison left her visitors sighing with delight and went to the hall. She returned seconds later, her face serious.

"Greg, it's for you... it's urgent." Mary watched her husband, mop his mouth with a napkin as he lumbered out from his seat.

Moments later Greg returned. Mark looked up at the chief, his expression changing to one of concern when he saw Greg's steel mouth set in a grim line.

"Problems Chief?"

"Seems so. Sorry, Mary, Callie, Debbie." He nodded at each of them in turn. " Keep the coffee hot. Looks like we'll need it, when we get back."

"But what about your desserts?"

"We'll have to finish them later. Can't be helped," he managed an apologetic grin. "We'll be as quick as we can. Ready Mark?"

Mark scooped a last mouthful of his lemon mousse and hastily followed the chief out of the room.

"You better drive Mark. I've been drinking," Allison growled but didn't speak further until they were both safely in the car.

"What is it?"

"Another body."

"What?"

"Same style of killing as the others. Looks like Clifton's work, but we all know he's inside."

"His mother?"

"Could be. But this time, semen samples have been taken from the girl at the scene."

Mark turned on the ignition,"Where to?"

"Gillot Road, Portland Road end."

The two detectives said nothing further until they arrived.

The victim was a young, white female no more than sixteen. Greg Allison lifted her head. there at the nape of the neck was the tell tale mark, a small sliver of flesh had been removed, cut in the shape of a cross. Allison rose from the pavement and gave the go ahead to the officers on the scene to continue their work.

"There's nothing we can do here, we may as well get back. I need a coffee. First thing tomorrow we'll both go and see Hurst." He called to the senior officer on duty, "Press ahead with the search for Grace Clifton, and contact Colin Brady, see if he's any news from his psychic girl. Come on Mark." A chill breeze began to play with Allison's hair and he hunched his shoulders against the wind. The thought of creamy desserts had vanished from his mind. Even when he returned home he would discover that he had lost his appetite for them also.

Grace Clifton, alias Dennis Grimes had booked into the friendly Portland Hotel for the night. A little too friendly as far as she was concerned. She preferred anonymity. The patrons of this hotel were far too kind and courteous. She didn't want them to remember her. She pleaded tiredness and a headache and hastily retired to her room deciding to check out before breakfast. She needed a safe base, but where? She needed an alibi for the last week. Where could she have been, undisturbed without contact for at least a week? Grace Clifton had the glimmer of an idea. She praised the Lord and smiled. The next day would take her to Worcester.

Greg Allison shook hands with Hurst. It had been a while since they'd met.

"Well, Geoff? what have we got?

"Same as the others, Greg except for one thing."

"What's that?"

"The DNA is different. Not the same as the other samples, either our killer has an accomplice or we've another copy cat on the loose."

"I can't believe that...Are you sure?"

"Positive. Come and look at this." Hurst led them both into a lab and selected a file on computer. "See? This is a strand of DNA from the Tony Clifton murders, all identical. This is from the murders after his arrest – from saliva... and of course you had the prints ... again all the same... And now this..." he paused as he brought up another bar code of information on screen along side the first. "This is from last night's murder. As you can see gentlemen, totally different."

Allison studied the two bar codes, there were no similarities. "Maybe from her last client?"

"Could be. It's a possibility."

By now the smell of the city morgue was beginning to have its usual effect on Mark. He started to breathe heavily and pin-pricks of sweat broke out on his face. Greg glanced at him, "Off you go, Mark. Get back to the car - get yourself a coffee or something. I'll be as quick as I can."

Mark nodded gratefully and began to leave but then paused by the door.

Greg Allison rubbed his bristly chin and snorted. "I don't like this. I don't like it at all... Tell me Geoff, last year the copy cat murder by Crabtree, didn't he use sperm he'd frozen?"

"He did."

"Is there any way of telling if last night's sample has been frozen and thawed out? And used in the same way?"

"There is, if it wasn't frozen correctly."

"How do you mean?"

"Well, Crabtree was clever – he had done his homework. Once he'd collected his samples he froze them quickly in liquid nitrogen and then stored them properly which meant there was no damage to or break down of the sperm. If however, the samples were frozen slowly then large crystals would accumulate surrounding them and cause damage to the semen which would make it ineffective and noticeable, to any technician in the lab's investigation. It was undetectable in Crabtree's case."

"And this one?"

"I have not personally examined the semen samples from last night's murder. Previous slayings after Clifton's arrest with the same MO revealed no semen, therefore we assumed there was no sexual motive. As you are aware we found traces of saliva and prints which matched Tony Clifton, giving the same DNA print out. That's where the problem starts. However, this time there is semen. And more... we also found a trace of faeces! One of the lab boys took the coding. I've not had time to read that report nor have I examined it myself. "

"Get hold of the lab boys who took the coding," ordered Allison, "straight away. And call me as soon as you have any news. I've a gut feeling that this time our killer has made a serious mistake." He glanced across at a green faced Mark still lingering by the door. "Come on Mark, let's get out of here, before you puke."

"If you hang on I can probably get that information for you now," interrupted Hurst.

Allison grunted and gestured for Mark to leave, which he did fairly hastily, whilst Greg took a seat to wait.

Hurst returned carrying a sheaf of papers and was busily scanning through it. He gave an excited shout.

"By George, Greg; you're right!"

Allison lumbered clumsily to his feet and craned his neck to peer over Geoff Hurst's shoulder.

"It's all here. The semen sample had been clumsily frozen, probably stuck in someone's deep freeze. The DNA strand was taken from some residue of faeces which appeared on the girl's stomach."

"Faeces? That's a new slant."

"Yes and it appears to be an old, not fresh sample."

Greg Allison smiled grimly, "Thanks Hurst. I think this is just the break we've been looking for... How long is the lab open for testing?"

"If it's urgent, I can do it today. What have you in mind?"

"I'm sending someone across, have you any sterile bottles, to hand, for samples?"

"No, but I can get you some. Wait there."

For the second time that day Allison found himself tapping his fingers while he anxiously waited. But this time he felt positive. So positive, he hankered after his sanity saving Mars Bar. He took out his substitute carob bar and gratefully bit into it. It took a little getting used to but he was sure it would satisfy him, eventually.

18

BREAKTHROUGH

PC David Taylor stood sheepishly before Allison.

"You want me to what?"

"You heard."

"But I can't just perform to order."

"Try!" Allison thrust three empty sterile specimen bottles across his desk to Taylor. "If you can't perform here, get along to Hurst's; he may have something to help you." Allison unsuccessfully attempted to suppress the grin that rose to his lips and the chuckle in his gravelly voice. Taylor snatched up the bottles and huffing with embarrassment quickly left the office.

"She's coming for me," murmured Holly as Paul helped her to the sofa.

"What do you mean?" queried Colin.

"The watcher, my grandmother, Mrs Clifton... I'm sure of it."

Colin knelt at Holly's feet whilst Paul sat anxiously at her side. Marcie handed her a glass of wine. Holly touched her cheek tentatively; a crimson welt had risen upon her skin.

"Things are coming to a head. I'm a part of this. There is going to be some sort of showdown. I feel it. I know," she said simply.

"If you're right, then there are things we can do," consoled Colin. "Let me ring, Allison. Warn him, tell him."

"Not yet. I have to think this through. I'm convinced this is something which has to happen." Holly sipped her wine. "This is something for me to figure out. Until then, let's get on with the evening." Holly smiled serenely, and ignoring all questions and protestations, removed herself from the sofa and returned to the kitchen.

The living room curtains fluttered lightly but no one noticed.

"You're right!," affirmed Hurst, "How did you know?"

"Just an inkling!" grunted Allison, "The old grey cells are still working...for the time being."

"What happens now?"

"Get the findings to me. We'll have to pull out all stops to secure Grace Clifton."

"What about her son?"

"I'm not sure... he may walk. He has an excellent team of lawyers. Once this gets out, we may not have such an air tight case against him."

"What about Sandra Thornton?"

"What about her?"

"Won't her evidence stick? Eye witness and all that?"

"Difficult to say. A clever lawyer could make her story inadmissible, we'll have to see."

"What happens then?"

"Tony Clifton won't be able to pee, without me knowing about it. He'll be watched, and if he puts a foot wrong I'll have him off the streets and inside faster than it takes to whistle."

Hurst acknowledged with a grunt and ended the call. Allison sat for a moment staring thoughtfully into space before replacing the receiver.

"Sir?" prompted Mark.

Allison lifted his bushy brows and met Stringer's eyes full on. "The DNA. It was Taylor's. Grace Clifton's been a little too clever for her own good. Get a search warrant, that house in Golden Hillock road is to be searched. Go through it, from top to bottom. Let's see what else we can find."

Grace Clifton swivelled her lizard eyes around the Wyre Forest woods near Kidderminster where she had camped. She knew exactly what she had to do. Soon she would move on to the Sukley Hills outside Worcester. She settled herself like a fox in its lair, waiting for the right time. Waiting for the night.

Holly sat cross legged on the floor in a half lotus. She breathed deeply and rhythmically. She had surrounded herself with floating candles which had flames that wavered uncertainly in the slight breeze escaping through the draught excluders surrounding the door. Incense pervaded the air, a calming, soothing scent of Ylang Ylang caught of the breath of an evening wind filtering through the landing and into the room.

The temperature in the room began to chill and fall. Holly redoubled her efforts to keep calm and in control. She focused on the centre of her being and tried to empty her mind denying the physicality of her surroundings.

Paul sat uneasily in a chair in the corner of the room watching.

Grace Clifton's plan was fool proof. Or so she thought. She had settled herself in the hills around Worcester. Hidden away from public view, if prying eyes observed her, she would claim she was a travelling protester, a public spirited conservationist, who had left the rat race to seek solitude. It would appear that she had outlawed herself from decent society to take stock, to become a recluse, a little old man with no family and no home. Grace Clifton no longer existed...

She had to find a way to stop Gillian, to prevent discovery, free Tony and live safely where the law could not reach her. But to do that she needed a passport and access to her money.

Grace was sure her accounts were still in order. No one would have frozen her assets. Using her banker's card and the hole in the wall over a period of time would give her enough cash to leave the country and to live until she found work. Her passport, that presented a bigger problem. The simplest thing to do would be to try and alter her Christian name to that of a man.... George or Gregory. Gregory would be easier, but then she couldn't be sure of doing it effectively so it wouldn't be noticed, she wasn't an accomplished forger. But she could get a new passport. If she checked in Births, Marriages and Deaths and could find a baby or child, born in the same decade, who had died young, it would be no problem to apply for a passport in that name. She could rent a room locally, have proof of her address using her rent book, use the new birth certificate and travel to Newport's passport office and wait while it was done. Yes, it would all be so easy. Now, should she maintain her disguise as a man? Or revert back to womanhood? That was a poser. But, there was no hurry. She was safe. First, she had to deal with Gillian; and then there would be no-one to stop her in her plans. Tony's freedom was sure to follow. She was certain of it.

"Well, Tony; it looks like the court of appeal will have to overturn the judgement. The evidence against you is in dispute. We have enough new information for there to be a reasonable doubt over the safety of your confinement" said the clipped tones of Tony Clifton's solicitor, Stephen Briggs.

"Enough for me to be free?" Tony questioned.

"As long as the doctors declare that you are mentally stable, there shouldn't be a problem."

With that the solicitor smartly closed his brief case and rose from the seat opposite his client.

Tony's magnetic blue eyes fixed on the lawyer's pale gaze, "What about my mother?" He asked.

"No news yet, I'm afraid. I'll keep you posted."

Tony's eyes followed Stephen's departing figure and his eyes glittered calculatingly. His prayer was being answered.

Mrs Clifton knew. She *knew,* like a pig waiting for its own slaughter. Her feral eyes, wild with insanity, roamed the landscape around her. She tilted her chin, and lupine like snuffed the air, as the old battle scarred tom cat had in that fateful alley two years previously.* Her instincts were closer now to animal, than they had ever been. She mewled softly, her nasal whine disturbing nocturnal creatures that scuttled through the night, aware of a mortal danger, not to them, but carrying with it the threat of violence.

The woman who had been Grace Clifton was scarcely recognisable. She lumped her way through the undergrowth near the race course and turned towards the spire. Gillian was in that direction and Gillian was waiting, that much she sensed.

Holly faced the window where the curtains streamed in the night breeze sending rippling shadows across the marble veined work top. She raised up her arms welcoming the soft, thick breath of midnight. Her inseparable attendant stretched across the floor like the crucifixion, and she closed her eyes focusing her whole being on what she knew would happen.

Paul stayed separated from her by a single door. Colin a few yards away close to handset recharging the mobile telephone. Both men were anxious. Both were silent.

The light breeze which had played so teasingly with the soft sway of lace at the window began to grow stronger. A fierce rushing of wind usurped the stillness of the dark. Tornado like, it swept across the garden picking up debris from the earth; twigs, leaves and soil dusted into a fine cloud which approached the house and rained on the window. The force metamorphosed into a bony knuckle which rapped authoritatively on the glass. Becoming more frenzied now, the insistent knocking, hammered the window pane until the menacing pressure of those fleshless phalanges cracked the transparent protection. The wind soughed in satisfaction and further blows frantically worked to make the crack a gaping fissure. Holly gave a frightened wail as the glass imploded. Cruel, flying

* See *Killing Me Softly*

bright needles of pain viciously embedded themselves in the wood of the pine kitchen, shattered on the tiled floor and searched for her soft flesh.

Paul roughly turned the handle of the door,

"I can't shift it Colin, it's stuck."

"You mustn't go in, not until she calls us."

"What if she's hurt? I can't risk it." Paul put his shoulder to the door.

"Leave it!" Colin ordered, but Paul took no notice and charged his bulk at the barrier once more.

Holly sank down to the floor. Splinters of glass showered her. She concentrated hard ignoring her fear, ignoring this unknown entity which had attacked her. She reached inside her for strength and control and was astonished to see a wisp of white issue from her and block the onslaught of the soldiering horde of glass that had threatened to engulf her. She watched as the pinpricks of spite dropped harmlessly to the floor.

The vision of yet another horror loomed closer. Holly could just discern the loathsome features of Mrs Clifton, crazed and mad, nearing the broken window, shrieking the name "Gillian!" Holly cried out for Paul.

He couldn't open the door.

Colin felt the receiver burn hot in his hand and let it fall from his grasp. He tugged at the sleeve of his sweatshirt, pulling it over his hand for protection and retrieved the phone. Using the message pen he keyed in the emergency numbers. The phone seared the skin around his ear. He held it away from him just managing to croak out his whereabouts and demand the message be passed on to Allison. The plastic handset began to sizzle. Colin dropped it once more. Astonished, he watched as the instrument began to melt. Blue sparks crackled and snapped rendering it useless.

The iridescent police siren lights blinked through the velvet dark; headlights harshly gleamed across the front lawn of the detached Worcester town house. The radios constantly crackled their distorted messages, neighbours peered through their bedroom windows at the unusual street scene. Mrs Clifton, handcuffed, and raving was led away to a waiting car, pronouncing,

"Cursed be he that perverteth the
judgement of the stranger, fatherless
and widow: and all the people shall
say, Amen."

Mark Stringer winced as another stream of invective hailed down on his ears.

"Is she referring to us or herself?" he mused.

"Who's to know?" replied Allison, biting into a carob bar, and swinging his huge frame inside the car.

"Whatsoever things were written aforetime
were written for our learning; that we
through patience and comfort of the
scriptures might have hope."

Allison's car door clanged shut.

Holly sat on the floor, wan faced, her knees up to her chin, hugging a milk chocolate drink. Her elbows resting against against Paul's legs, who was sitting on the settee.

"Well, what happens now?"

Paul gently massaged her neck and shoulders and addressed Colin,

"Yes, what's the next step?"

"She'll be placed in a secure unit, to allow time for a proper medical examination. That being done, I expect she will be committed to live out her life locked away from the rest of society."

"Will Holly have to do anything?" asked Paul anxiously, still kneading Holly's shoulders.

"Statements and the suchlike. I doubt she will have to give evidence in court, if that's what you mean."

Holly shuddered, "I couldn't go through with that, people would think I'm a raving loony."

"I was coming to that; I think, for official purposes, if questioned, you bend the truth a little. Make out it was a straight forward attack, leave out the details."

"Nobody'd believe me anyway."

"Talking of which... what did happen in there? "

"You don't want to know, let's say that I now believe the old adage.... *there are more things in heaven and hell....*"

"Isn't that Shakespeare?" questioned Paul.

"Mmm, Hamlet, if I'm not mistaken," said Colin.

"Said to Horatio, I think," added Holly.

"When *are* you going to tell us? asked Colin.

"When I can deal with it... Maybe never."

"In all my life, I've never experienced anything like I witnessed here tonight. It was like something out of a Stephen King novel," murmured Colin.

"Worse," said Paul, "We were involved in it. It was actually happening. Happening to us."

"But at least it's over now." sighed Holly gratefully.

"We can't be sure of that, though... Can we?" said Colin tentatively.

"What do you mean? Mrs Clifton's been caught, when the t's are crossed and the i's dotted, it'll be over."

"I don't think so, Paul," whispered Colin. "I don't think so, by a long way."

"Why? You can't mean that?" said Paul astounded.

"I think I know what he means..." affirmed a subdued Holly.

"Paul, Holly has to learn to live with her new found powers, her increased sensitivity. This episode has recharged her batteries, so to speak. She is more acutely aware than she's ever been. She has untold talents waiting to be developed and heightened."

"Can't she just ignore it and let us go on as before?"

"Her inner visions will be hard to ignore.... more like impossible.... Holly will never be the same again."

"Can you cope with that?" Holly raised her eyes questioningly and turned to look back at Paul. "Can you deal with it?"

Breakthrough

The blond viking sat flustered in disbelief for a moment before committing himself, "I will always be there for you." "That's what I'd hoped," smiled Holly gently, "Maybe I am ready to tell you, after all." Holly began her story.

Allison slurped the last of his tea, and replaced his cup on the saucer. He eyed Mark carefully.
"What are you thinking?"
"Sir?"
"Well, you're so deep in thought, I thought you must have come up with a solution to curb Birmingham's crime rate once and for all," joked Allison.
"No.. not that."
"Well?"
"I was just thinking how strange life is. You think you know who you are, what to expect out of life, then wham something comes and hits you in the face to turn your whole life upside down."
"What are we talking about here?" asked a puzzled Allison.
" I don't know... all sorts. That poor girl, Holly. Believes she's settled and then it turns out her close relatives are lunatics, murderers."
"I think young Holly will be all right. She's tough enough. It's environment that matters more than heredity. She's had a caring, loving upbringing."
"She inherited her grandmother's psychic abilities." Mark argued.
"Yes, and she'll either harness them in the right way, get proper help and advice, or subdue them, so they don't interfere with her lifestyle. She's surrounded by love," reasoned Allison.
"So were Bonnie and Clyde."
"Wrong example, Mark. Their love for each other couldn't change what they were."

"Maybe you're right. Young Ronnie Soper promises to turn out OK."

"You're forgetting he had a good home until the death of his twin. That's when he started to go off the rails. A reaction – quite a dramatic one, but fortunately for him the family has come to its senses. Ronnie will be fine."

Mark sighed, and changed the subject. "Debs wondered if you and Mary were up to a night out, a week on Saturday."

"What have you in mind?"

"A meal and a show..."

A knock on the office door interrupted them. Pooley popped his head round,

"Sir, we're setting up a collection for young Taylor and his bride to be. What shall I put you down for? A fiver?"

Allison nodded and gestured to Mark who offered,

"Me too, when's the happy day?"

"They're undecided yet, but think it'll be sometime in June."

With that Pooley closed the door. Mark scrutinised his finger nails before continuing,

"Do you know what really scares the hell out of me, Chief? "

Allison stared quizzically at his subordinate.

"Tony Clifton's conviction... that is, his confinement in a top security hospital. I'm worried it might be seen as unsafe. That he may walk."

Allison had no answer, no platitudes, no philosophy. He stood up from his desk and gazed out of the window at the bustling scene outside the General Hospital.

Vencat smiled, even with the gold tooth gone, there was a more than a hint of menace in his smirking lips. He looked at the suitcase of cash in front of him. His diligence had paid off. He congratulated himself. The deal he had made with the South West farmer would more than amply satisfy his customers' needs for cannabis. And his courier system, was working brilliantly and he was never short of volunteers anxious to make a quick buck. He didn't take risks himself, that was the secret. Now he could attend to more pressing matters, that of changing his appearance enough to avoid recognition, enough to allow him freedom in Britain. He wanted to return, for good. Vencat picked up the telephone and dialled.

"So what are you going to do now?" asked Marcie.

"I've decided to face up to my responsibilities," replied Holly, looking better and brighter than she had for months. "I've promised Colin, that he can test me as much as he wants. I have this talent, this gift, and if possible I want to harness it to help others. I'm spending a week at a centre in Shropshire where research into the paranormal is carried out. Not only that, I will meet others, like me, who have a heightened sixth sense."

"Paul won't like that."

"Paul has actually encouraged me. He needs time to finish his designs, this opportunity is perfect. I can learn to understand myself, Paul can complete his work."

"Aren't you afraid it might separate you?"

"Who? Us? We've been through too much together. We'll survive."

"And what about your grandmother?"

"What about her?"

"Are you going to follow that through as well?"

Holly paused for a moment to think... "I've spoken to mum and dad, they don't feel so threatened now, so... yes. It's time I learned more about Hilda Fisher and my biological mother, Ellie. Yes," she said more definitely as if finally making up her mind. "Yes, I have a need to know. Sharing my love doesn't mean there won't be enough to go round. It just means I give more."

Marcelle scrambled up from her perch on the floor and gave her friend a hug. "You're doing the right thing. I'm sure of that."

"Who's the instinctive one now?" laughed Holly.

"Come on, let's forget the tea and crack open a bottle of wine."

"But it's only eleven o'clock," protested Holly.

"So?.. We've a lot to celebrate."

"Is there something you're not telling me?" questioned Holly, turning the angle poised lamp on her friend and switching it on.

It was Marcelle's turn to laugh, "Sort of..."

"What do you mean, sort of?"

"Well, with everything that has been happening, I've been taking stock of my life. I've decided to give it a go with Colin."

"Oh Marcie!" Holly hugged her friend, "I'm so pleased. You won't regret it, I'm sure. That's brilliant news! Let's get the wine!"

Tony squinted in the bright sunshine as he walked down the worn, stone steps, in the company of his solicitor.

The predatory press pack pounced, vying for position, to confront the newly released Tony Clifton. Stephen Briggs raised his hand to still their questions and read the prepared statement.

"It is a day of mixed emotions. Sadness that Tony's mother has been incarcerated for crimes and for which Tony stood accused. And gladness, gladness that justice has been done. The recognition that my client is innocent and that the balance of his mind was disturbed due to the accusations levelled against him coupled with the tragic death of his girlfriend, Amy Calcutt. A full enquiry has been ordered to investigate the West Midlands' Police Force actions in this case and the possible tampering of evidence. Tony has regained his equilibrium according to the psychologist's report and now just wants to get his life in order. His old firm, have reinstated him in ......" Stephen Brigg's voice droned on and Tony took a gulp of the fresh air he had been denied so long. He was free – FREE! A female reporter, identified herself and pushed her way forward to the front of the crowd and thrust a microphone under his nose badgering him for a comment on how he felt and what his future plans were. His calculating, well modulated tones answered her crisply and politely. Stephen Briggs urged his client forward to the waiting car.

As Tony settled back in his seat, a movement caught his eye. The fluttering of a long, Isadora scarf, held his attention and he was filled with a deep yearning. Tony perused the face of the reporter who had asked the last question. He recalled her name and place of work. He would remember her.... he wouldn't forget. Then, he smiled.

Edward Gaskell *publishers*
DEVON

AUTHOR'S ACKNOWLEDGEMENTS

Firstly, I would like to thank everyone who wrote to me after the first novel, *Killing Me Softly*. The sequel *Prayer for the Dying* has taken a little while to produce, but I hope it was worth the wait.

I'd like to thank my husband, Andrew Spear who has made it possible for me to write full time. Without his love and support I wouldn't have made it!

Special thanks to my son, Ben Fielder who always provides me with a light moment in my day when spirits are flagging and to my Dad who has always been there for me.

I couldn't go on without a mention for my publisher, Edward Gaskell who makes me believe all things are possible and more importantly gives me belief in myself. His team are of paramount importance particularly Bill, and his talented partner, Norma Finn, who is the inspiration behind the artwork on the cover.

Finally, the friendship of some very special people, Heather Maxwell whose encouragement has been fundamental to my writing progress as has the support of Tim Prescott, Val Smith, Gill Nathanson, and Bill Buffery whose great insight has helped me enormously in writing in other fields. My internet friends, zany Catherine Pinkney and Brian Harris, better known as Cat and Snowleopard – who always make themselves available for a chat whenever I need one.

I hope you like the result and want to read the next, because there's more.

see overleaf for other titles available

Other titles available from *Lazarus Press* and Edward Gaskell *publishers.*
All titles are available to readers post free quoting reference RT/3330
Please send cheque to cover cost of book(s) only to *Lazarus Press*
Unit 7 Caddsdown Business Park Bideford Devon EX39 3DX or telephone
01237 421195 • Fax 01237 425520 • email bookwove@aol.com.
Trade orders welcomed

fiction

isbn	title	author	
1-898546-19-3	*Sekunjalo*	Gill Jackman	£14.99

hardback • thrilling adventure set in the declining years of African apartheid

| 1-898546-20-7 | *My Dear Soul 'an Days* | Les Terry | £6.99 |

paperback • by turns sad and hilarious; a poignant tale of war time Devon

| 1-898546-18-5 | *New Mrs Fox* | Peter Kunkler | £14.99 |

hardbackback • the romantic new life of widowed farmer Edward fox

| 1-898546-09-6 | *Las Fuentes* | Peter Kunkler | £5.99 |

paperback • the twists and turns of a Canadian girl's pilgrimmage to Brittany

| 1-898546-06-1 | *Killing Me Softly* | Elizabeth Revill | £5.95 |

paperback • highly popular, if terrifying account of a Birmingham serial killer

| 1-898546-07-X | *Jacobs' Kingdom* | AA Hasker | £6.99 |

paperback • fast moving nautical saga featuring Capt. Aaron Jacobs

| 1-898546-28-2 | *The Exposed* | John Hollands | £15.99 |

hardback • acclaimed account of post war Japan by this best selling author

| 1-898546-35-5 | *The Dresden Vases* | R.J. Ellis | £7.99 |

paperback • the moving war time story of Jewish refugee Rebecca Radstone

| 1-898546-06-1 | *Prayer for the Dying* | Elizabeth Revill | £5.95 |

paperback • by popular demand! The Birmingham serial killer is back

poetry

| 1-898546-36-3 | *Stranger on a Strange Planet* Jeremy Bell | £5.99 |

non-fiction

isbn	title	author	
1-898546-01-0	*The History of Bideford*	John Watkins	£24.00

hardback • reprint of 1792 History • oldest extant • considered definitive

| 1-898546-03-7 | *Memorials of Barnstaple* | Joseph Gribble | £24.00 |

hardback • reprint of 1830 History • oldest extant • considered definitive

| 1-898546-05-3 | *Policeman in Palestine* | Colin Imray | £8.50 |

paperback • autobiography covering turbulent years in Palestine

| 1-898546-08-8 | *North Devon History* | Peter Christie | £7.50 |

paperback • highly popular account of north Devon's colourful history

| 1-898546-16-9 | *Clouds & Rainbows* | Ursula Madden | £14.99 |

hardback • one family's way of dealing with early-onset Parkinson's disease

| 1-898546-22-3 | *Wear Gifford* | Peter Coad | £9.99 |

paperback • educational history of a north Devon village (rare photographs)

| 1-898546-23-1 | *My Personal War....* | David Grainger | £4.99 |

booklet • one-man's war against Parkinson's disease • illustrated non-fiction (continued)

isbn	title	author	
1-898546-25-8	*Slaves of Rapparee*	Patrick Barrow	£9.99

paperback • discovery of a 1796 slaveship's wrecking at Ilfracombe (Ills.)

1-898546-26-6   *British Colonialism*   Harry Arrigonie   £15.95
hardback • autobiography covering turbulent years in Palestine and Africa

1-898546-27-4   *Nothing Ventured....*   Chris. Pantall   £19.00
hardback • autobiography of a Herefordshire born self-made millionaire

1-898546-29-0   *To Horty From Rose*   R. Symes-Earle   £6.99
paperback • amazing account of frequency healing across two continents

1-898546-31-2   *The Way of a Transgressor*   Negley Farson   £23.00
hardback • reprint of best selling biography of the 1930s (first illustrated)

1-898546-32-0   *Our Miss Wadland*   Shane Wadland   £15.99
hardback • biography of a Devon village schoolteacher (rare photographs)

1-898546-33-9   *How to Enjoy Your Children...* Monica Head   £9.99
paperback • *..and have an easy life.* 50 years of childcare experience

1-898546-34-7   *One Man's Boer War*   Ed, S Pine-Coffin   £19.00
hardback • the amazing diary of a Boer war hero • many rare photographs)

1-898546-38-X   *Pixy-Led in North Devon*   Z.E.A.Wade   £19.95
hardback • illustrated reprint of fascinating 1895 genealogical Devon history

1-898546-39-8   *The Dawn Stand-To*   Chris. Hiscox   £19.95
hardback • autobiography covering turbulent years in Kenya

1-898546-40-1   *Knights of Raleigh Manor*   Pat Barrow   £15.95
hardback • amazing discovery of a medieval jousting site in north Devon

1-898546-17-7   *More North Devon History*   Peter Christie   £6.95
paperback • by popular demand more of north Devon's colourful history

1-898546-30-4   *Even More N. Devon History* Peter Christie   £7.50
paperback • further accounts of north Devon's colourful history

1-898546-21-5   *Barnstaple's Vanished Lace*   Gahan & Christie   £7.50
paperback • Barnstaple's vanished lace industry (rare photographs)

1-898546-37-1   *Journal of a Nature Lover*   Stewart Beer   £7.99
paperback • by the author of Exultation of Skylarks • beautifully written

0-9523062-2-0   *My Life on Lundy*   Felix Gade   £23.00
hardback • autobiography covering turbulent years in Kenya 0-9521413-1-0
Lundy an Island Sketchbook Peter Rothwell   £12.95
hardback • delightful, illustrated tour of the island and its secret places

0-9521413-4-5   *Lundy Island: a Monograph* John R Chanter   £15.00
hardback • beautiful reprint of the 1895 history. Illustrated by Peter Rothwell

0-9530532-0-2   *Island Studies*   R.A. Irving *et al*   £15.00
hardback • illustrated study celebrating 50 years of the Lundy Field Society

0-9521413-3-7   *The Play's the Thing*   Frank Kemp   £14.95
hardback • history of theatre in north Devon (many rare photographs)

0-9521413-2-9   *A Book of Georgeham*   Lois Lamplugh   £7.95
paperback • beautifully written village history illustrated by Peter Rothwell

* * * * *

full catalogue available upon request

1 -898546 -41 -X